PERFECT LIVES

PERFECT LIVES

Lauren Loos

First published 2017

ISBN 978-0-6480196-0-2

Copyright © Lauren Loos 2017

All rights reserved. No part of this book may be reproduced or transmitted in any form or by any means without prior written consent.

Cover design by Drop Dead Designs

Printed by IngramSpark

For Tim & Jack

CHAPTER ONE

'When are you going to grow up?'

The words rang in Kate's ears. She'd heard it all before. Many times. And, in a haze of stale beer and day-old smoke, with the glare of the sun forcing her eyes into a squint and accentuating the mascara that was everywhere but where it was supposed to be, this was not the time to have this argument again.

Kate was killing it. She had fun. There's so much more to life than jobs, cars, houses and relationships. Kate partied and took chances and lived in the moment. Acting like an adult (whatever that means) was completely overrated.

'Are you listening to me, Kate? You're thirty-bloody-four. I know that your breakup with Jake was hard, but you were only together for two months. I'm glad that you're trying to move on from Peter, but as per usual, missy, you jumped in too quickly. Who moves in with some bloke after knowing them a week? And now you're living with me. Again. What are you doing with your life? Getting tarted up and acting like a floosy every weekend seems a bit bloody ridiculous at your age. You need to take some bloody responsibility for your actions. You need a plan.'

A plan.

'My plan is to eat some toast, down a Gatorade and get *some* sleep before I have to be at work.'

'Fine. Go to bed. But we're going to discuss this later.'

Kate had already flung her stilettos to the corner of the room and discarded her sequinned clutch. Her simple, tight red dress left little to the imagination. Her long legs looked like they could belong to a teenager – a little bit awkward and slightly too thin. Her breasts, although small, vied for attention with the help of a push up bra and a low neckline. Her fingers and toes were painted a high gloss red, matching her pouting lips.

Kate was unapologetically confident. The picture that she presented to the world was one of a vapid, superficial lady-child who didn't know how to act her age. This was partly true – Kate seemed incapable of acting like a woman in her thirties. The notion that someone – a woman who looks a certain way – must be stupid and have nothing to contribute was something that Kate was ambivalent about being saddled with. If people wanted to underestimate her, that was their problem.

From a distance, the biggest giveaway that Kate was older than her outfit implied was her arms. They were long and lean, like her legs, but had the toned, hard look that thin women over a certain age get when they don't allow an extra kilo or two to soften them. This hard look is usually reserved for women much older than Kate, but Kate's over exercising and under-nourishment had led to this early onset. Up close, Kate still looked beautiful, but much older than her thirty-four years. And on mornings like this, after nights like the one just gone, Kate looked *very* much older than her age. Excessive alcohol and cigarettes had etched premature lines under her eyes. Being slightly undernourished and lacking sleep gave her a hollow, hardened look. And she was always undernourished and lacking sleep. This morning the effect was accentuated by last night's eye makeup that sat in the creases beneath her eyes.

Kate prided herself on the fact that strangers were often surprised when they learnt her age. She dressed and acted like she was in her early twenties. She had become more and more reluctant over the past few years to mention her age to the men she met. She couldn't quite put her finger on why. She still felt happy that she could pass as being much younger (when, in fact, in any sort of lit arena, this was not actually the case). Maybe it was because the age gap between her and potential suitors was continually getting bigger. Or maybe because the surprised reaction was less to do with her youthful looks and more out of pure astonishment that a woman of that age would be dressed like that in a nightclub, acting so foolishly, dancing, flirting like that. Or maybe, when these conversations occurred in the harsh light of day, the reaction was surprise that those bony arms, hollow cheeks and harsh wrinkles belonged to someone as young as Kate. Kate only caught glimpses of this now and then and she never let her mind dwell on it. But mostly, she still felt happy that her life was so much more fun and fulfilling than those women who wasted their lives getting married, having babies and settling... down.

Kate only managed an hour of sleep before she dragged herself out of bed to go to work. She was thankful on days like this that her job required no brainpower. If only she could wear sunglasses at her desk.

'Fuck!'

'What's up?'

'A girl I went to school with just got engaged.'

'Oh.' Gemma looked around, bored. She wasn't in the right frame of mind to deal with the drama of yet another thirty-something chick having a melt down over being past her prime. Kate was still staring intently at her phone.

'Don't worry, hun. You'll find someone soon,' a little half-heartedly from Gemma, as she looked at her nails.

'Argh! God, no! I'm happy being single. I just feel like all these girls that I went to school with are so obsessed with getting married. Why would you want to limit yourself like that? Once they're married, their lives *just stop*. They never go anywhere or do anything remotely interesting. Next she'll be popping out kids, her Facebook feed will be all about her ugly children and she'll be constantly talking about her kid's shit.' Kate waived her phone for emphasis and then said intently to her phone screen, 'I honestly don't care what your kid took a shit on or the texture of that shit. And I don't want to have to pretend that your spawn is actually cute. It's not. I'm yet to see a baby that doesn't look like a tiny Vladimir Putin.'

'Facebook? God, you're so old,' Gemma muttered under her breath, as she turned to pick up the ringing phone on her desk.

Kate wondered if Michelle had seen this Facebook post. She could always count on Michelle to share in a joke at the expense of their married friends.

CHAPTER TWO

'Do you know where my car keys are?' Mike asked, mouth full, clearly not having looked for them. 'Georgie's spilled the milk,' he added casually, without looking up from his cereal.

'Your keys are on the kitchen bench. I'll grab them for you in a sec,' Rachel said as she finished tying her shoe laces and picked the horizontal milk bottle up from the table. She felt a twinge of annoyance at her husband, but swallowed it quickly. He and Georgie needed her and that felt good. She worked hard to maintain the perfect household and the perfect life. Mike was a good husband – caring and loving – but sometimes it did feel as though he slipped in to the role of another man – a man who took his wife for granted. A man who didn't pick up a carton of spilled milk. Just sometimes. But Rachel always dismissed those thoughts quickly. Those feelings were for a lesser woman – a lesser family unit. Having any sort of grievance about her husband told of imperfection. There simply wasn't room for that in her life. Her life was perfect.

As she walked toward the kitchen, she moved with the intense focus of a woman who has planned each step to gain optimal efficiency and perfect posture, all whilst engaging her core, just like her personal trainer incessantly lectured all of his clients to do. Her pert butt was accentuated by her exercise tights and her pony tail bounced with each step.

Rachel handed her husband his keys before cleaning up the spilled milk. Always busy with an internal checklist of things to do, she grabbed the mail from the hall table to quickly sort before taking Georgie to her swimming lesson. The bills were added to her filing system in the study. Junk mail went straight into the recycling. Who has time for that? Except a catalogue for office stationery that caught her eye. They were having a sale and Georgie was running low on craft supplies. Rachel mentally added that to the list of things to do that week.

Amongst the bills was a large gold envelope, handwritten and addressed to her. Just her. With her usual precision, Rachel slid the letter opener into place and sliced the envelope with a quick incision. An engagement party for Fiona Masters. A brief feeling of excitement swelled within Rachel. It would be lovely to see all the girls again at a party! Why is it they don't catch up more often? It had been years since they had all gotten together. Though there was a brief underlying twinge of annoyance – why wasn't Mike invited? He was her husband. And Fiona had met him plenty of times.

Rachel immediately began planning. She would need to add the date to her diary and ensure that Mike was available to look after Georgie or find a sitter. Buy a card to RSVP. Or should she send a handmade card? It's far more personal (she had spent years perfecting the art before ever giving a homemade card – you simply couldn't give handmade things unless they were perfect... or perfect in their handmade imperfection). Yes, she would pick up supplies when she bought Georgie's craft supplies. And of course she'd need to arrange an engagement gift.

This was going to be so much fun!

CHAPTER THREE

Alex walked through the door of her apartment carrying four large bouquets of flowers. Tiger lilies, irises, daffodils and sunflowers filled her arms, and she struggled to shut the door behind her with her foot.

Alex – and her bright flowers – looked out of place in her home. She lived in an old industrial building that had been transformed into exclusive apartments. Daniel and Alex's decorator had designed the interiors and furniture to make the most of the industrial look. The exposed wooden beams in the lofty ceilings and the bare bricks on one wall gave only the slightest hint of homely warmth to an otherwise cold, impersonal decor. Everything within the apartment seemed to fall somewhere on the spectrum between black and white. The decorator had used so many different words to describe what were marginally different shades of grey. The floor to ceiling windows flooded the apartment with light, which was the only aspect of the apartment that Alex actually loved. Polished concrete floors and stainless steel kitchen bench tops offset any warmth gained by the sun, filling the rooms with a cold and sterile gleam.

Alex's home looked like it came right from the pages of a magazine. It didn't look lived in. And it certainly didn't look like it would be home to someone like Alex. Looking around the apartment, the only hint of Alex that could be seen was the flowers. The bouquets in her arms would be added to the masses of flowers that filled every available space. Alex loved them: the more colourful the better. But Daniel had allergies, so the only time that Alex could have her beloved flowers was when he was away. She cherished those times without him. More than she cared to admit.

Alex threw the bouquets onto the stainless steel countertop, opening a draw and fishing around for a pair of secateurs. The pair she found were in a custom leather slip, high carbon stainless steel, with a wooden handle, specifically created for a lady's hand and handcrafted in Japan. Daniel had bought them for her and still, two years later, persisted in prompting her to talk about them – how thoughtful the gift and how exquisite and expensive they were – on the rare occasions she joined him at his work functions. Alex began expertly snipping the ends of the stems and placing them in a vase, tilting her head to one side and critiquing the arrangement, shifting a stem here and there, plucking another out and replacing it to ensure the perfect combination of colour, positioning and overall shape of the arrangement. In another life, Alex would have been a skilled and no doubt happy florist.

Alex was short and curvy, with a style that she would call simple, classic and elegant. Most people would call it boring. She had a large bust that could easily make her look a little on the plump side if she didn't wear the right thing for her figure, which she never did. Alex's round face showed off her youthful, olive skin, but her clothes aged her. Her smile was undoubtedly her best feature; it could light up a room and when she laughed, everything else faded into insignificance. But when her face wasn't adorned with that magnificent smile, she was a little bit plain.

Daniel would be away for another week. He travelled a lot for work and Alex only occasionally joined him. She loved to travel but she also loved the solitude she found when Daniel was away – the times when she could read, surrounded by the fragrant aromas of her arrangements.

Over the last few years Alex had become a loner. She rarely spent time with anyone other than Daniel. She no longer had any close friends and found socialising to be an anxiety-ridden chore that was best avoided. There were a lot of social functions for Daniel's work, which she seldom attended, even when she took the overseas trips with him. Both of them preferred it that way – Alex didn't need to worry about making small talk or finding a dress that she would inevitably hate, and Daniel didn't need to feel embarrassed about his fat wife's social ineptitude.

Alex glanced at the engagement party invitation that was stuck to the front of the built in glass-door fridge. She wasn't excited at all about the prospect of seeing her old friends. Times had changed. They had all changed. There was a reason they didn't see each other anymore – they led different lives. She always felt self conscious when talking about her life to strangers. And let's face it: these women were practically strangers now. She always felt as though people thought she was bragging when she talked about her home and the overseas holidays and her incredibly handsome husband. Or worse – she worried that they thought she was lying. She saw the looks on people's faces as they looked from Daniel to her and back again. She knew he was out of her league. His looks. His money. His charisma. She was sure that most people immediately started wondering what Alex brought to the table. It clearly wasn't her looks. And then she felt there was pressure on her to be funny or witty, which wasn't really her thing. That kind of pressure just made her feel even more socially awkward.

Alex had resigned herself to go to the engagement party despite her reservations about seeing her old friends. Hopefully it wouldn't be as bad as she imagined.

CHAPTER FOUR

Sitting in the lounge, Michelle glanced up from her laptop to the screen above where the word *delayed* flashed. Typical. She continued to type. Her phone buzzed with a new message. From Kate Harris. They hadn't spoken in ages. Curiosity distracted her from an email, mid-sentence.

OMFG! U c FB? Fiona Masters is engaged???

Michelle groaned inwardly and rolled her eyes. Another one bites the dust. She and Kate were the only unmarried ones left amongst their group of friends from school. They were destined to be old maids together; getting to their forties and going to nightclubs to try pick up men half their age; owning a dozen cats between them; and forever talking about the good old days when they used to be *really* hot and were turning men down. Although that had never truly been the case for Michelle. Michelle knew that her assets didn't lie in her looks, but that didn't faze her. She was comfortable in her own skin.

Michelle glanced back at her phone. Who has time to be on Facebook mid-morning on a Monday? Kate, that's who. She's probably between jobs again.

Michelle quickly pulled up Facebook on her laptop. Fiona's feed boasted photos from an engagement shoot, showing a man standing behind Fiona, with his arms awkwardly wrapped around her, and her holding her left hand unnaturally across her chest, to show off the huge rock that shone from her finger. Michelle punched a reply to Kate.

Engagement shoot = tacky

In the past, Michelle would have felt slightly bitter about a girlfriend's engagement. But this time she felt a little less so. Things were going really well with Andrew. She was actually – secretly – hopeful that her time would come soon. Sure, she had always mocked the whole marriage thing. Over the last couple of years, this shared contempt had been the glue that had bonded her and Kate. She'd said she didn't really want to get married. Who had the time, anyway? And she'd sworn black and blue that if she ever did, she wouldn't be involved in one of those staged engagement photo shoots, where you looked lovingly at your partner in the most artificial way possible, showed off a ring and plastered the whole thing on Facebook just to rub your *true love* in the faces of everyone you know. She was certain that that was the entire basis for the success of Facebook – people wanting to show everyone they know (but never see) how fucking fabulous their lives are; people like Rachel with their Stepford style perfect fucking lives.

But who was Michelle kidding? She did actually want to get married. If she was honest with herself, she knew she'd jump at the chance. She'd be the first there with a huge engagement party, photo shoot, big white dress. She would have it all. And for once in her life, it almost seemed like it was within her grasp.

Michelle's brash nature and self-assuredness were often mistaken for independence – the kind of independence where a person doesn't need or want another person. And, yes, Michelle did function well alone. She was always so busy with her business, she was financially independent, and, frankly, she was used to being alone. But none of that stopped the aching that she had felt – the need for companionship, the desire to feel loved and to love. And now she had that.

Her business was going well. She had a boyfriend. A serious boyfriend. (Although she did prefer the term *partner*. She wasn't in high school, for fuck's sake. It felt absurd for a woman in her thirties to be talking about her *boyfriend*.) She was making really good money, which mattered a lot to her, mostly because it meant that her business was dominating the market. A sure fire sign that she was winning. For once, she was killing it in every aspect of her life.

Michelle wasn't a pretty woman; not ugly, but not pretty. Her jaw line was a little too strong and her nose a little too big. She was very tall and athletic looking, with no curves to speak of and the butt of a fourteen year old boy. Despite her athletic looks, she had never really excelled a sports and wasn't particularly coordinated. Regardless of that, she was training for her first marathon. Not because she wanted to get fit, or achieve some sort of life goal – a bucket list item – but because a partner in her marketing firm was doing the marathon and she wanted to beat him. She couldn't wait to see the look on that smarmy dick's face when a woman (because apparently that's somehow relevant) kicked his ass.

Michelle was driven to achieve, to succeed, to win. If she didn't think she would win, she wouldn't play. She knew what she wanted and was intensely passionate about getting it. These qualities, embodied in her oversize frame, and unencumbered by an internal filter, made her incredibly intimidating, particularly to members of the opposite sex. She was generally well liked, but men tended to avoid her romantically. And her female friends were limited to like-minded successful women. And her school friends, whom she'd mostly grown apart from.

Michelle really didn't have anything in common with Kate, Rachel, Alex and Fiona. The only real commonality was a shared past. The five school friends had grown apart over the years. Michelle had moved to Sydney immediately after finishing a marketing degree. She had worked for a short time – very hard – at a small marketing firm before deciding with two other juniors that they could do it all themselves. And in true Michelle style, she had worked her ass off and made an absolute success of something that would have seemed – and been – impossible to most people.

Rachel had stayed in Brisbane, gotten married and started a family. Michelle thought this a waste of an intelligent woman. Rachel had always been smart and had been reasonably successful – not in the same league as Michelle, but successful nonetheless. Rachel was a perfectionist through and through – so long as something could be achieved by perseverance and hard work, Rachel would achieve it. Michelle found that kind of attitude admirable, making it even more disappointing to Michelle – a shame, really – that her friend hadn't done more with her life; that Rachel had settled for being average – just another *mother* – when she could have been so much more.

Like Michelle, Alex had also moved to Sydney. Michelle didn't know when that had happened or what drove the move.

She only really knew that Alex was there because Kate had told her so. Michelle and Alex had not kept in touch at all. Alex wasn't active on social media (though she secretly used it obsessively, voyeuristically), not that that would really make a difference because Michelle never had time for frivolous things like Facebook. Social media was a marketing tool to Michelle, and Michelle was not in the business of marketing herself, just her clients, and did not want or need a way to broadcast her life to the masses or catch up on what old friends were up to.

For the most part, Alex had completely kept to herself since they had all lost contact somewhere in their early twenties. None of the others were really aware of what Alex was doing with her life. They hadn't even been invited to Alex's wedding, which had seriously miffed Kate, despite not being a fan of weddings. Rachel had been quite understanding and leapt to Alex's defence – weddings were expensive, you can't possibly invite everyone, even if they had been great friends for so long. Michelle, on the other hand, couldn't have cared less about an invitation to a wedding. She didn't have enough time to be worried about social events that she didn't even need to attend.

Kate was really the only one who had stayed in touch with everyone – texting and emailing each of them every so often with updates on what they were all up to, gossip about other girls they had gone to school with and – only to Michelle – gripes about their friends who'd gotten married and started families. Kate had even managed a few catch ups now and then with Fiona, Michelle and Rachel – usually separately. Kate's ability to stay in contact was probably, or so Michelle thought, due to an abundance of time. In reality, it was more than that: it was in Kate's nature; she loved her friends dearly. She at times felt disappointed that they weren't still as close as they once were and often contacted them in an attempt to rekindle that closeness. Unlike Michelle and Rachel, she had the time to think of others; and unlike Alex she had the confidence to keep in contact.

In Michelle's opinion, Kate was a flake. She was actually reasonably intelligent, or at the very least, competent enough that she should be able to hold down a half-way decent job. But she never seemed to. Michelle figured that it came down to the fact that Kate prioritised everything else above work: simply put, she just didn't give a shit about her work. Rather than thinking it a shame, Michelle often just felt the need to roll her eyes at Kate's flakiness and shake her head at Kate's ridiculously long work history. Michelle loved Kate fiercely, but would that girl ever grow up?

CHAPTER FIVE

Rachel's suggestion of meeting up before the party and arriving together had been either dismissed or disregarded by the other three. Kate thought it was a fantastic idea, but wasn't planning on arriving at the party until later. Apparently for no particular reason.

Michelle was flying in just before the party started, so didn't have time. And Alex made no real excuse; she had just said she'd catch up with them all at the party.

So Rachel entered the party alone. Fiona's parents' home had always seemed grand, but on the evening of the engagement party, it was spectacular. The ten foot ceilings made the house seem more open and cooler than what you would expect for the unseasonably warm night. Rachel's heels clicked noisily on the wooden floors that were polished to a high shine.

Shadows were cast by the warm glow of tea lights that were scattered around the house, the overhead lights were dimmed and the rooms were filled with white peonies, giving off a subtle fragrance and giving the home a romantic feel.

'Rachel! How are you? I'm so glad you could make it! This is Isaac.' Fiona launched into the conversation at a break-neck pace. She was always cheerful, never lost for words but excitement and nerves had gotten the better of her, and her speech was practically giddy.

'Nice to finally meet you, Isaac. Fi, you look beautiful. And the place looks amazing. I'm so happy for you.'

'Thank you! We're just so excited! Can I grab you a drink?' Fiona looked around, distracted, obviously anxious to ensure that she hadn't missed welcoming any guests. For a brief moment the stress was visible on her face. Isaac firmly placed a hand on Fiona's shoulder blade, subtly reminding her that he was there for her, in a bid to calm her nerves.

'Fi, I can get my own drink. You've got hostessing duties.' Rachel hugged Fiona and exchanged knowing smiles with Isaac.

'Thanks, hun. I'll catch up with you a bit later on tonight.'

Rachel walked through the bi-fold doors that opened out to a deck, where most of the guests were congregating. The deck had several round, elbow-height tables scattered around it, each covered with a crisp, white linen table cloth, with tea lights and vases of peonies in the centre of each table. The deck sat only a foot or so above the perfectly manicured lawn and gardens. Two large steps ran the entire length of the back of the deck, leading down to the lawn. Paths through the grounds were lined with more tea lights on either side, inviting guests to explore the large gardens.

Rachel scanned the faces looking for one she recognised. She was always punctual and this was the downside – she was usually one of the first to arrive and this almost always either led to awkward solitude or more awkward small talk. To Rachel's relief and delight, Alex was already there. Making a beeline for Alex, Rachel grabbed a glass of wine from a waiter en route.

There was a stark contrast between Rachel and Alex, in both their outfits and mannerisms. Rachel wore a fifties style dress – fitted bodice, sweetheart neckline, flaring from the waist to a voluminous skirt – with a large floral print in vivid pinks. The dress didn't give any indication of Rachel's toned body beneath, but was perfectly suited, nonetheless, to her petite frame. Rachel, as always, walked with confidence and focus. Her long, blonde hair was in a chic pony tail, with a curl at the end that bounced as she walked. She was gorgeous, but in a subtle way that didn't initially draw attention.

Alex's shoulders were slightly rounded, her posture terrible. She wore a shapeless loose fitting plain black silk dress that made her look a lot larger than she was. She was, in fact, only slightly larger than average, but her dress implied otherwise. She wore barely any makeup, which suited her perfectly brown skin; and her dark, shoulder-length hair was ironed straight – the only hairstyle she could manage on her own. Her big brown eyes were framed by her long dark, and naturally curled, eyelashes. Her eyes had always been mesmerising – so warm and friendly. But now they just seemed like they belonged to a frightened deer – large and innocent; terrified, trapped and staring into the headlights of an oncoming car. Her face showed an unusual mixture of boredom and panic. She clearly didn't want to be at the party.

'How are you?' Rachel warmly wrapped her arms around Alex, and lightly brushed her lips across Alex's cheek.

'Really well thanks. You?'

'Great. When did you fly in?'

'Oh, I arrived last night. Thought I'd take the opportunity to catch up with family.' Alex twisted her wedding band around her finger nervously.

Rachel immediately noticed that something was off. Alex had always been the bubbly one – the life of the party, but she seemed oddly subdued, like a faded facsimile of her former self. Alex's smile didn't quite seem as bright as Rachel remembered it. It was a little forced. The conversation wasn't flowing so easily. She seemed exhausted. Rachel hoped that was all it was.

They say that you can be apart from your true friends for years and instantly, on seeing them again, pick up your friendship without missing a beat. If that was true, Alex was facing the uncomfortable thought that these people may not be her true friends. The conversation felt stilted. Alex felt uneasy, trying to remember the usual small talk questions.

'What are you doing for Christmas?' *Damn it!* Alex should have thought that through first. Whenever you ask a question like that, you'll end up having to answer it yourself.

'We're staying in town. The grandparents get upset if we're not around. But we're going away to the coast for New Year's with some friends. I'm really looking forward to having a nice beach break.' Rachel smiled brightly.

Alex's mind immediately went to the beach. Wearing swimmers. A bikini. That sounded like her worst nightmare. But if she looked like Rachel…

'What about you?' Rachel interrupted her train of thought.

Can this question be dodged? 'We're going away for Christmas and New Year's,' Alex answered a little too briskly.

'Where are you going?' Rachel, ever perceptive, noted the cagey answer and pushed.

Here it comes. 'Paris.'

'Oh my goodness! Paris,' Rachel gushed. 'Have you been before? I've never been but I've always wanted to go. And for Christmas. How romantic! You must be so excited!'

Rachel didn't have that look in her eyes – the look that combined jealousy with disbelief and veiled anger. Alex wondered for a moment how much of her reluctance to share details of her life with people was born of paranoia. Maybe Alex could get through this conversation without looking like an arrogant jerk.

'Oh, ah, yeah. I'm really excited. Daniel's family isn't particularly close, so he likes to go away for Christmas every year.' *Why did I say every year? Quick, change the subject before it comes out that Paris is a pretty frequent occurrence and that last Christmas was New York and the one before that Vienna.*

'Do you catch up with the girls ever?'

'Oh, no. Kate sometimes, but not often at all. I guess we've all gone our separate ways. How about you? You and Michelle are both living in Sydney, right? So you'd have the opportunity.'

'No, I haven't seen anyone from school in years.'

'Well, I'm a little concerned about Kate. Hopefully this engagement doesn't affect her.' Rachel was always concerned about other people. Her life was so perfect and it was painfully obvious that very few other people could say that. She wished that all of her friends had found the happiness that she had with her little family.

At that moment, Michelle walked onto the deck. Alex

exhaled and her whole body relaxed. It would be a lot easier to fade into the background of the conversation with Michelle there. Rachel's perceptive looks, her digging, pushing questions wouldn't be pinpointed directly on Alex.

The women exchanged greetings, hugging, and Michelle grabbed three glasses of wine from a passing waiter.

'So, fill me in on what you two have been up to for the past – how long has it been? When did I see you both last?' Michelle waved her hand, dismissing the question. 'Anyway, what have you both been doing?'

'Well, you know I've got a daughter, Georgie. She's turning three soon. She basically takes up most of my time.' Rachel smiled warmly thinking about her chubby little princess.

Michelle had to force herself not to roll her eyes. Rachel had been so smart and driven. She had so much potential. And to just throw away that on being a stay at home mother. What a waste.

'What about you, Michelle?' Rachel hadn't noticed how unimpressed Michelle had been with her response.

'Well, my business is going really well. We just took on two new partners. Our growth strategy is pretty aggressive, but I think it will work despite what the economy is doing at the moment. We're considering expanding interstate. We're just at the initial stages right now. Looking at small firms that we might take over and putting feelers out for key staff that we might headhunt.'

As Michelle continued talking about her business plans, Rachel smiled and nodded with a vague look in her eyes, while imagining having a growth strategy that didn't relate to her daughter's shoe size. She had given up her career to have Georgie. Sometimes she thought about what her life would be like if she hadn't. Would she be running her own business too? She briefly wondered what Michelle must think of her, being a stay at home mum; but she knew that no one would choose a career over a child – *obviously* Michelle would be jealous of *her* – though in the back of her mind there was just a hint of doubt about that. Wouldn't it be wonderful to have it all? To have a career and a child. How did people do that? It didn't quite fit with her idea of the perfect family – at least not with Georgie being so young. But she did like the idea of stepping up to the challenge of being the working super-mum and perfecting something new.

Michelle registered the vague look on Rachel's face and the disinterested expression that Alex was wearing. Rachel was politely nodding along, but she clearly wasn't listening. Michelle was accustomed to this. She generally tried to limit her business talk at social events, but sometimes her excitement got the better of her and she rambled. 'And I'm training for a marathon at the moment. It will be my first.'

'When is the marathon?' Rachel spoke. Alex was still attempting to fade into the background of the conversation.

'In April. In Paris.' Michelle smiled broadly. 'It's a bit inconvenient to take so long off work, especially given that one of my partners is doing it as well, but I'm very excited. I've actually never been to Paris before.'

'Oh, that's just wonderful. And what a coincidence. Alex was telling me just before you arrived that she's spending Christmas in Paris.'

Alex began to squirm, thumbing the well-worn patch of

skin on the outside of her pointer finger. She didn't want to discuss this. She didn't want to be part of the conversation. Why couldn't they just respect her natural place as a wallflower?

Michelle began firing questions at Alex. 'Have you been to Paris before? Where are you staying? Will you travel around at all or are you just sticking to Paris?'

'Ah –' Alex wasn't really sure which question to answer first. 'One of Daniel's friends has an apartment that he's not using over Christmas, so we're staying there.'

'Whereabouts is it? Which arrondissement?'

'Umm... It's in the Fifth.'

Michelle bit her lip and thought for a moment, trying to remember the map of Paris she'd been studying. 'The Fifth... Is that where Notre Dame is?'

'No, the apartment's near the Sorbonne.'

'Kate's here!' Rachel was practically giddy with pep.

As she approached, Kate smoothly exchanged glasses, empty for full, with a passing waiter and was halfway through the fresh glass by the time she reached the other women.

Alex was amazed at the way Kate looked. She had seen photos of Kate's transformation over the last few years on Facebook but had suspected that good lighting and filters had been behind the photos. In high school, Kate had been very pale, with freckles and mousy hair and had been that awkward kind of skinny, like a foal with legs so long that it can't quite work out how to control them yet. And the last time Alex had seen her, Kate had come into her own – she'd had a few blonde highlights, but nothing too drastic, and had put on weight, with a little too much around her middle. Kate had looked good back then, but this was something else. Kate was now the girl that had every man in the room watching. Literally, Alex could see the men turning or glancing, most peripherally, some blatantly. Kate was skinny, probably more so than what she had been in high school. She wore a tight, black dress that showed off her inordinately tiny waist, with a plunging neckline and an outrageously effective push-up bra. Her hair was champagne blonde, parted in the middle, with loose waves cascading from her chin all the way down to below her breasts. Kate was already blessed with height, but with her enormous silver stilettos, she towered over all the other women (except Michelle, who looked like a footballer next to Kate), and some of the men at the party. She wore heavy makeup, with long false eyelashes and red lips. Everything about Kate commanded attention.

Watching Kate, Alex felt a little part of herself wither. Alex longed to be that thin; to be that girl that everyone looked at. She imagined Daniel's reaction if he looked up from his phone one day to see her looking like that – how differently Daniel might treat her if she dressed like that – walked with that confidence. Alex resolved there and then to go to the gym, to take her dieting more seriously and to do whatever it took to become that girl. She tried to remember what she'd eaten that day, attempting to mentally add up the calories already consumed (she knew the calorie count in most foods off the top of her head, from years of crash diets, obsessing about food, counting calories and depriving herself only to binge later). Within minutes Alex's resolve had wavered. Who was she kidding? She would never be that thin. And she could never have that confidence. Never.

Immediately she reached for another glass of wine and started looking for the waiter with the canapés.

'Kate, where are you working at the moment?' Rachel didn't mean to have a dig at Kate's constant job changes by using the words *at the moment*; it just came out that way. She blushed at her own words and hoped that Kate hadn't noticed the implication behind them.

'I'm at a law firm in the city. It's crap.' Kate looked bored just talking about it.

'What don't you like about it? Is the workplace crap? Or is it your particular role?' Rachel registered Kate's sceptical expression. 'I mean – is there a way you can work your way up to something that you find more fulfilling?'

Kate knocked back the rest of her drink. 'The only way to do that is to fuck your way to a better job. And I have far too much self respect to do that.'

Michelle raised an eyebrow. Kate wasn't the type to sleep with someone for any motive other than to have a good time; however, self respect wasn't the first thing you thought of when you looked at her. Sure, she had an abundance of confidence, but half the time she was shamefully pissed – not exactly synonymous with self respect. And the men she slept with all seemed to be losers (by Michelle's standards, at least), implying that Kate really didn't have that much self respect at all.

Kate mistakenly took Michelle's look to mean that she was dubious that this was in fact the only way to gain a promotion. 'It's true. This hoe that I work with is fucking the boss. And she's managed to get a pretty significant pay rise for her trouble. And she keeps bragging that they're going to give her a company car.' Kate scoffed, took another swig of her drink and muttered, 'Keep dreaming, slut bag. Your vag ain't worth no car.'

Michelle's eyes went wide and she made a subtle gesture, shaking her hand across her neck, indicating for Kate to cease that conversation immediately. However, Kate didn't notice.

Kate shook her head. 'Sleeping with the boss is so fucking trashy.'

Rachel cleared her throat and frowned. It wasn't Rachel's usual disapproving frown, lips pressed together to form a thin line with the corners of her mouth slightly twitching downward. This time her eyebrows were furrowed, and her eyes glistened with a self conscious kind of hurt. 'The pay rise mightn't have anything to do with this girl seeing your boss.'

'Ummm.... actually, it has everything to do with it. And it's definitely the only reason why she's fucking him. He's disgusting. And he's married. He's like thirty years older than her, *really* overweight and has all this nose hair.' Kate screwed up her face and stuck out her tongue. 'The thought of *that* lying on top of me makes me puke a little in my mouth.'

Rachel sighed. What felt like a lifetime ago, Mike had been her boss. Well, to be precise, her boss' boss. She had worked in HR at a pharmaceutical company and he was the general manager of the Brisbane office. He was so good looking, in that ruggedly handsome, salt-and-pepper-hair, older man kind of way. The first time she saw him was her first day as a graduate HR officer. She had been shown around the office and was given a cursory introduction as they passed by his office. She had managed to utter a nervous sounding *nice to meet you*, but had actually felt a bit weak at the knees just looking at him. It had thankfully come across as though she was just a nervous kid on her first day in the real world of work. But that had definitely not been it. She had always considered hot older men to be unicorns; the George Clooney's of the world were fantasies that only existed in Hollywood. But Mike's gorgeous smile; those straight teeth, made to look even whiter against his tanned skin; the big rough hands that completely diminished her own when they shook; broad forearms showing below his rolled up sleeves, giving the impression of a muscular body hidden beneath the rest of his shirt – these things were not a fantasy. This was a beautiful man. She should have known better. She worked in HR, for goodness' sake. But she couldn't help herself.

They had kept it a secret for a while. At first it had been fun. Sneaking around, sharing looks as they passed each other in the halls. It had been – and was still – totally out of character for her. Rachel had always done the right thing. She'd always played by the rules; done what was expected of her; been the good girl, who never strayed from the path that she was expected to follow. Not this time though. And it felt great. Until it didn't.

Someone had seen them together, somewhere, sometime – they weren't sure who, or how that person knew – and rumours started to spread. It wasn't long before she was on the receiving end of contemptuous looks. Whispered voices would abruptly stop every time she entered a room. She had felt as though the whole world thought she was a slut. She had felt ostracised. Mike had assured her that it would all be fine. Once they were certain of where things were going, they could tell everyone. But there was no point if it turned out to be just a little fling. He wanted to be sure that he wasn't risking his reputation for something that would fizzle out after a couple of months. And once it was out in the open, there wouldn't be anything for people to whisper about. Everything would be okay.

But it hadn't quite worked that way. The company had a policy about office relationships, particularly relationships that weren't disclosed immediately. Mike had nearly lost his job. In the end, the easiest thing to do had been for her to quit.

Rachel had felt vindicated when their relationship had become serious, when they'd gotten engaged, married, had a baby. But Kate's gossip about the *hoe* that she worked with had touched a nerve with Rachel. She knew Kate wasn't taking aim at her. She knew that her friends would never think less of her because of it. She knew that Kate's big beef with the situation was the unknowing wife sitting in the background, while her dirt-bag husband disregarded their wedding vows – and her – just so he could get his rocks off. But knowing that didn't help Rachel. It still marred her perfect life with Mike, her perfect work history, her perfect reputation. And it still stung. Even after all these years.

Kate, still completely unaware of the relationship between the topic and Rachel's life, sniffed with indignation – she knew she was definitely right, and was a little miffed that her friends hadn't jumped-in in agreement. 'That's somebody's husband. And, if nothing else, it really lacks class.'

'Michelle!' A tall man waved and walk towards the women.

'Cute. Who is he?' Kate said quietly, wiggling her

eyebrows suggestively, but by that time the man was too close for Michelle to discreetly reply.

'Hi ladies. Look at you all – you haven't changed a bit.' He gestured around them. 'Fi Fi's done a great job, hasn't she?'

A look of recognition passed over Rachel's face – no one calls Fiona Fi Fi. 'My God, John! I didn't even recognise you!'

'It has been a very long time.'

Rachel hadn't seen Fiona's brother since Fi moved out of home at nineteen. At sixteen John had been awkwardly tall, with bad skin and the kind of puppy fat that made him look like a giant twelve year old.

'Michelle does give me updates on the three of you though.'

'John and I work on some projects together, so we see each other a fair bit.'

'You live in Sydney?' Kate seemed more interested in getting the waiter's attention to have her glass refilled, than she did on the conversation.

'Yeah, I moved there six months ago. Michelle has actually been great. She's introduced me to a heap of people and taken me to all the cool bars – not that I fit in at any of them.' He chuckled. 'It's great to have a real friend down there.' John, distracted, waved to someone inside the house. 'I've got to go help Dad with some drinks emergency. I'll catch up properly with you all later.'

As soon as he was out of ear shot, Rachel looked pointedly at Michelle, feeling gleeful at the thought of Michelle in a serious relationship – maybe even getting married – *and* with Fiona's brother. That would be just wonderful – perfect even. 'You're a *real friend*?'

'Does that mean like a sex friend?' Kate added, wrinkling her nose and wiggling her eyebrows.

'We're just friends. I'm seeing someone, remember?'

'Too bad. He's gotten really good looking.' Kate's attention was back on the conversation, now that she'd had her drink refilled.

'Are you seeing anyone, Kate?'

'Nope and I don't want to be.'

'Oh, really?'

'Really. Since Peter, I've had only one relationship. It lasted two months and we lived together. It was a huge mistake. Peter was a huge mistake. And, you know what, I like myself better single. I can do what I want, when I want and don't have to consider anyone else.'

'Just because things have gone badly in the past, doesn't mean you should give up. You just haven't found the one yet.' Rachel squeezed Kate's arm and looked at her friend, head tilted, eyes wide with sympathy.

Kate shrugged off Rachel's pity. 'That's not really it though. I'm happy. And I don't need a partner to validate me as a person. For some reason people seem to think that all women need a guy to make them happy. It's just completely untrue. I'm whole without a man. And having to compromise on being myself just for the sake of having someone to cuddle in bed at night just isn't worth it. Not for me, at least.'

Alex was dumbstruck. The thought of being alone terrified her. She couldn't imagine feeling so at peace with herself. And to want to be your own company all the time – you'd really need to like yourself a lot. Alex wasn't sure that she did. Who had that kind of confidence to be able to walk through life alone and be happy about it? Kate, that's who. Alex imagined how it would feel to be so sure of herself that she could just *be single*. It sounded really lonely but more than a little bit inspiring.

'So you'd be happy living a life of celibacy, is that what you're saying?' Michelle laughed – she wasn't buying a word of it. Michelle was a confident, self-sufficient, successful woman. And despite all that, before she had met Andrew she had longed for a partner. She felt with absolute certainty that no one preferred to be alone. She called bullshit.

'No. Definitely not. I'm saying I don't want a serious relationship. I still want to have flings and flirt.' Kate wrinkled her nose and wiggled her eyebrows. 'And fuck. That's fun. I just don't want the serious stuff.'

Rachel noticed the tension building between Michelle and Kate. Michelle clearly didn't believe Kate and Kate knew it. Rachel also thought that Kate's words were a show of bravado, but she was being a bit more discreet in her disbelief. She truly believed that Kate was in a bad place and needed their support not scepticism. Sensing this and Alex's reluctance to join the conversation at all, Rachel decided to lighten the mood a little.

'Do you guys remember when Alex had that huge crush on Troy?'

'Troy? Which one was Troy?' Michelle frowned trying to remember.

'Oh my God! How could you forget? Troy Ward. Remember that time at the rock pools?' Kate's voice was full of mock outrage. 'I was scared out of my mind! The whole fiasco is permanently imprinted on my brain.'

Michelle laughed, 'It is hard to remember all of Alex's

crushes. I don't think I could even keep up with them at the time.'

Alex's face went red with embarrassment, but she was laughing as well. Her earlier apprehension was easily waning with the conversation. 'I wasn't that bad, really.'

'You were totally boy crazy. A complete fiend,' Kate laughed as she grabbed a new glass of wine from a passing waiter.

'The boys were just as crazy for Alex.' Rachel looked at Alex, one eyebrow arched and gave her a knowing smile.

Kate remembered it all too well. She'd been such an ugly duckling in high school. And Alex had been the gorgeous one; the confident, vivacious girl, with perfect olive skin (so unlike Kate's natural pasty, freckly skin), who boys went completely berserk for. Kate loved Alex dearly but had always been so jealous of her and had felt totally overshadowed by Alex's confidence and popularity. Things had changed so much since then.

'What happened at the rock pools?' Michelle asked.

'Troy and his friends were jumping off the waterfall. I wanted to seem cool, so I convinced Kate that we could jump off too.'

'Seriously Michelle, how do you not remember this?' Kate took another long sip of her wine. 'You did it too. One of the guys – I can't remember which one – said you were too chicken. So you climbed up, ahead of everyone else, and jumped. Meanwhile, I'd already agreed to be Alex's moral support. We got to the top and the guys were all doing flips and stuff into the water. Alex jumped –'

'And I lost my bikini top when I hit the water. I was so embarrassed!'

'I don't remember that bit,' Rachel chimed in.

'Because I recovered it pretty quickly. Troy saw, which I think may have been the only reason he ended up asking me out,' Alex laughed.

Kate continued, 'And there I was stuck at the top by myself. It was so high. I was so scared, I couldn't move.'

'Oh I remember now!' Michelle exclaimed. 'You were up there for ages. You wouldn't jump and you wouldn't climb down. How did you end up getting down?'

'Rachel came up. She tried to convince me to climb down, but I just couldn't do it. I was shaking so much.' Kate smiled to herself at the memory. Rachel had always been such a good friend. It was so sad that they hadn't all stayed close; Rachel was still that concerned, selfless friend that she had loved back then. Kate felt a warmth growing at the thought that maybe the engagement party would rekindle their friendship. She missed them – really missed them – and hadn't really realised until that moment.

'Eventually I convinced you to jump.'

'Yeah, we jumped in holding hands. I was so scared I think I actually peed a bit.'

'What happened to Troy? We used to hang out with those guys all the time,' Michelle said.

'He knocked up Chastity Myers straight after high school. I think they've got a few kids together. Pretty sure they're divorced now though,' Kate shrugged.

'That right,' Michelle exclaimed. 'Didn't he end up breaking up with you, Alex, because he'd gotten Chastity pregnant? What a dickhead.' Michelle shook her head slowly. 'You totally dodged a bullet there.'

'Chastity. What a fucking joke. Least chaste girl I've ever fucking met,' Kate muttered.

Kate kept calling the waiter over to refill their glasses. Neither Alex nor Rachel was accustomed to drinking much at all. Thankfully both of them were sensible enough to refrain from going round for round with Kate. Nevertheless, they were both getting quite tipsy. Michelle was drinking pretty heavily, though that was standard for her, and didn't make a dent in her outward appearance. Kate was also well accustomed to drinking excessively, so the effects of so much alcohol were gradual; she was slowly but steadily getting louder and laughing more.

'Do you guys remember that time Michelle challenged that guy to a push up contest?' Kate laughed. She was enjoying reminiscing about the good old days, remembering why they all became friends in the first place. She was, of course, glossing over some of the less favourable memories and some of the frankly horrendous times that occurred in their teen years. But who didn't have some angst ridden teenage memories, full of stupid decisions and regret?

'Push up contest? Let me guess, Michelle won,' John said, sidling up to Michelle and giving her a friendly nudge with his elbow. 'You've never been one to lose anything,' he said with a cheeky grin.

Kate looked at Michelle slyly and raised an eyebrow. There was no way nothing was going on between those two.

'Nope, she didn't win. It was a dismal loss, in fact,' Kate replied, cheerily.

An indignant look came across Michelle's face. The loss still stung a little (as with any occasion where she wasn't the victor), but, even she would admit, it was funny. 'It wasn't a dismal loss. He misrepresented himself because he wanted to be challenged.'

'Because there's nothing manlier than beating a girl at doing push ups?' John chuckled. Michelle was never a gracious loser.

'Because he wanted an excuse to take his shirt off,' Michelle retorted, indignant.

'Well, if I remember correctly, his strategy worked.' Kate laughed and gave Alex a mischievous grin. 'Right, Alex?'

Alex had drunk enough by this point that she had relaxed and felt quite comfortable. So much so, that she seemed to momentarily slip back into the role she had played in the group as a teenager; a persona that she hadn't worn in many, many years. The old, confident Alex was boy crazy – completely in love with being in love, funny and a little sassy. Since then Alex hadn't so much grown out of being these things, but she herself had faded, she was now a shadow of her former self. But not in that moment; that night at the engagement party, as the alcohol created a little buzz and she laughed with her friends, Alex had a feeling of ease growing within herself – a confidence – and it felt good. Momentarily, Alex remembered why she loved these girls: they were fun, made her feel good and when she was with them she had just a little bit more love for herself.

A slight pink came to Alex's cheeks, a twinkle in her eyes, she smiled deviously and shrugged. 'He had a six pack.'

Kate laughed heartily and as she did, she caught John's eye

and he gave her a warm, goofy smile. Something seemed to shift inside her. Kate felt her breath catch in her chest and a glowing warmth swelling inside her. This was a feeling that Kate hadn't had for the better part of a decade. She liked this guy – properly liked him. There something about him. This felt like much more than a crush. But that was crazy. He seemed to have something going on with Michelle. And he was Fiona's brother. And she didn't even know him – certainly not well enough to have proper feelings for him. But more importantly, Kate was happily single. Relationships only ended in compromising parts of yourself that never should be compromised. They led to hurt feelings and, ultimately for Kate, disaster. That was not something she needed in her life ever again. And definitely not with the Fi and Michelle complications. Although, that did pretty much guarantee that anything with John would never get far enough to be disastrous. Either way, Kate pushed the feeling aside and tried to forget about it.

****

'Mmmm... he's cute!' Kate gestured towards the young man she'd been eyeballing for the last five minutes.

'The one with the stubble and the really tight jeans? He's about twenty,' Rachel said, horrified.

'Who cares how old he is. He's hot and I'm single.' Kate downed the remainder of her nearly full glass of wine. 'I'm going to talk to him.' She walked off grabbing a fresh glass on her way.

Rachel had an apprehensive look on her face as she watched Kate walk away. 'I'm really worried about her.'

'You're right to be worried. She's a train wreck waiting to happen,' Michelle looked equally as concerned.

'What are you talking about? She looks amazing! And she looks like she'll be going home with that hot guy.' Alex burst out, seemingly out of character, given how restrained she'd seemed all night. 'Sorry. Maybe you're right. But she seems like she's just having fun.'

'Maybe it's just a little fun, but she's had way too much to drink. And, honestly, I think it's a coping mechanism.' Rachel's piercing gaze moved to Alex. She was concerned about Kate, but her instincts (and her natural impulse to meddle) were also telling her that Alex's response was cause for alarm. And why was Alex so quiet and distant? She'd always been the life of the party and – apart from a brief glimpse of the old Alex as they reminisced about boys – she no longer seemed to be able to even muster a genuine smile. Focus, Rachel. One problem at a time.

CHAPTER SIX

Kate woke the next day with a feeling that she knew all too well. Her head felt foggy and besieged with a dull ache that wasn't going to subside any time soon; her mouth was dry and tasted revolting and a little bit furry; her stomach was churning in a way that told her that food would fix everything, but she knew from past experience that that was a lie. Kate rolled over and barely managed to part her eyelids enough to see – her mascara and fake eyelashes sticking her eyelids closed. And then fragments of memories from the night before began to hit her.

'Oh, God,' Kate muttered into the pillow.

'Hey.'

Oh no! What is this guy's name? He looks way younger than I remember. How many people saw me leaving with him last night? Kate felt regret welling in her stomach, along with bile. Then she noticed something else. Her ankle was throbbing.

'Ahh...Is it ok if you give me a lift home?' *I have no idea where I am, and I probably can't afford the cab fare.*

'Sure.' The nameless man-boy pulled on a pair of shorts. 'How's the ankle feeling?'

'Not great. I can't quite remember...' Kate searched for a

less embarrassing way to ask what in God's name had happened last night.

'You fell down the stairs.'

Suddenly an image came back to her – lying in a heap on the lawn at Fiona's parents' house, with a crowd looking down at her. She'd fallen down the two stairs that ran the length of the deck. *God, I hope I didn't flash everyone.* It would be that absolute epitome of embarrassment if – on top of being a fall-down-drunk mess – Fiona's father had seen her vagina. Why had she chosen to wear such skimpy underwear?

'Those stairs are really dangerous. They should have a handrail,' Kate said quietly, equal parts embarrassed and annoyed.

Kate dressed quickly and grabbed her things. She carried her shoes in her hand, in the hope that the stiletto that had broken in her fall the night before could be fixed. Kate limped after her nameless companion from the bedroom, through the house to the garage. It was quite clear that he lived with his parents. Kate was sure that she would feel ashamed later, but right now her horrendous hangover was taking up all of her energy. She noticed the P plates on the car. *How old was this kid?*

'So, ahhh, how do you know Isaac and Fiona?' Kate buckled her seatbelt and wished that she'd put sunglasses in her bag.

'Isaac is my uncle.'

No hangover was big enough to stop the shame onslaught that that response elicited.

'How old are you?' Kate didn't really want to know the

answer, but the question had popped out of her mouth before she could think.

'Ummmm...yeah, I lied last night. I'm actually nineteen.'

Kate remained silent for the rest of the car ride, with the exception of a few words to provide her driver with directions.

How many people saw me with this kid? How bad is my ankle? Did I do anything else that I need to be worried about? What the fuck am I doing with my life? What am I doing with my life?

As Kate got out of the car, she decided that she needed to spend the day lying in bed, wallowing in her hangover and humiliation. Just as she was getting comfortable in bed, her phone rang. Rachel.

Kate had an internal conflict over whether she should answer the phone. She really wanted to know how bad the situation was – how much she'd embarrassed herself – but at the same time she didn't think she was currently in a state to handle examining her loss of dignity. Curiosity won out in the end.

'Hello.'

'Hi Kate, it's Rachel. Michelle told me about your ankle. I was just calling to find out how it is.'

'Pretty sore, but it's ok, I think.'

'What did the doctor say?'

Doctor? It's 11am on a Sunday. When would I have gone to the doctor?

Kate's silence forced Rachel to prompt further. 'You did make it to the hospital last night, didn't you?'

Kate wracked her brain. She was certain she didn't go to hospital. There's no way she could have forgotten a whole hospital trip. Plus she was sure a hospital would have at least bandaged her ankle. Sure, she'd forgotten a few things from the night before, but she hadn't been completely black-out-drunk.

'No, I didn't go to hospital. My ankle was feeling a lot better and I didn't want to wait around half the night in emergency.'

'Kate, I'm really worried about you,' Rachel paused, slightly uncomfortable to be having this discussion. She cleared her throat and continued. 'We – that is, Michelle and I – are worried that Fiona's engagement has brought up bad memories for you. No one would blame you if you weren't entirely happy for Fiona, given your situation.'

'My situation? You can say divorce – it's not a dirty word.' Kate barely stifled a laugh. 'I was married to a cockhead. I don't want to be married. Why would I be jealous of Fiona?'

'Well, if you're sure.' Rachel was clearly not convinced. 'Michelle and I were going to catch up for lunch today. Would you like to join us?'

Kate felt terrible and the thought of leaving bed didn't particularly excite her. But she was painfully curious about just how much she had embarrassed herself last night.

'Argh, ok. Where and when should I meet you?'

As she hung up the phone, Kate wondered what her friends thought of her. She was amazed that they actually believed she would be jealous of Fiona getting married. She had been there, done that. It didn't work. She may not have her shit together, but she was much happier without Peter in her life. If she was jealous of anyone, it was Alex. She would have given anything – except maybe single life – to have travelled. Kate never had enough money to do anything. She had been overseas once with Peter. A trip to Thailand when she was twenty was now a distant memory. She longed to see the lights of Paris, to dine in fancy restaurants in London, to shop in New York, to lie on a beach in the Maldives, to dance at a beach party in Goa, to go snowboarding in Japan. Alex was the one who was living the life that Kate had been destined for. Amazing holidays paid for by a rich husband. That was the kind of husband Kate was jealous of – one that provided finance for everything that she could want. And if Kate could have that kind of life without the husband, that would be even better.

Her marriage to Peter had been a huge mistake. They had been together since they were fifteen, engaged at twenty and married by twenty-one. Kate had been so wrapped up in the romance of it all when Peter had got down on one knee on the beach at Phi Phi, she hadn't really considered whether it was a good idea or even if it was what she wanted.

By the time they were in their late twenties it was clear that they wanted different things from life. They had nothing in common. Their every interaction felt strained. The next few years were spent trying to make it work; trying to get along and find some sort of common ground. Neither of them were happy but neither of them had the courage to end it.

Kate's thirty-second birthday was the day their relationship finally ended. At that point in time they had been trying hard for a number of years to make the marriage work, or so Kate thought. In a last ditch attempt to repair something that seemed to fundamentally not work, they had begun marriage counselling.

Following prompts from the counsellor, Peter was making

an effort for Kate's birthday. He had forgone working late for once and had come home early to Kate. Peter greeted her with a long kiss, which was unusual for him. As she got ready to go out to the dinner they had planned with friends, Kate began to wonder if possibly things would get better with Peter. Sure, they didn't see eye-to-eye on having children and she could never understand why he was so dedicated to his job. But despite all that, she did love him and maybe the counselling was working. If you love someone, nothing else matters, right?

While Peter was out picking up the cake from the bakery before it shut, Kate applied her makeup and daydreamed about them getting back to the way they used to be. Kate could hear Peter's phone ringing. He was always so absent minded, it wasn't unusual for him to forget his phone. Kate rushed to pick it up but missed the call. But right there on the screen was a text message from someone named Jessica. The whole message previewed on the screen. Kate didn't even need to open the text to see the end of her marriage.

Can't believe u ditched me for that bitch's b'day. Looking fwd 2 u making it up to me tmw. Love u

Love u. Love you. Love you. Jessica loves my husband. That was the part that stood out to Kate. Peter was cheating on her. But, more than that, they loved each other. After almost two decades together, two words – one of them not even a real word, just a letter – were enough to finally and permanently end it.

Everyone who knew Kate had heard the story a thousand times. How clichéd it was to find out the way she did. And how it had happened on her birthday. And how Peter had kissed her properly that night for the first time in years. And her musings about whether Peter had left his phone behind that night – maybe even on a subconscious level – because he wanted to be found out.

Everyone who knew her thought that she was having a meltdown in the months following her thirty-second birthday. Her mother claimed that she'd never liked Peter in the first place and that they had gotten married far too young. Kate knew her mother's heart was in the right place, but found it hard to not snap 'If it was so fucking clear to you, why didn't you tell *me*?' every time her mother said it.

A part of Kate felt glad that Peter had cheated, simply because it was the catalyst that finally ended their terrible marriage; but a much bigger part of her hated him for ruining their relationship and betraying her trust so devastatingly.

Kate had never done much of anything while she was with Peter. Their trip to Thailand being the only thing that Kate felt was noteworthy. She never drank or partied, bought herself nice things or even bothered making much of an effort with her appearance – their mortgage and strict budget didn't really allow for any of that.

In the two years since they had separated, Kate had begun a journey to experience the things that she'd forgone. She now partied a lot and prioritised her appearance above almost everything else. She had always been slender, but she'd lost five kilos and was now gaunt. Her mother constantly worried that Kate had an eating disorder. She didn't though – she just didn't care to waste money on food, when it could be spent on clothes and alcohol.

Kate had also discovered men. At the age of thirty-two, she had only ever slept with one man. At the age of thirty-four, she would need to sit down with a calculator to tally the number, but she wouldn't be able to list the names.

She knew it made her seem vapid to care so much about appearance and fashion and men, but she didn't really care if people thought she was vapid. She knew she wasn't. She knew that she was a woman of substance, no matter what other people thought of her.

Despite all the suspicion that Kate was suffering some sort of breakdown, she felt liberated. She was making up for lost time; doing exactly what she wanted – at least, what she wanted within the confines of her credit card limit. Kate had honestly never felt so good in all her life, which is why she was baffled – and slightly offended – that her friends thought she was jealous of Fiona getting married.

Kate quickly showered, dressed and put on her makeup. Her head was still pounding and her ankle throbbing when she left for lunch. Maybe she *should* see a doctor.

Michelle and Rachel sat at a table out the front of the cafe. The street was always bustling with shoppers, pedestrians and other cafe goers, which made these tables prime for people watching. Kate approached with a limp. Her long legs accentuated by her high waisted cut-off denim shorts, sandals showing her perfectly painted toes. Oversized sunglasses managed to hide the bags under Kate's eyes, and disguised her hangover reasonably well.

'Hey.' Kate flung her enormous handbag on the floor and flopped onto a chair.

'How are you feeling?' Rachel's voice was full of concern.

'Okay. My ankle is a little sore, but I'll live.'

Michelle gave Kate a knowing smile. 'I'm amazed that you're feeling up to lunch. You were pretty crazy last night.'

'Hmmm...' As curious as Kate was about what actually had transpired the night before, this conversation was making her uncomfortable. She needed to work her way up to hearing all the gory details. 'Where's Alex?'

'She had an early flight back to Sydney.'

After the waiter took their coffee order, Rachel leaned in. 'So tell us – did anything happen with John last night?'

John? Is that the kid's name? 'Umm... Nope.'

'If you want, I can suss him out next time I see him,' Michelle added.

What is she talking about? How does she know that kid? And why would I want to see him again? He's a child!

Michelle registered the confusion on Kate's face. 'He lives in Sydney. I do some work for his company.' She spoke slowly, as though she was talking to a dimwit.

It slowly dawned on Kate. She meant Fiona's brother. 'Oh, no! He's cute, but I can't hook up with Fi's brother.'

'I don't think Fi would mind,' Rachel said with a mischievous smile.

'Really?' Kate clearly didn't believe her. 'You think Fi would be fine if I slept with her brother?'

'I think Fi would be okay with you dating her brother.'

'Dating? I have no intention of dating anyone. I'm happily single, thank you very much. I'm not interested.'

'Well, you seemed pretty interested last night.' Rachel raised her eyebrows knowingly.

'Ugh. What did I do?' Resigned to a fate of humiliation,

there was no use avoiding it; she just wanted to know exactly what she had to be embarrassed about.

'Nothing really.' Rachel was holding back.

'Pfft! Nothing?' Michelle leaned in and turned to face Kate. 'You and John were flirting pretty hard.'

Fragments of memories began to come back to Kate. John gently – subtly – brushing his hand against her arm as he said something, making her feel all hot and bothered; her drinking; him smiling his gorgeous smile; her drinking; him being sexy as all hell; her saying something about her underwear – oh God!; him saying something interesting, though she couldn't remember what, but she definitely had a strong recollection of him being interesting and smart; her drinking and laughing. Loud laughing. Throw your head back laughing. Obnoxious laughing.

'Did I make a total fool of myself?'

Michelle and Rachel both answered at once. Rachel, 'No.' Michelle, 'Yes.'

Kate rolled her eyes and turned to face Michelle. 'Just give it to me straight – exactly what happened.'

Rachel began, 'You and John were flirting. You were drinking quite a lot. But I'm not sure exactly what you two were saying to each other. You seemed really cosy, but I don't think that there was anything to be embarrassed about. Not that I saw anyway.'

'Falling off the deck's a bit embarrassing though,' Michelle said as she pulled a face.

'How did that happen? I'd already left by then. Michelle only told me you'd hurt your ankle, she didn't say how.'

Kate shrugged and looked at Michelle for answers.

'Kate, do you seriously not remember anything from last night? How drunk were you?'

'Just tell me what happened,' Kate said impatiently.

'You were flirting with that kid –'

'Hayden,' Rachel interrupted.

'Yeah, Hayden – and you were –'

Kate now interrupted, 'Wait. I was flirting with John *and* Hayden? I was really on fire, wasn't I?'

'To be fair, you were chatting to the kid pretty early on in the night, but nothing serious. You spent most of the night with John. But when he left to drive his grandma home, you started flirting pretty hard with Hayden.' Michelle paused. 'You were really drunk by then, though.'

Kate groaned, put her elbows on the table and pressed her forehead into her hands.

'At least John wasn't there to see you flirting with Hayden.' Rachel patted Kate's arm reassuringly, then turned to Michelle. 'He wasn't, was he?' The corners of Rachel's mouth twitched down slightly in her trademark disapproving, slightly judgemental (in a caring kind of way) frown, which she was attempting to hide from Kate; right now Kate needed a sympathetic friend, not disapproval.

Michelle shook her head, trying hard to suppress a grin.

Suddenly Kate looked up. 'Hang on. He drove his grandmother home? So he was sober?'

'Yeah,' Michelle said very slowly and grimaced. Michelle paused while the waiter served their coffees. 'So, you were talking with that kid, then – I think – you decided to demonstrate how good you are at walking in heels. Apparently you're not as good at it as you think,' Michelle took a deep breath, trying to contain her laughter, 'but to be fair, you did make it look pretty easy right up to the point you fell off the edge of the deck.'

'Oh, honey, that deck has always been super dangerous. It looks great, but without any railings, someone was bound to fall off it one day.' Rachel patted Kate's arm again.

'So I was just walking on the deck and fell? That doesn't sound too bad.'

'You were trying to walk along the edge of the deck like it was a tightrope. I think you said that you could walk a tightrope in stilettos and that you probably should run away and join the circus.'

'You seem to be taking some sort of perverse pleasure in my humiliation.'

Michelle could no longer contain it and began shaking with laughter, snorting a few times before controlling herself enough to speak. 'Sorry, but it is actually hilarious.'

'Thanks.'

CHAPTER SEVEN

'Good morning,' Alex said brightly as she walked into through the front door.

'Morning.' Daniel barely glanced up from his laptop. 'How was the trip?'

'Really good, actually. It was so nice to catch up with the girls. I never really realised before how much I've missed them.' Alex spoke quickly, excitedly. 'How was your weekend?'

'Hmmmm,' Daniel said, clearly not listening.

'Do you feel like breakfast? I was thinking that we could go to that new cafe on Elizabeth Street. I really feel like bacon.'

This got Daniel's attention. He turned from his laptop towards Alex, with a look of displeasure on his face. 'You don't need bacon. I thought you decided you were going to lose weight. You drinking last night won't have helped either.' Daniel pointedly looked her up and down. 'Maybe you should go to the gym this morning instead.'

Alex's shoulders dropped, her smile froze and slowly dissipated; her cheerful mood seemed to vaporise almost instantly. Alex folded her arms instinctively across her stomach – a reaction that had been second nature to her for a long time – in an attempt to hide her plump belly.

'Yeah, that's a good idea. I'll go to the gym.' Alex's voice was quiet, dejected. A stark contrast to what it had been only moments earlier.

Alex considered Daniel to be the most attractive man she'd ever met. His bright blue eyes with long black eyelashes gave him a young, innocent quality, and those eyes were still mesmerising even after three years of marriage. His strong jaw line gave a sense of masculinity to his otherwise boyish facial features. His dark blonde, wavy hair and bronze skin made him look like a surfer, though he didn't actually go to the beach at all. What Alex failed to recognise was Daniel's size – what had started out as a little bit of podge around his middle had turned into a full blown beer gut; he could easily rival a full term pregnant woman in stomach size. Even if Alex ever noticed this, it wouldn't make a difference – Daniel was still extremely attractive to her and a little bit of extra padding around the middle would never change the way she felt about him.

Alex took her bags into the bedroom and changed for the gym. Standing in her gym clothes, she assessed herself in the mirror, critiquing every inch of herself. She thought that Daniel was right – she was disgustingly overweight. It was truly amazing that he could love her given the way she looked. Alex imagined the way Kate had looked the night before; she pinched her belly fat, stood on her tip-toes and imagined Kate standing next to her, with Kate's legs reaching Alex's armpits and Kate's thighs being smaller than Alex's flabby, tuckshop lady arms (which was certainly an exaggeration created by Alex's imagination). Alex's shoulders slumped. She pinched her belly fat again. Hard. She was disgusting. Hideous.

To anyone else looking, disgusting would not be the word used to describe Alex. Sure, she wasn't slim, but her slightly larger frame would not evoke such a response from anyone with perspective. Daniel had unrealistic expectations and Alex took his criticism on board and made it her own.

Alex thought back to the conversations from the night before about all the boys she had chased, crushed on and dated. She wondered if she had always been this unattractive. Boys did used to like her. She was sure of it. When did it happen that she became ugly, fat and... old? Maybe she had always been this way (apart from the old bit, of course). Maybe all those boys back then had only liked her because they thought she put out. It was certainly possible. Teenage boys would do anything to get laid, including dating a fatty. Alex figured it didn't matter anyway. Either way, she was fat now. And Daniel didn't love her properly because of it. And that's all that was relevant to her life right now.

CHAPTER EIGHT

Michelle walked from the elevator to her office. She passed Sarah as she walked through the door. Sarah's round belly elicited a pang of longing in Michelle. Yearning. Emptiness. It was too early in the day for this and she felt overwhelmed by these sudden emotions. It wasn't the first time. And it was just so clichéd; admitting these feelings to herself weighed her down with self-betrayal.

She was jealous. Jealous of Sarah's growing belly. Jealous of all the pregnant women that she saw on the street. Jealous of all the women who had babies. Jealous of Rachel. Jealous of Rachel! Rachel: the woman who had wasted her talents – her life – on having a family. Rachel, who could have done so much more; could have been so much more. Michelle felt sorry for Rachel, being stuck at home with no goals or career; it just didn't make sense that Michelle could feel some sort of – envy, she supposed – of Rachel's life.

Michelle wished that her belly was growing rounder every day. She wished that she could feel movement – kicks – inside herself. She could imagine hearing a heartbeat on a monitor; feeling an inexplicable, undeniable love for a person that she had never met.

When Sarah had announced her pregnancy, Michelle's

reaction had appeared exactly as it should have. She congratulated Sarah and was warm and chatted about the exciting times ahead. Michelle had been the perfect example of a boss reacting to such news. HR would have been proud. Inwardly, however, Michelle had been shocked. Annoyed at the inconvenience. Annoyed at herself for the jealousy she felt. Painfully aware of her own ticking biological clock.

The next time they met on the subject was a different story. Michelle had begun to explore this jealousy and the resulting meeting was far from the realm of what HR would deem appropriate. Michelle had been terse, blunt and outright rude, firing questions at Sarah about the timing of her leave. Pushing with questions that couldn't yet be answered. Her tone full of hostility. 'We need to know when you'll go on leave. You'll need to provide us with an end date, and we must stick to it. And you really can't be doing this job if you're unwell, so you'll need to factor that in to your decision. We can't have you changing your end date because you're not feeling well. We'd rather you took your leave early than have you calling in sick, so please make sure you choose your end date wisely.' Michelle was completely unprofessional, which was very much unlike her. She came across as a bitter woman, which was completely out of character and yet completely accurate.

In the nearly six months since that meeting, Michelle had researched IVF and sperm donation. She'd weighed up pros and cons. She'd debated the subject over and over and over again in her head. And met Andrew.

Andrew complicated the decision – the decision that was already the most complex problem solving exercise she'd ever undertaken. She loved Andrew. Maybe. He was a really great guy and he was so supportive of her and he was successful. They were so happy together. Was she really willing to give that up for a baby? She had waited her whole life to find a guy like Andrew and now was she really going to throw it away? Being a single mother and balancing a career was of course another major consideration for Michelle. With her business expanding, it would be terrible timing. But was there ever a right time? She also had to consider how this could impact any future relationships. The decision would surely end things between her and Andrew, which was honestly the only thing really holding her back. How do you tell someone you've only just started dating that you're going to get yourself pregnant and you'd like to keep dating? It was the plot to a clichéd romantic comedy, but in real life she wouldn't end up getting the guy. Was there actually potential for a baby with Andrew? Was it worth the gamble? She wasn't getting any younger. What if, in two years' time, she and Andrew broke up? She'd be two years older and exponentially further from being able to conceive.

With all these what ifs, she hadn't actually broached the subject with Andrew. Or anyone else, for that matter. Michelle wasn't accustomed to needing help in making a decision. In business, she sought the opinion of experts when it came to things like the accounting and the legal side of things, but she always ultimately made the decision herself. And that wasn't a responsibility that she had ever shied away from. With this decision, she had the facts, which was usually enough. But this time she wasn't sure.

As she walked out of her office for the day, she wrestled

with the idea of discussing children with Andrew. This had been a problem that she'd struggled with for months. Just having the conversation was an incredibly difficult decision. She – surprisingly – had always avoided commitment related conversations when dating. She'd never been lucky in love, so she tended to try to delay an inevitable breakup by postponing discussions that may just make a man run in the opposite direction. It seemed to her to be a logical approach, rather than a weak one. This time though, she felt she should bite the bullet and have the conversation. If breaking up was just a foregone conclusion (which, deep down, she felt it almost certainly was... maybe), the *tick tock* told her that she needed to know sooner. But her heart told her otherwise.

Michelle and Andrew sat on cushions on the floor at a low table at a new Japanese tapas fusion restaurant. Michelle had made up her mind – they were going to have the discussion. And when Michelle had her mind set on something, there was no beating around the bush – she would lay her cards on the table. If this meant it was over between her and Andrew, so be it.

'I know we haven't been together long, but I think that I need to be straight with you about what I want.' She paused briefly. 'There's no point in either of us wasting our time if we aren't after the same thing.' She paused again, deftly picked up a piece of sashimi with her chopsticks and popped it into her mouth. Michelle wanted to give him the opportunity to interject and opt out – she didn't want to have this conversation if he wasn't even interested in hearing her out. He remained silent and waited for her to continue. 'I want children. And I'm not getting any younger. Statistically speaking, I should aim to fall pregnant within the next year or so. After thirty-five, fertility decreases, and the rate of miscarriage and Down syndrome increases significantly.'

There was a long pause before Andrew finally spoke. Michelle held back the urge to keep talking – to give him the statistics and babble about the risks, the likelihood of multiple births and the research she'd done on IVF.

'Michelle, I really do love you, but I don't think I'm ready for that kind of commitment. But I can't tell you how I'll be feeling in a year's time.'

'Do you want kids?'

'Yeah.' He shrugged noncommittally.

'The logical answer is that I begin trying to conceive now. With or without you.' Michelle had emotionally tapped out of the conversation and was just talking facts now. 'It can easily take more than a year to fall pregnant, which I need to anticipate given my age. And if I want to get pregnant before thirty-five, it just makes sense.'

He took a moment to process. 'But logic also tells you that you're not going to become suddenly barren overnight on your thirty-fifth birthday. So giving it a few months is unlikely to do any harm.'

Andrew was a good match for Michelle. He understood that this was a decision that needed to be made with the heart and the head. He understood her position and wasn't going to run away from it. Nor was he going to jump in if it wasn't exactly what he wanted too.

'Why don't we reassess in two months' time? That will give us both time to decide if this is what we want. You need to think about it too. You shouldn't let wanting a baby dictate who you're bound to for the rest of your life. You need to be certain that you actually want me too. Not just a baby.'

Michelle had already considered that point. And she was still unsure if she wanted Andrew. But the point of this conversation was to find out what he wanted. She had assumed that it would be far too soon for him and he would jump ship immediately. His response had thrown her a little. Now she would need to do a lot more soul searching about what she really wanted.

CHAPTER NINE

'Why, all of a sudden, are you such good friends with this woman that you need to go out for drinks? If she's that important, why haven't I ever heard you mention her before?' Daniel spoke to Alex like he was talking to a naughty child.

'Well, yes.' Alex didn't know how to justify this to Daniel. She just wanted to have drinks with Michelle. Did she really need a reason? 'I guess I didn't mention her because I haven't seen her in so long.' She knew for a fact that she'd spoken about Michelle to Daniel many times. But Alex lied to save him the embarrassment. Or maybe to keep him calm. Or maybe both.

'And is this the shit that you get up to while I'm away *working*? Do I need to be worried while I'm at work that you're going out drinking all night and getting up to God knows what?'

'No, I tell you everything.' Alex couldn't meet Daniel's cold stare. 'Why don't you come too? I know Michelle would love to meet you. She could bring along her boyfriend and we could make it a double date.' Alex sounded chipper but her eyes told a different story; they stung with unshed tears, her eyebrows knotted together in a pleading frown, begging him to let her to do just this one little thing – just this once.

'Well, I don't really want to waste a night on this. If you have to go, maybe I'll stop by the bar and say hello.'

****

Seeing the girls at the engagement party had reminded Alex of what it was like to have friends; to have fun. And seeing Kate made Alex want to be just like her. She knew in her heart of hearts that she'd never look that good. But the way that Kate looked, the way men looked at her and the way she exuded confidence had Alex daydreaming of being like that – of being *that* girl.

In a bid to emulate Kate – but only in a very small way – Alex had decided to wear bright red lipstick. She wore a plain black dress and low black heels – an outfit that she'd worn a thousand times before. But she felt a little sparkle within herself – a small spring in her step – wearing the lipstick.

The open-air bar was packed with an after-work crowd who all seemed determined to soak up the sunlight afforded by the long summer days. Alex clumsily negotiated her way through the mass of people, narrowly avoiding wearing a few patrons' drinks in the process. After a full ten minutes of searching, she finally found Michelle sitting at a table in the corner. Michelle had clearly just come from work. She was wearing a semi-sheer white silk blouse, a grey pencil skirt with the matching jacket flung over the other chair at the table, and a pair of towering black heels, adding to Michelle's already intimidating height.

Michelle grabbed her jacket from the chair. 'Here, I saved

you a seat.' She pulled a wine bottle from an ice bucket on the table and poured a glass for Alex.

'You look really good.'

Alex blushed and smiled. 'Thanks.'

Michelle was amazed at the transformation in Alex. She wasn't quite looking like the old Alex, but her eyes were brighter and her smile a little less nervous and a little more genuine. Michelle wondered if maybe Alex had just been feeling a little off at the engagement party. Maybe she hadn't changed as drastically as Michelle had first thought.

The two women quickly polished off the bottle of wine and bought another. As they poured themselves drinks from the new bottle, Daniel spotted them.

As he approached, Michelle took the opportunity to survey him. She was surprised and a little impressed that Daniel was everything that Alex had said he was. He was gorgeous; a little overweight, but gorgeous nonetheless. She thought that Daniel was completely out of this Alex's league and then immediately chastised herself for thinking that about her friend. Alex was beautiful, she just seemed to lack the confidence she used to have. Alex's laughter and smile had been what made Alex so attractive; although she did seem much happier tonight, she still wasn't quite like she used to be. But then again, were any of them quite the same as they had been a decade ago?

As Daniel got closer, it became obvious that he was annoyed and very drunk. He immediately launched without engaging in any pleasantries, 'Why don't you ever answer your fucking phone? I've been looking for you for ages.'

Alex's cheeks flushed and she suddenly seemed nervous

and embarrassed. 'Uhh... Sorry. I mustn't have heard it over all the noise.' She paused briefly, 'This is Michelle. Michelle, this is Daniel.'

'Hi. It's nice to finally meet you.' Michelle extended her hand, which Daniel ignored.

Daniel reached across the table and grabbed Alex's drink, which he proceeded to finish off and pour himself another.

'You look different.' Daniel's eyes narrowed as he scrutinised her appearance.

Alex's hand instinctively darted to her face and hovered in front of her mouth, conscious of the lipstick.

Daniel shrugged and turned his attention to Michelle. 'So what do you do?' This was an interrogation, not a social chat to get to know his wife's friend. He wanted to know if this woman was worthy of his time. Not that that was likely – what woman was? He wanted ammunition against Michelle that he would use to justify why *his* wife shouldn't be spending any more time with this woman.

'I'm in marketing.'

'What type of marketing? Like TV ads or something?'

'No, that would be advertising.' Michelle's tone was a little terse. This guy might be Alex's husband, but he was really drunk and seemed like a dick. 'My business specialises in indirect marketing. We do a small amount of direct marketing, but for a TV ad, we would work with an advertising agency.'

Daniel wasn't really listening. Essentially, this Amazonian woman was using a lot of redundant words just to say that she sold stuff. He'd met these kinds of people before. They work in some flaky business that seems to be based on dressing well in trendy clothes (not that she did), seeming cool (not that she did), getting drunk and talking vague shit about harnessing consumer interest and creating demand. Based on what he could see of this woman, she obviously couldn't be very successful – she simply wasn't good looking or cool enough.

Daniel abruptly turned to Alex. 'Lipstick. That's what's different about you. There's some saying about that, isn't there? Something about putting makeup on pigs.' Daniel laughed heartily at his own joke.

Alex cringed and her eyes began to water slightly. Michelle's jaw muscles visibly clenched, her eyes narrowed and she glared at Daniel.

Daniel looked from one woman to the other, clearly bewildered that neither of them thought his joke was funny. 'Well, I'd better be off. I wasted so much time looking for you – I really hadn't planned on staying long in the first place.' Daniel wandered off into the crowd.

'Alex.' Michelle looked at Alex, a little lost for words.

'I'm so embarrassed. What a terrible first impression. He's never usually like that. He's just really drunk.' Alex clearly flustered, grabbed a tissue from her handbag to wipe her lips.

'You are not taking that lipstick off.' Michelle pulled the tissue from Alex's hand. 'I can't believe he said that. And I can't believe that you would take that kind of shit from your husband. Or that you are actually acting on such ridiculous criticism.'

'He's probably right. I don't think I can pull the lipstick off.'

Michelle wondered if Alex was telling the truth. Was this sort of thing really out of character for Daniel? She assumed not. However, the truth was something far more complex. In fact, Daniel rarely criticized Alex so directly, and he never spoke like that in front of anyone. Behind closed doors he sometimes made jokes at her expense and he would give her helpful suggestions on how she might improve – challenge her to be a better version of herself – all while slowly picking away at her sense of self-worth.

Michelle's phone buzzed. She glanced at it and quickly said before picking it up, 'Hope it's alright – I asked John to meet us here.'

Michelle proceeded to give directions to their exact location within the bar. A few minutes later John appeared through the sea of corporates at the other side of the bar and waved. He, like Alex, seemed unaccustomed to the bar scene. He awkwardly manoeuvred his way through the throng of bodies.

John was dressed in a Mad Men style blue suit, with a crisp white shirt, no tie. His beautiful blue eyes contrasted against his dark hair and strong jaw bone; while not the best looking guy in the room, he wasn't far from it. His looks, together with his great dress sense, didn't seem to fit with how socially awkward he appeared to be.

'Hey, how are you both? I'm just going to grab a drink. Would you like anything from the bar?'

Michelle held up the empty bottle of wine. 'Another of these, please.'

While John was at the bar, Alex took the opportunity to look around, to check that Daniel wasn't still anywhere nearby. She wondered if Michelle's boyfriend minded her going out drinking with John. She was sure that Daniel would be really annoyed, especially given how drunk he was tonight.

'Do you two usually catch up for drinks? I thought you just worked together.'

'Oh, yeah – not long after John moved down here I saw him in a meeting. He didn't know anyone and was basically living the life of a sad little hermit, so I took him under my wing.'

'I can't imagine him being a hermit.'

'I know. For some reason he's not great in social situations. He lacks confidence. The girl that lands him soon will be very lucky indeed – getting in before he finds out how good looking he is and gets an enormous ego.'

'Who's got an enormous ego?' John appeared at the table with drinks.

Michelle shook her head. 'Just some guy who was trying to chat us up earlier.'

'Well, I'm not surprised guys are trying to chat you two up. You're both looking great.' John looked at Alex for a few seconds longer that what seemed normal. 'And you look different. What is it?'

Alex blushed. She didn't want to have this discussion again. Why did she let Michelle stop her from wiping off that stupid lipstick?

'It's your lipstick. That's it, isn't it? It looks really good.'

Alex turned a deeper shade of crimson. Of course he said it looked good. He's not exactly going to say, '*What's different about you? Oh, it's your lipstick. That looks fucking terrible.*'

'You have a really nice smile. The lipstick really makes it noticeable.'

Alex felt a little dumbstruck. Was he flirting with her?

Surely not – he was way out of her league. Plus she was married. God, this was awkward.

John was feeling a little self-conscious too. He realised as soon as he'd said the words that they sounded awkward – and a bit like he was flirting – but he was just being honest.

'So – ahh – what are you guys planning for Christmas? Going back home?'

Michelle grabbed John's clumsy attempt to recover the conversation, 'Yeah, I'm flying back on Christmas Eve. I'm taking Andrew with me. It's our first Christmas together and the first time he'll meet my family.'

Alex was a little surprised by the excitement in Michelle's voice. Michelle had never been one to get giddy over a man. Not that she seemed quite giddy – but this was the most excited she'd ever seen Michelle over anything that wasn't a competition; grades, work, promotions were the only things that seemed to be really important to Michelle in the past. Andrew must be really special.

'And Alex is going to Paris for Christmas. You two can talk about how incredible that's going to be while I duck to the bathroom.'

John turned to Alex, 'Wow that would be amazing. Where are you staying?'

'We're staying in an apartment in the fifth arrondissement.' Alex was still wary about discussing her travel. She wondered if she would feel this way if she was paying her own way. Probably not. She felt bitter about being a kept woman, and simultaneously felt guilty for not appreciating how good she had it.

'You don't sound particularly excited about it.'

'Oh, I am,' Alex replied vaguely.

'I guess it's hard being away from family at Christmas time, even if you do get to spend it in Paris. But Paris will be amazing and you can spend next Christmas with your family.'

Alex exhaled loudly, 'But I won't get to spend next Christmas with my family.' She immediately regretted saying it. She must have had too much to drink; she didn't usually say things like that.

'What do you mean? Why not?'

'Oh, we go away every year for Christmas.' Alex paused and exhaled audibly again. 'I know I'm going to sound very ungrateful in saying this but I just wish that I could spend it with my family for once.'

'I don't think I understand. If you don't want to go away, why do you?'

'Daniel – my husband – doesn't like to see his family for Christmas.'

'But that doesn't mean that you can't see your family.'

'I know. It's just – well – I guess he doesn't really want to do that either.' Alex could feel herself opening up to John. She didn't like that she was being so honest with him, but she couldn't seem to stop herself.

'But what about what you want?'

And with that the floodgates opened. 'I don't earn any money. And – let's face it – I'm so incredibly lucky to have someone like Daniel. I don't really contribute much.' Alex shrugged. 'So what he wants is more important.'

'That's insane.' Seeing the look on Alex's face, his tone became gentle, 'No one person in a relationship is more important than another. You need to value yourself more.

Has Daniel actually said to you that what he wants is more important?'

'No.' Alex said the word slowly, stretching out the one syllable.

'Did you just decide that what he wants goes? Or have you actually told him what you want?'

'No.'

'Well, tell him. Tell him what you want.'

Alex started to think. When had she started to feel like what she wanted didn't matter? Why did she feel like this? She vaguely remembered a time when she was happy and confident. She used to be a lot more like Kate than what she was now. Where did that go? She used to wear lipstick and not feel self-conscious about it. When did that change? And why? Was she thinner back then? Or prettier? Alex didn't think so. She searched her memory for images of how she used to look. No, she definitely didn't think she was thinner back then. But that must be it, mustn't it?

Alex was in her own little world for the rest of the night. And Michelle wasn't much better. She couldn't help thinking of what Daniel had said to Alex. *Something about putting makeup on pigs.* And the look on Alex's face. It just didn't sit right with Michelle; it was really eating away at her.

As she left the bar, Michelle texted Rachel and Kate: *We need to talk about Alex.*

****

'What's wrong with Alex?' Kate wondered to herself what

could possibly be wrong with Alex. Having to decide between summer in the South of France or the Hamptons? She rolled her eyes at her phone and was immediately thankful that her friends couldn't see her face – she was sure it would betray what she was thinking.

'Well...' Michelle wanted to find the most delicate way to express her concerns. 'I met her husband.'

'And?'

'We went for drinks last night. He made a comment that basically – indirectly – called Alex a pig.'

Rachel waited for Michelle to elaborate. As usual, Rachel didn't like to jump in with comments until she had all the information. Kate was not so reserved.

'What the fuck? A pig?'

'Alex also let slip that he almost didn't let her come out with me.' Michelle waited a moment for what she was saying to sink in. 'He seems very controlling. And not like a particularly nice guy.'

'Oh, God! Do you think that this is what's up with her? She's changed so much. She just seems so... dull now.'

Rachel clicked her tongue disapprovingly.

'Not like she's boring. I mean – she used to be so... effervescent. She was always the life of the party, but the other day she seemed like her sparkle had just disappeared.'

'She has definitely changed.' Rachel's words were measured; she didn't want to rush to conclusions. And she certainly didn't want to say anything disparaging about their friend.

'What do you think we should do?' Kate asked eagerly.

'I don't think that we should do anything. Obviously we

should be there for her if she needs us but we shouldn't get involved based on a few harsh drunken words and because you think she seems less sparkly. A marriage is too important for us to be jumping in without all the facts.'

'You're right. I don't think we should do anything about it. I just thought I should tell you guys.'

'I completely disagree.' Kate was firm. 'Emotional abuse can be really damaging. I've read a lot about it. You wouldn't ignore the situation if you thought he was hitting her, would you?'

'But he's not hitting her. That's not the issue.'

'Emotional abuse is still abuse and can be just as harmful.'

'I really think that we're jumping to conclusions here. We don't know that there's anything wrong with their relationship at all or how he treats her. Abuse is a really strong word to be throwing around without any facts to back it up. As far as we know, the poor man has done nothing wrong.'

'I'm going to talk to her about it.'

'I guess if you did it subtly...' The feeling in Michelle's stomach about Daniel was gnawing away at her. She couldn't quite maintain her stance of not interfering.

'I don't think you should. What would you say?' Rachel was determined to stand her ground. This kind of gossip was really destructive. And they really shouldn't act on some inkling that Michelle had from one offhand comment.

'I heard your husband's a dick. I can hook you up with a good divorce lawyer.'

'Kate!'

'Of course I'm not going to bloody say that. I'm not

actually an idiot. I'll get her drunk and ask her about him. I'll just let her do the talking.'

'I don't see any harm in it.'

'I still think it's a bad idea. Anyway, when are you going to have this drunken discussion? Alex said the other night that she's not planning on coming back to Brisbane anytime soon.'

'Oh, you guys could come down to Sydney. We could have a girls' weekend.' Michelle immediately started thinking of which bars they could go to, where they would eat, where Rachel and Kate could stay, where she would take them shopping.

'That does sound fun.' Rachel sounded hesitant; she didn't want her agreement to imply that she wanted any part in the plan to interfere in Alex's marriage.

'Sorry to be a downer, but I can't afford to go to Sydney for a weekend.'

'That's a shame. I'm sure there'll be other opportunities for us to catch up. Michelle – you'll be in town for Christmas, won't you?'

Michelle ignored Rachel's question. 'It's just that you can't afford it?'

'I would love a girls' weekend in Sydney. But, seriously, my credit card is absolutely maxed. I could start saving and we could maybe plan it for sometime around Easter.'

'Easter?' Michelle scoffed. 'No. Let's do it. I've got heaps of frequent flyer points – more than I'm ever going to use. I'll use them for your flights.'

'Really? Are you sure?' Kate was practically jumping up and down with excitement.

'Of course. Aaannnnddddd.... you can see John while you're here.'

Kate stomach did a little flip at the mention of his name. A flash of the memory came back to her of that goofy grin he had given her. *Fuck, he was sexy.* 'Still not interested in John. But, oh my God! You're the best! This is going to be amazing.'

CHAPTER TEN

'Daniel,' Alex's voice was confident, though she wasn't really feeling that way. She had given a lot of thought to what John had said. He was right; how could she expect to ever have things her way if she didn't articulate exactly what she wanted.

Alex began again, 'Daniel, I just wanted to talk to you about Christmas. I know we usually go away. And it's great. I mean – I really appreciate our trips. It's just – well – I really miss spending Christmas with my family. I know that we've planned to go away this year, but I thought maybe next year we could maybe see my family.' The last sentence sounded more like a question than a statement.

'Hmm... You know I hate spending Christmas with family.'

'Yes. You're right, but I thought maybe, we could...' Alex's voice trailed off.

'I don't think so.'

'But – it's just that it's not really fair if I can't spend Christmas with my family just because you don't like your family.' In her head she sounded churlish. She didn't know how to articulate this like a grown woman.

'Maybe you could organise some sort of pre-Christmas get together with your family.' Daniel seemed to be barely paying attention. His response was an attempt to end the conversation.

Alex nodded eagerly. It wasn't really what she wanted, but it would be a nice compromise. They could fly her family down for a weekend. Or maybe she and Daniel could go up there. She was so excited that Daniel was willing to do this – he didn't usually do family things, particularly not with her family.

'I'm away for work mid- December. You should organise it for then.'

'You mean you're not going to come?'

'No, I'm not interested. This is your thing.'

'I just thought that maybe you would come too.'

Daniel seemed to have already checked out of the conversation and was looking at emails on his phone.

Alex tried again, remembering what John had said – she needed to articulate exactly what she wanted. 'I'd really love it if you came too.'

Daniel replied without looking up from his phone. 'Hmmm... I don't think so.'

CHAPTER ELEVEN

Kate and Rachel left for Sydney on the Friday morning. Kate had taken the day off work. She had, actually, called in sick – she didn't have any leave days accrued and couldn't afford to not be paid, especially given how much she would probably spend over the course of the weekend.

Rachel had shed a tear as she'd said goodbye to Georgie. This wasn't the first time she'd been away from her, but that didn't make it any easier. Rachel's mother was looking after Georgie for the day, then Mike would have her to himself all weekend. At least it would give him a chance to have some really good quality time alone with Georgie. This weekend would be amazing and definitely worth it – Rachel just needed to keep reminding herself.

When Alex picked them up from the airport in her sporty little Mercedes, Kate immediately felt a pang of jealousy but brushed it off quickly. Having a nice car was not high on Kate's priority list – it would be amazing, but even more than that, she'd love it if she had the money that that little car was worth to put towards a holiday.

'I just want to reiterate – we need a social media blackout, as far as I'm concerned, for this weekend. My boss can't see that I faked a sickie to come to Sydney.'

'She said this five times before we even boarded,' Rachel laughed.

'No problems.' Alex pulled out of the airport car park. 'So, Michelle has a meeting or something. We'll head to lunch and she'll meet us for drinks afterwards.'

The three women caught up on each other's news over lunch. Rachel talked about Georgie and the Christmas play that she was organising with the kids from her music class, in which Georgie would be playing a key role – possibly even the lead role, but Rachel hadn't quite decided if it was worth getting all the other parents offside just to make her daughter the star of the show. Rachel was quite torn on the matter – objectively (or so she told herself) Georgie was the clear choice – she was the cutest, the best at following instructions, the best at remembering the lines and she had a great singing voice (or really as great a voice as was possible for an almost three year old – she could pronounce the words and say them roughly in time to the music). But if Rachel gave her the part, she knew it wouldn't be seen as an objective decision at all.

Kate tried hard to listen to Rachel's boring story about her boring child and an even more boring topic – a children's play – but it was very difficult concentrating. She did manage to look interested and nod at the appropriate times. Kate wondered whether Rachel actually found her life interesting or if she was just stuck in this rut of mind numbing child stuff and couldn't think of anything better to contribute to the conversation. Kate hoped that Rachel was genuinely content with her life. Kate really did want nothing more than her friends to have happiness, except possibly for this incredibly boring story about a children's play to end.

Alex talked about her trip to Paris. She felt a lot more relaxed with her friends now; she wasn't even feeling particularly self-conscious about the topic. So relaxed, in fact, she didn't even notice the looks of envy passing over Kate's face. And even, to a lesser extent, Rachel's. Alex, oblivious to her friends' thoughts on the topic, talked about where they were going to stay, what they planned to do on Christmas day, the restaurants she wanted to eat in, the trip to Chamonix they were taking after they had seen in the New Year in Paris. Alex wasn't a particularly confident skier; and Daniel snowboarded, refusing to go out on the slopes with her. Every time they went to the snow, she would take a beginner's lesson for a few days then spend the rest of her time drinking hot chocolate by a fire. Daniel was always so critical (not that she mentioned that to her friends) about her continual need to have lessons each time they went to the snow, but she just wasn't confident enough to do it by herself. He was also very critical of her skiing. Apparently skiing wasn't cool enough for his liking.

There was the slightest hint underlying Alex's words that described a husband who didn't treat her particularly well, mocked her and made her feel bad about herself. But her friends didn't hear that. No one ever heard that. All they heard was that Alex was going on a holiday that most people would give their right arm to experience. The subtext was subtle – Alex's friends may have noticed it – but their jealousy obstructed any chance that they might pick up on the true relationship she had with her husband.

Kate talked about her apartment hunt, which was going nowhere. To her embarrassment, she really couldn't afford to move out of her mother's house. But maybe something would come up – a reasonably priced share house. Maybe. Kate chatted about an incredible party that she was going to on Christmas Eve. And another on New Year's Eve.

Alex, again, felt the pangs of jealousy twist in anxiety laden balls in her stomach – she wished she could go to fabulous parties and spend time with fabulous people. But who was she kidding – even if she knew about these sorts of parties and knew those sorts of people, she would never have the confidence to go. She was just not one of the fabulous people. She was nothing like Kate.

****

The three women had only just finished lunch when Michelle joined them. They had been too busy talking to be distracted by food, and from the time they were seated it had taken them quite a few hours to finish their meals.

'Fill me in on what you three have been gossiping about while I was hard at work.'

'I just have to say no social media this weekend. Okay? I called in sick to come here.'

'We know,' Alex laughed.

'Well, not all of us can just take a day off at such short notice.' Kate was indignant.

'Ah, yeah. I – um – didn't take a day off. I don't actually have a job.' Alex's cheeks flushed red.

'What? You don't have a job? Why?' Rachel's voice was gentle; her face was full of concern, the corners of her mouth twitching down in a slight frown that often seemed to be adorning her face.

'I travel a lot with Daniel, so it would be difficult,' Alex said weakly. Her cheeks turned a slightly darker shade of red. She wondered why she had voluntarily told them that she didn't work. No one had even asked.

Kate immediately started daydreaming about having Alex's life – substituting Ryan Gosling for Daniel, but the rest wasn't fantastical. Not working – amazing. Travelling so much that you couldn't possibly work – amazing. Driving around in that shiny little Mercedes – amazing. Alex was living the dream. Kate did wonder why Alex didn't wear better clothes though; she clearly had enough money to dress really well.

While Kate was imagining herself behind the wheel of a Mercedes, Michelle was wondering what Alex did all day. What was the point of her life? How could someone choose not to work? It seemed crazy to her. How could a person thrive without the sense of accomplishment of achieving career goals or the pressure of a deadline or the high of winning a new client? She wondered that about the other two as well – at least Rachel was sort of doing something, she supposed. Looking after a child didn't seem like particularly fulfilling work, but at least – she imagined – it would keep you occupied, if not mentally stimulated.

Kate, on the other hand, completely baffled Michelle. How could she possibly go to her dead-end job every day, knowing that she was just a tiny, unimportant and completely replaceable cog in a machine? That just sounded soul destroying to Michelle, and yet Kate didn't seem to even care.

Rachel's voice cut through the others' daydreaming. 'Alex,

is that really it? Couldn't you work in a casual role and still travel?'

Alex's feeble excuse and her discomfort had sent alarm bells ringing for Rachel. It just didn't feel right, so Rachel prodded, in her perceptive, pushy, caring way. And Alex squirmed in her chair.

On seeing how uncomfortable she'd made Alex, Rachel back-pedalled. 'I'm not criticising you. If you've made the decision to not work, that's great. I'm sure everyone would love to be in a position where work was a choice. You just don't seem… committed – confident – in your decision, and I thought that maybe there's more to it.'

Alex sighed. 'Honestly, sometimes I do kind of wish that I had a job. It's just that, well, Daniel doesn't really want me working.'

'What?' Kate was suddenly outraged. It would be incredible not to work, but no one has the right to make that decision for you.

'He just thinks that if I worked, it would mean that he can't look after me properly – that he doesn't earn enough money.' Alex looked around the table at her friends' faces and quickly added, 'And the travel thing too. That's definitely true.'

Kate and Michelle exchanged looks and Kate turned back to Alex. 'Alex –' Kate's words were slow and deliberate, '- don't you think that it should be *your* decision if you want to work or not?'

'It is my decision. Daniel probably wouldn't stop me if I really wanted to. I just don't really want to work that much.'

Kate had her doubts about this, but who was she to argue

that Alex actually *wanted* to work. Given the opportunity, Kate would quit her job in a heartbeat and never work again.

Michelle and Kate exchanged looks again. They both still wanted to have the discussion with Alex about her relationship with Daniel. But both of the women recognised that this wasn't great timing. Alex had barely had anything to drink and she didn't seem like she was quite in the mood to be forthright with them right now.

Michelle made the decision to change the topic. 'So, Kate, I invited John to have dinner with us tonight.' She winked at Kate.

Alex jumped at the change in topic. 'Ooo-ooo,' she said in a sing-song voice, 'Your boyfriend's going to be there.'

'Seriously guys – I'm not interested.' A slight blush crept into Kate's cheeks in spite of herself.

****

Kate, Rachel and Alex piled into Alex's Mercedes and they headed back to Alex's apartment to drop off their bags and get ready for dinner. The decision had been made for the girls to both stay with Alex, because she had more room, and because Daniel was going away for the weekend. And Kate really couldn't afford a hotel.

'Now, just to let you guys know, Daniel doesn't leave until tonight. He might be there when we arrive.'

'That's great! I'd really love to meet him.' Rachel said cheerily from the backseat.

'Mmmm... me too.' Kate sounded far less cheerful, but she was quite looking forward to meeting this *pig* of a man.

As the three women walked through the front door, Daniel swooped; he wrapped an arm around Alex's waist and kissed her on the lips. He turned, looked Kate directly in the eyes and gave a warm smile, 'Kate, right?' He turned to Rachel, 'And you're Rachel.'

'It's really nice to meet you.' Rachel's smile mirrored Daniel's.

'Let me grab your bags. I'll put them in the guest rooms while Alex shows you around.'

Once Daniel was out of ear-shot, Rachel whispered, 'Alex, he's *really* nice. And so good looking.'

Alex grinned, pleased that her friend thought so. 'I know.'

Kate was still not won over. It took more than just a pretty smile to charm her. Kate's mind was quickly torn away from her suspicions; her jaw dropped as she took in the apartment; it was huge, immaculate and the style was so on trend, it looked like it had come straight from a magazine. She had no idea that Alex had such great taste. Kate immediately thought that it must actually be Daniel; she loved Alex, but there was no way Alex was behind this apartment.

'Your apartment is amazing.' Kate was clearly in awe. 'I love this rug. Did I see this lamp in the latest Vogue Living?' Kate didn't know where to look or what to comment on first. It was all spectacular. Immediately she started day dreaming about living in this apartment. She wondered how big the wardrobe was. There was probably an entire wardrobe dedicated to shoes.

'Can I get you ladies a drink?' Daniel had walked back in to the living room.

'Please.' Kate didn't look up from the monochrome painting that hung above the dining table.

'Alex tells me you're both white wine girls. I've stocked the fridge. There are a few different options that should keep you all reasonably buzzed the whole weekend.' Daniel laughed. He poured three glasses of wine and distributed them to the women.

Kate had moved on to looking through the kitchen. She looked up at Daniel. 'Did you decorate this apartment? It's amazing.'

Daniel laughed. It was warm and genuine. He just oozed charm but in the kind of way that seemed absolutely sincere. 'I would love to claim that I had something to do with it, but alas no, it was all done by a professional.'

'So you just hire someone and they decide what you'll have in your home and how it's all going to look?'

'It does sound really clinical, doesn't it? But it's not as bad as all that. The designer showed us pictures of heaps of different styles, we picked the one we liked best and talked her through what we actually liked about the picture. She then took us to some shops and showed us different options for things like the couch. We picked what we liked with her guidance. I guess it was a collaboration but I know we never would have come up with anything this cool if we'd done it ourselves.'

Despite herself, Kate found that she liked Daniel. She had been hit on enough that she wasn't suckered in by a handsome face and a smile. But Daniel seemed genuine. He seemed likeable. He was absolutely charming. Nothing about him gave even the slightest impression that he was the kind of man that Michelle had described. Maybe what she had witnessed was just a bad day fuelled by too much alcohol. And maybe Kate had it all wrong.

'Excuse me. I better finish packing then I can get out of your hair. Leave you ladies to gossip and do whatever it is that you do when men aren't around.' Daniel gave a wink and a laugh and left the room.

'Sorry – I'm just going to go help him pack. He always ends up forgetting something.' Alex set her wine glass down on the kitchen bench and left the room.

'He seems really nice, doesn't he?' Kate was a little sheepish.

'Yes. I bet you're glad you and Michelle didn't have that chat to Alex over lunch. You'd feel a little foolish now.'

Kate sighed loudly and rolled her eyes. 'Yes, you were right, Rachel. As usual.'

Alex walked into the bedroom behind Daniel and shut the door behind herself. He turned to her. 'I don't like you spending time with that slut. And I especially don't like you spending the whole weekend with her, drinking, while I'm not around.' His voice was quiet and his tone angry; his eyes seemed darker than usual.

Alex's face fell. She knew from previous experience that there was no point in saying anything. Nothing she could say would have helped.

'I suppose at least I know no one's going to be looking at you with those two around.' Daniel gestured toward the kitchen.

Alex immediately began to make a mental list of all the ways in which Kate and Rachel were more attractive than her. She simmered. In that instant she despised them both for being everything that she wasn't. For being everything that she wished that she was. Especially Kate. In that moment her shortcomings – real, exaggerated and imagined – were all Kate's fault. If only she weren't so ugly, Daniel would love her more. If only she weren't so fat, Daniel would find her more attractive. If only she weren't so disgusting, she wouldn't be stuck with Daniel. *Stuck with Daniel* – did she really just think that? She wasn't stuck with Daniel. She was lucky to have him. Incredibly lucky.

****

Alex, Kate and Rachel arrived at the restaurant late; too caught up in gossiping and trying several of the bottles of wine that Daniel had bought them, they'd all lost track of time. John and Michelle were already seated at the table, deep in conversation. John was leaning in close to Michelle and saying something that caused her to throw her head back in laughter.

As they approached the table, Kate chuckled, with only the slightest undertone of jealousy. 'Tell me those two are *just friends.*'

'Bit jealous, are you?' Alex's remark wasn't friendly – it had a little too much bite to it. She seemed annoyed; not at all like the fun, vivacious Alex that they used to know, or like the reserved, nervous Alex that they'd seen lately. Rachel turned to look at Alex, shocked, looking for meaning – reason

– behind Alex's comment and mood; but Alex just ignored her penetrating gaze. Outwardly Kate seemed not to notice, but she wondered what she'd done to Alex to warrant a comment like that.

There were a flurry of hellos and kisses, as the three women reached the table. Kate felt a little awkward with John, which was unusual for her. She had become accustomed to dealing with men post-one-night-stand or flirtation, so this wasn't a unique situation for her. Nevertheless, she felt shy; she didn't quite meet John's eyes; she briefly laughed nervously when she said hello. When he smiled at her, she felt the blood rise to her cheeks. Did she actually fancy this guy? Properly fancy him? She hadn't really felt that way about anyone since Peter. Sure, she had moved in with Jake, but, honestly, that had been a bit of a whirlwind, and a little bit more to do with convenience than she cared to admit – even to herself. She had been adamant for so long now that she didn't want a relationship; she was happy alone; she was an independent woman, who didn't need a man in order to feel fulfilled. And she was sure that that was all true. But she might just like this guy. Really like him. But relationships were hard. And disappointing. And she really didn't want to go through the pain – anguish, jealousy, hurt, despair – that she had felt with Peter. Never ever again. And with that thought, she dismissed her feelings for John. It was much easier to stick with guys that she didn't really like all that much. That did feel a little bit like a cop out to her. But surely being so self aware was a good thing. And not giving in to her gut instincts meant she was exercising self control – again, a good thing.

Only spending time with men who were unimportant – to her, at least – didn't quite feel like a good thing, though.

Alex watched John and Kate exchange greetings. Her earlier feelings of jealousy simmered away inside her. Men didn't ever look at Alex the way that John was looking at Kate. Daniel definitely didn't look at Alex that way. Alex hated the way she looked. But, more than that, she hated herself for feeling this way. Being jealous of her friend for being the focus of flirtation was ridiculous, petty, high school stuff, yet she couldn't stop feeling that way.

Alex and Kate sat either side of John, while Rachel sat across from Kate, next to Michelle. Alex immediately felt unhappy about her position at the table. She bitterly thought that the seating arrangement was apt – her being a little off to the side, not in the midst of the group, missing parts of conversations and not quite being included – it was just like how she felt in life, generally. Alex wondered why she had even bothered with this weekend in the first place.

John turned to Alex, quietly, 'Did you talk to your husband about Christmas?'

'Yes. I'm just going to do a pre-Christmas thing with my family.' Alex felt a little uplifted that John had remembered their previous conversation. Maybe she wasn't quite as much a wallflower as she thought. She knew John wasn't interested in her – and she was happily married, so she definitely was not interested in him – but it felt nice to pretend that that this was a little bit of a flirtation. That maybe if she weren't married...

'That would be nice. Will you do Christmas day with your family next year?'

'Ah, well, no. Daniel wasn't keen on that. We'll go away

again next year.' Alex realised how it sounded and quickly added, 'But we'll do a pre-Christmas thing with my family next year too. It doesn't really matter if it's on the day. Seeing them is the most important part.' The glow Alex had been feeling from John's attention quickly faded.

'I guess so. It's not much of a compromise though.' John immediately regretted saying it.

Her face made it clear that she agreed. The expression she wore gave away her true feelings on the subject. She felt anger swell inside of her; for some inexplicable reason it felt to her as though it was all John's fault. And Kate's. Kate's long legs and blonde hair and red lips. It was Kate's fault. As her resentment grew, she knew her feelings were misplaced; she knew she was being absurd; she hated herself for her jealousy and nonsensical anger toward Kate. The logical part of Alex's brain told her to calm down. There was no point in feeling annoyed with Kate all weekend for Alex's own inadequacies. A part of her still resented Kate, but she pushed those feeling deep down inside herself and didn't think about them; she just let them brew away out of sight.

Alex smiled at John; a big, fake smile. 'Enough about my boring life. What have you been up to?'

'Not much, really. Michelle's been away and I don't really know anyone else in Sydney.' John paused, his eyes narrowed. 'Is that your phone ringing?'

By the time Alex had fished her phone out of her handbag, it had stopped ringing. John glanced at the screen. He didn't mean to, but there clear as day, nineteen missed calls from Daniel. He knew he shouldn't say anything, but he just couldn't hold his tongue. 'Unless someone has died, I think you've got a stalker.'

Alex looked flustered. 'I better call him back,' Alex said, as she stood and walked out of the restaurant.

****

After dinner the group walked to a bar nearby. As they entered, Rachel was blown away by the decor. This was easily the coolest place she'd ever been. There were kitsch knick-knacks lining the bookcases. The chairs were all mismatched and looked like they had come straight from the 1950's. The bar was crowded and most of the super stylish patrons seemed to be sipping cocktails from mason jars. Every male, besides John, was sporting a beard and tight pants. This place was a hipster's paradise.

'I'll grab us some drinks.' Michelle had to shout above the music, which was coming from a jazz band in the corner of the tiny bar.

Despite the massive crowds, Kate managed to find them a table. You don't go out in six inch heels without becoming an expert at sizing up when people are about to abandon chairs.

They lowered themselves onto some khaki lino chairs and a tapestry covered settee that looked like it belonged in a grandma's house, and Michelle returned with the drinks. She set down on the coffee table in front of them a tray containing a teapot, covered by a crochet teapot cosy and five miniature teacups.

'Tea?' Rachel felt very confused by the choice of drink.

'Silly, it's teapot shots.' Kate laughed.

'Shots don't need to be kept warm. Why is there a teapot cosy?' John yelled. Only Michelle seemed to hear what he said over the music; she rolled her eyes in response.

Kate and John sat next to each other on the small settee, in such close proximity to each other that Kate could feel his warm breath against her skin. The blaring music and the collective noise of all of the people in the bar were prohibitive to a group conversation. Instead, Kate bowed her head close to John's in order to talk. Michelle leant across Alex toward Rachel, to somewhat facilitate a three-way conversation. However, Alex was missing most of what was being said, thus cementing her earlier feelings of being the odd-one-out.

'Do you love marketing?'

John looked at Kate with a quizzical expression. 'What?'

'Do you love working in marketing?' In Kate's experience, people who work in marketing tend to love working in marketing. Or at least saying so. A lot.

'I'm not in marketing.'

'What? But don't you work with Michelle?'

John registered what she meant. 'Oh, no. Michelle's firm does the marketing for the company that I work for. I guess I'm technically her client.'

'Oh.' Kate paused briefly, searching for something brilliant to say. Why was she having some much trouble talking to him, when she was usually so good at this? Because she liked him, was the answer. But she didn't want that thought hanging around in her head, so she pushed it aside. 'So, what do you do then?'

'I work for a software developer.'

'That sounds really cool. Do you love that?'

'Not really.'

Kate could feel a small section of goose bumps appear on the back of her neck, where his warm breath met her skin as he talked. *They were talking about work, for fuck's sake. This wasn't sexy. Why was it giving her goose bumps? Get your shit together, Kate.*

'Oh, that's surprising. You strike me as the type who'd be all passionate about work. And work stupidly long hours and say it was your dream job and you'd do it even if you won the lotto.'

'Hardly. And those people who say that are lying to themselves. Just trying to convince themselves that their lives are what they want and not driven completely by money.'

'I always thought that. It's such a stupid thing to say. But so many people say it. Sometimes I wonder if I'm the only one who just works for money.'

'Nope. You're definitely not the only one.' John smiled.

Kate felt the muscles in her back twitch, and goose bumps threatened to rise again.

John continued, 'So what job will you be quitting when you win millions?'

'I'm an admin assistant.'

'And I'm guessing you don't love it.'

'No. I absolutely hate it.' Kate shrugged. 'But I've grown accustomed to a fairly glamorous lifestyle,' she gave a cheeky smile. 'Money is kinda a necessity. Especially when you like wine as much as I do.'

'Then why do you do it? That job, I mean. You can get money from doing other things.'

'Why do you do a job you hate?'

'I never said I hate my job. I just don't love it. There's a difference.'

'I don't know.' Kate shrugged again. 'I'm not qualified to do anything.'

'And what would you do if you were qualified?'

'I dunno.' Kate shrugged, wrinkled her nose in thought, then pouted. 'Something to do with fashion, maybe.'

'So, you want to design clothes? How do you get into that?'

'Not fashion design. I'm not that creative.' She gave a short, self-conscious laugh. 'I mean like being a stylist or working for Vogue. Or being a buyer or something.'

'A buyer? Buying clothes? That sounds more like the reason why you need to *have* a job.'

'Yeah.' Kate laughed, in an attempt to seize the opportunity to brush past this topic. Despite what some people thought, she generally didn't like talking about herself much; and definitely not about her career – or lack thereof – and what she was and wasn't doing with her life.

'But, seriously, I would think that there are a lot of jobs in fashion that you don't need to be qualified to do. They may not be the exact job that you want, but surely something peripheral to your dream job is better than a job you hate.'

'Hmmm... You know sometimes I feel a little envious of Michelle. She's always known what she wants. And she always has a plan on exactly how to get it.'

'That's true. But there's nothing stopping you from making your own plan.'

Kate's mother was always harping on about getting a plan. And now John. Maybe having a plan was actually a good idea.

But you need to know what you want before you can plan how to get it. The thought of having a five year plan seemed daunting; and a little bit like a cage that you've locked yourself into. Kate preferred to be breezy. It suited her personality much better to fly by the seat of her pants. But it wasn't helping her get what she wanted out of her job – or, more accurately, her career. She despised using the word career. It always reminded her that what she did was going nowhere; that she felt trapped by her lack of qualifications – though when she was honest with herself, she could admit that it wasn't a lack of qualifications that held her back, it was a lack of confidence in her own abilities and a fear of rejection. And whenever she felt trapped like that, she would panic and change jobs. But always to something equally as stifling, which would just make the whole experience worse, knowing that job after job after job felt the same. She always tried to dismiss these feelings though. She wasn't one to dwell on this sort of thing. Having a job was a means to an end. Her life didn't revolve around her work. And she loved that. Ultimately she felt that was the most important thing. And so she was happy that she was right in rejecting the pursuit of anything more.

'So what's *your* plan?'

'I don't have one. I like feeling unfulfilled and having a life that's just a wasteland of forgotten dreams and rusty ambition.' John laughed at his own words. As much as he joked about it, he did wish that he'd pushed himself further; had actually done what he loved rather than taking the easy – and more lucrative – road.

****

Kate was the last out of bed the next morning. Michelle had already made her way to Alex's apartment and the three women were sprawled across the lounge when Kate ambled out of the bedroom.

'Morning.'

'Thank God you're finally up,' Michelle groaned. 'I'm starving and apparently –' she shot Rachel a look – 'we couldn't eat breakfast without you. So hurry up and get dressed.'

'Argh... okay. I had planned on going for a run, but I *am* feeling pretty dusty. So I guess I'll just skip it.'

'Yes, yes, we're all feeling hung over. Get your shit together so we can shove some bacon in our faces and feel better.'

'Okay. Jeez. Can we go to Bondi? I want to lie in the sun for a bit – it always makes me feel better after a big night.'

Michelle sighed loudly. 'It's Saturday. And December. The traffic there is going to be fucked. And it'll be packed with tourists and wankers. Anyway, under all that fake tan, you're the whitest person alive. You shouldn't be lying in the sun.'

Kate rolled her eyes. 'I'm not an idiot. I'll wear a hat, sun cream and a kaftan.' Which she had no intention of actually doing.

Rachel recognised that Kate and Michelle were a few nasty words away from a full blown cat fight. 'Why don't we go somewhere close by for breakfast and then we can talk about Bondi. I'm sure we'll all feel better once we're eating.'

Kate got her way and, after breakfast, they made their way

to Bondi. As Michelle had predicted, the beach was heaving with a mass of sticky, sweaty, bare skinned, sunburnt people. Michelle and Alex, being the two who no longer resided in hot humid Brisbane, began complaining about the heat as soon as they arrived at the beach.

'I'm going to find a cafe – preferably one that isn't completely packed – and get a cold drink. You can stay here and work on your skin cancer.' Michelle was still unimpressed about the decision to go to Bondi.

'I'll come with you,' Alex piped up. She had no intention of getting into her swimmers. And just being in this kind of proximity to so many scantily clad people had her feeling uncomfortable and more than a little down about herself.

Kate and Rachel stripped down to their bikinis and lay down on their towels in a tiny patch of free sand that they found amongst the throngs of people.

It didn't take long before two, much younger men approached. 'Hey, how are you doing?'

Kate barely glanced up from her magazine. 'Hi.' Everything about Kate screamed that she didn't want to have a conversation. She wasn't interested.

'What are you two doing after?' One man spoke, the other hung back a few paces, obviously not too keen on doing any talking.

'We're pretty busy. Have a great day though,' Kate said dismissively without looking up.

'Oh, so you're one of those bitches.'

Kate put her magazine down. 'Excuse me?'

'You're one of those hot girls who knows their hot. Pity.'

The man had Kate's full attention now. 'You know what is

actually pitiful? You. Thinking that there's something in some way lesser about a woman who values herself. Let me guess, you like women who don't know their own worth. I assume they're the only ones who would touch you with a ten foot pole.'

As the first man began to say, 'I'll show you a ten foot pole,' his friend who was hanging back began to laugh. 'She's totally got your number, man. Always going for the low hanging fruit.'

Kate's line of fire moved to the other man. 'Low hanging fruit? Don't talk about women like they're inanimate objects. We're not fucking fruit waiting to be picked. Not even the ones with self-esteem issues. Fuckwad.'

Kate was clearly done with this conversation and turned back to her magazine. The two men walked off, muttering obscenities and insults under their breaths.

Once they were out of ear shot, Rachel spoke up. 'That was a little harsh.'

'Whatever. They should show a little more respect toward women.'

'I thought that was amazing. You're officially my new hero.' A young twenty-something girl with a thick Irish accent, who was lying on a nearby towel sat up and leaned toward them. 'I'm Sally.'

Kate and Sally instantly clicked and spent the next thirty minutes chatting about boys, magazines, fashion and travel. Sally had just spent three months in South East Asia and was planning on making her way up the east coast of Australia. Kate couldn't get enough of Sally's travel stories. The thought of spending a year abroad, living out of a backpack, meeting new people, seeing new things was just incredible. Kate wondered if she was too old to do it. And – more importantly – where she'd get the money to do it if she tried.

Rachel finally interrupted them. 'Kate, I'm going to go find the others. I don't think I can handle much more sun right now.'

Kate begrudgingly left her new friend. They exchanged Facebook details, with a promise that they would catch up in Brisbane when Sally made it up there.

It took the four women quite a while to find each other. When they finally did, they all were fed up with the crowds and heat.

'Let's get out of here.'

'Oh, I was hoping that we might go to the Opera House for a drink this afternoon.' Rachel had heard fantastic things.

Michelle agreed that they'd go back home, shower, then head to Opera Bar for a drink and some dinner. It wasn't really what she had planned for them, but Bondi hadn't been on the weekend's itinerary either. She had resigned herself to ditching all of her plans.

'So Bondi's too touristy for you, but the Opera House is okay?' Kate was unimpressed. It sounded naff to her. She wanted to go to some amazing bar she'd been told about in Surry Hills. And maybe to The Cross afterwards.

'Umm.... Kate?' Alex looked up from her phone. 'I thought you didn't want it on Facebook that you're in Sydney.'

'I don't...' Kate reached for her phone and saw a notification. There it was. Sally had tagged her in a post.

Just met my new idol Kate Harris on #BondiBeach. Absolutely slayed the misogynist trying to hit on her. Fuckboy had no idea what was coming – totally brutal #AussieChicksRule #DoingItForTheSisterhood #WomenArentInanimateObjects #WereNotFuckingFruit

'Fuck! Fuck! Fuck!' Kate quickly deleted the post from her Facebook feed. 'I hope no one from work saw that or I'm fired.'

****

'Drinks?'

Kate shook her head at the stewardess. The last thing she needed was another drink.

'That was such a great weekend. Opera Bar was fun.' Rachel smiled. She missed her baby girl so, so much, but it really was nice to spend some time with friends, being an adult. And it was good for Mike to have alone time with Georgie.

Kate had lobbied hard for them to skip the Opera House. But in the end, the group had ruled against her. And Kate was a big enough person to admit when she was wrong, which she definitely was in this instance. They had sat at tables by the water, looking out towards the Harbour Bridge. Sitting outside, drinking cocktails, they had absorbed the gorgeous view and the delicious gently warming sunlight (which, unlike Brisbane, didn't feel scorching hot. No one was drenched in sweat and oppressive humidity wasn't making it difficult to breathe). They had stayed there until just after sunset, which didn't happen until eight pm! (Long summer days were definitely Kate's thing. Why was it that Brisbane didn't have daylight savings?) As it got darker, they watched the lights turning on in the apartments on the other side of the harbour, the bridge lighting up, the reflections of the lights twinkling on the surface of the dark still water. It was magical. This was a beautiful city.

Kate had laughed heartily at Rachel's delight at being hit on. A few men over the course of the afternoon and evening had shown more than a little interest in the group of women. Rachel clearly wasn't accustomed to that (Kate did wonder why – she supposed it was simply that Rachel didn't get out much, she certainly was hot enough to warrant a *lot* of male attention).

After Opera Bar, they had headed to Surry Hills to the bar that Kate had heard fantastic things about. Not even one metre through the door, Alex had declared that she was tired; she'd had enough and wanted to go home. The bar was exceptionally trendy and Alex had felt entirely out of place. Rachel was even uncomfortable. Unlike the amazing eclectic retro bar from the previous night, there wasn't kitsch decor to hold Rachel's attention. Instead she was focused on just how fashionable and unwelcoming all of the other patrons looked. One particularly cool androgynous-looking woman looked their group up and down, rolling her eyes before turning away. That was the last straw for Rachel. Unlike Alex, it didn't make her feel bad about herself, she simply thought that this bar wasn't going to be that fun if it was filled with those kind of judgemental people.

Noting the look on Alex's face, Rachel brightly suggested they leave. 'I think this place is too trendy for me,' Rachel had laughed, in an attempt to ease some of the harsh self talk that Rachel could see was going on inside Alex's head.

Kate had put up a brief fight, until she had realised just how miserable Alex was as the prospect of staying.

'Did you see that chick rolling her eyes at us? Best Justin Beiber lookalike I've seen! What a tosser,' Kate said, and they left the bar in fits of laughter.

They had whittled away the rest of the night in an old fashioned English style pub, laughing about old times and drinking far too much.

Now sitting on the plane on their way home, Kate didn't feel too well; she regretted some of the many, many, many drinks she'd consumed. 'Yeah, it was fun.' Kate's voice was vague and non-committal.

'I think that we should make this a regular thing.'

'Mmmm...' It had been a fantastic weekend. Kate would love to go away regularly, but she couldn't imagine how she would ever be able to afford it. She had spent an insane amount of money just on drinks over the course of the weekend. Her liver definitely couldn't cope with this becoming a regular occurrence. At least she'd be convincing at work on Monday, when she would have to fake having spent the whole weekend sick in bed.

CHAPTER TWELVE

Kate sat across the desk from her boss. This wasn't good. She knew it. He had called her in to his office and was now making her wait while he finished up some email or something (typing painfully slowly with two fingers). She sat on the edge of the chair, back straight – rigid, nervously twisting one of her rings around her finger.

That post had been on Facebook for less than an hour. It seemed so unlikely that anyone would have seen it. And then that person would have had to dob her in for it. And there was only one bitch here who hated her enough to do that – Kylie Bennett. Surely Kate's luck couldn't be that bad, could it?

As Tony continued to type, Kate tried hard not to stare at that nose hair. Maybe that was the wrong tact. Maybe she should get the staring out of her system now, while he wasn't watching. It was so gross. How did this guy have a wife *and* a girlfriend, and neither of them had ever suggested he trim that shit? Though Kate imagined that both women probably avoided looking at him as much as possible. But that hair just couldn't be avoided. It sprouted out at all angles. Some of it was grey. It was like a car wreck – you just couldn't seem to look away. *Oh my God*, there was a booger.

'As I understand it, Kate, you were unwell on Friday.'

Kate cleared her throat. 'Yes, that's right.'

'Kate, as you are aware, we've had some issues with your performance.'

Fuck. 'I – ahh – well...'

Tony Nose Hair held up his hand to silence her. 'And your attitude.'

Kate stared despondently at his nose hair. And that booger. Part of her wanted to reach across the desk and pick the booger out of his nose hair – it was too hard to just *see* it; but at the same time, she could feel her breakfast rising in the back of her throat just thinking about touching it – and the nose hair.

'We've been informed that you were in Sydney over the weekend.' He was careful not to actually accuse her of faking sickness.

There was a long pause. Tony Nose Hair was possibly waiting for Kate to say something. But she remained silent, thinking about how much she couldn't afford to lose this job. She'd never move out of her mother's house. And all of her credit card debt – it was one step shy of feeling insurmountable now, and that was with a steady income

'Is there anything you'd like to say?'

'I know about you and Kylie Bennett.' The words shot out of her mouth before she really had time to think about them. Her gaze nervously darted from his nose hair to his eyes and back again.

This time it was Tony's turn to be lost for words. His mouth opened and shut a few times. No one was supposed to know. He was sure that no one had known. His face twitched stupidly as his mind played out the doomsday scenario. His wife would leave him. All of his assets were in her name. It was supposed to be a precautionary measure in case he was ever sued. When he'd done it twenty years ago, he'd never given any thought to them ever divorcing. They were so in love back then. She would take everything. He had visions of those crazy stories you hear of scorned wives selling Ferraris for a dollar. Not that he had a Ferrari, but, oh God, his Range Rover. As these thoughts passed rapidly through his mind, all Kate saw was trembling nose hair.

'Right.' Nose Hair had composed himself. He just needed to handle this and his wife would never find out. And he needed to give some serious thought to a better asset protection structure. He considered bluffing, but he thought better of it. 'Well, your job is safe.'

Kate's mouth was still ajar. She couldn't believe she had just done that. She had just blackmailed someone. Blackmail so that she could keep a shitty job she hated. What a fucking stupid thing to do. Though he did deserve a lot worse than that.

CHAPTER THIRTEEN

Alex wildly rummaged through her handbag for her ringing phone. She really did need to clean her bag out – there was way too much stuff in there. She finally located her phone and answered the call from an unknown number just before the call was bumped to her voicemail.

'Hello.'

'Hi Alex. It's John. Ahh... John Masters.'

Alex wasn't able to mask her surprise. 'Hi?'

'Michelle gave me your number. She's out of town at the moment. And I just thought that maybe you'd like to catch up for a coffee. I don't really know anyone in Sydney. And – well – it's hard to make new friends as an adult.' John's honesty and awkwardness was endearing and immediately made Alex feel at ease.

'Sure. Why not?'

They arranged to meet later that day and Alex instantly began wondering what she would wear. There wasn't enough time to go shopping to buy something new. Though, who was she kidding, it was incredibly difficult to find anything that was her size, let alone something that she liked and felt comfortable in.

As she tried on a third outfit and sized herself up in the

mirror, it struck her – why did she care this much? She never really bothered with her clothes. She used to. For Daniel. But she realised it had been years since she had gone to these lengths for him. He never really noticed when she made an effort. Or, if he did, he made her feel silly – as though she was trying unsuccessfully to be something she wasn't. Why was she going to so much trouble for *John*? Did she maybe have a little crush on him? That was crazy – she was a happily married woman. And, really, John was extremely good looking. Why would he even look twice at her? It had been a complete fluke that she had somehow caught the eye of someone as gorgeous as Daniel; that certainly wouldn't happen again.

There was no harm in trying to look nice though. She decided on a red shift dress, with cap sleeves and a pair of black sequinned ballet flats. The outfit was a little out of the ordinary for her – she rarely wore bright colours. In fact, she wasn't sure if she'd ever actually worn the dress before. The red set off her olive skin and dark hair – she did look quite beautiful, especially when she practiced her 'confident' smile in the mirror. The shape of the dress, however, like most of her wardrobe, was far too loose and not flattering at all for her figure.

Impulsively she decided to have her nails done. She deliberated over the colour of the polish for a long time at the salon, eventually deciding on a shade of pink so pale that it was almost sheer.

The nail artist noted how long Alex took in deciding her colour. 'Is it an important occasion, sweetie?'

'Not really. Just seeing a friend this afternoon and I want to look nice.'

'Lovely. What are you wearing?'

'This.' Alex looked down at her red dress and began to panic – had she made the wrong decision? She didn't have time to go home and change before she saw John.

'Hmmm... With that dress, I'd probably do a red.' The woman turned and surveyed the rack of polishes, pulling one off the shelf and holding it up against Alex's dress. 'This one would be perfect.'

'Do you think? It's not too... bold?'

'Trust me, he'll love it.'

'Oh, no, it's not... umm... okay.'

As Alex approached the coffee shop, she felt very unlike herself. Or maybe she felt more like herself than she had in years, she wasn't sure. Either way, she felt good – about the way she looked, and just good in general. She felt a little brave meeting John like this. There was something bold about making new friends, and going out for coffee, especially given that this new friend just so happened to be a man.

The cafe wasn't nearly as trendy as any of the places that Alex had frequented over the girls' weekend that they'd had. It was tucked away in a back street, but not in the it's-so-hidden-you-have-to-be-incredibly-cool-to-know-about-it kind of way. John was already sitting at a table inside, toward the back. The harsh fluorescent light ruined any atmosphere that might have been created by their out of the way table.

'Sorry. I realise this isn't the coolest place around. They do good coffee though.'

Alex was secretly glad that he hadn't picked a chic coffee house. She knew she would have felt more intimidated if he had. This was much more her speed.

The waiter came to take their orders and John craned his neck to see the cabinet filled with pastries and other sweet delicacies. 'I think I'll have a lemon tart.' He turned to Alex, 'Will you have something? I'd offer to share with you, but the sweets here are just too good, I think I'd resent you for it,' John laughed.

Alex felt a little self-conscious. If she ordered dessert in front of Daniel, he would look at her, lips pursed and eyes full of judgement, and she would usually call the waiter back and say she'd changed her mind or just leave the dessert untouched on the plate. It felt unusual for someone to be encouraging her to consume calories. But she supposed that John didn't have any personal interest in her figure. She considered it for a few minutes, then declined.

John and Alex chatted over their coffees. He talked about his frequent trips back home to Brisbane and admitted that, although they were technically for work, he mostly arranged them because he missed home so much. He hadn't made many friends in Sydney, hadn't put down any roots.

'I haven't even furnished my apartment yet. I want to do it properly – matching furniture, cushions, rugs and all. But I have no idea where to even start.'

Alex laughed. 'I think the style at the moment is to not have your furniture matching.'

'See, I have absolutely no idea what I'm doing. I need help!'

'I actually have heaps of books and magazines on decorating. We ended up getting a decorator, so...' Alex shrugged. 'You're welcome to borrow them.'

'Thanks. That would be great.' John smiled. 'Do you get back to Brisbane much?'

'Not really.' Alex wanted to change the subject. She always seemed to talk too easily to John; she had no idea what he must think of her immediately divulging her personal problems without any prompting. 'In one of your many trips back, are you going to take Kate out on a date?' She teased John like he was an old friend.

'Well, I don't know. I had thought about asking her out. But I'm not sure if...' He trailed off as he registered the look on Alex's face. 'What is it? Did she say something?'

'Oh, no, it's nothing.' Alex squirmed. She was shocked that anyone would have any hesitation at asking Kate out. And equally, she was a little jealous that this gorgeous man was interested in her friend.

'But you don't think I should ask her out?'

'No, that's not it at all,' Alex said guardedly.

'Then what?' John changed to a lighter tone, 'Come on, you can tell me.'

Alex stared into her coffee. 'I'm just surprised that you're so hesitant.' She smiled broadly. 'Kate's stunning.'

'Mmm...' John nodded in agreement. 'But looks aren't everything.'

'But she's also fun and confident and nice and cool.' Alex laughed in a bid to dial back the intensity that she was conveying. 'Well, I could list her better qualities all day. But you get the point.' She laughed again, this time sounding a bit less nervous and a little more natural.

'Sounds like you've got a little bit of a girl crush.' John's smile lit up his whole face.

Alex's face went red. 'Yeah, well, not quite a crush exactly,'

Alex stumbled over her words, and then muttered, 'She's just perfect, is all.'

John laughed and shook his head. 'Kate's definitely beautiful and fun and confident and nice and cool. And she probably is a lot of other things that you haven't listed. But she's not perfect.'

'She's pretty bloody close.' She felt childish and immediately regretted her words, but, as always with John, she couldn't seem to keep herself in check – the words just jumped out of her mouth before she'd had a chance to think about them.

John's expression was a mixture of amusement and confusion. He began to shake his head.

Alex, despite her embarrassment, couldn't seem to contain herself. 'It's just – I don't know – she's so beautiful.' *Stop talking. Now.* 'And to have someone like you interested in her – she's so lucky.' *Oh god! I can't believe I just said that.* 'Her life is just amazing. She's always going to amazing parties and hanging out with cool people and doing fun things.' *You sound like a sulky child! Why are you still talking?*

The look on John's face changed from amusement to something like pity. 'Alex, you're a beautiful woman. I'm not sure why you can't see that. You're a much more natural beauty than Kate.'

Alex felt a wave of heat reach her cheeks. He thought she was beautiful.

'Don't get me wrong – I've had a thing for Kate since I was twelve. I think she's gorgeous, fake tan and all. And about her life – it's all smoke and mirrors, surely you can see that. You can't compare your life to what you see on her Facebook feed.

It's just not real. Everyone has their problems; you just can't see them from the outside.'

Alex cleared her throat awkwardly. She didn't know what to say. She was so embarrassed. A part of her wondered if he was right about Kate. Maybe her life wasn't as amazing as what Alex thought it was. Maybe Kate had problems too. She couldn't imagine what problems could possibly weigh you down when you looked like Kate. Or had Kate's confidence. Though the logical part of her mind knew that was silly.

'Sorry. That escalated quickly, didn't it?' Alex laughed nervously, and then slumped her shoulders despondently. 'I just get a little bit jealous of Kate sometimes,' Alex said quietly while staring into her empty coffee cup.

'You don't say,' John laughed. 'Should we get some more coffees?'

Alex nodded. 'Hang on – you've had a crush on Kate since you were twelve?'

It was John's turn to look sheepish. 'Yeah.'

'Well, you have to ask her out then.' Alex said emphatically, her composure now completely regained and her embarrassment pushed to one side.

'Okay, okay, if you're going to twist my arm.'

After another few hours of chatting, they decided to walk to Alex's apartment together so John could borrow the design books. They talked as they walked and Alex felt so comfortable that she began to wonder if she really did have a thing for John. She didn't think so, but knowing that he thought she was beautiful made it all very confusing.

As they walked through the door to the apartment, Alex's

face dropped. John instinctively looked around for the cause of her alarm. It wasn't immediately obvious.

'Hey, I'm home early. I had -' Daniel stopped dead in his tracks as he walked into the living room. The shock that was written across his face quickly turned to fury.

'Who the fuck is this?' He gestured wildly at John.

'Hi mate, I'm John. My sister's -'

Daniel cut him off, turning to Alex and slowly closing the gap between them, 'What are you doing with him when I'm not here?' His voice was quiet and simmering with pure rage.

As he spoke, Alex instinctively recoiled. Her full body tensed and pulled as far back from him as she could, pressing herself against the wall.

John saw Alex's response and immediately stepped between Daniel and Alex. 'You need to calm down. Alex and I are friends. Nothing is going on.' John attempted to placate him while maintaining a physical barrier between Daniel and Alex.

'I think you need to get the fuck out of my apartment.' Daniel's voice remained quiet – almost calm. Almost.

'Mate, you're pretty upset. I'm not leaving Alex here with you until you calm down.'

'John, it's fine. Please go.' Alex's voice was meek.

'Yes, please leave.'

'Are you sure you're alright alone with him?' John sounded unconvinced as he turned to Alex.

'Of course. He's my husband.'

A brief look of victory passed over Daniel's face.

John turned and walked out the door. As he did so, he felt ashamed for leaving Alex. He felt weak for taking the easy road and not standing his ground. He should have done something more. He wasn't sure what but anything would be better than doing nothing. He felt sure that asshole hit her. The way she recoiled was like she was anticipating it. John sat on a park bench around the corner from Alex's apartment and replayed in his head what he had just witnessed. Was he imagining things?

He decided to call Alex to check that she was alright.

The phone rang for a long time. John was about to hang up when Alex finally answered.

'Hello.'

'Hi, it's John. I just wanted to check that you're alright.'

'Yes. I'm fine.' Alex's tone sounded stilted and artificial.

'Are you sure? You don't sound fine.'

'Yes, but I can't really talk now.'

'Okay. Well, can we catch up sometime soon?'

'Sure. Okay then. Bye.'

'Wait. When are we going to catch up?'

Alex sighed. 'Monday – next week. I've got to go. Goodbye.' She hung up before he could say anything further.

CHAPTER FOURTEEN

The doorbell rang and Rachel felt a wave of panic rise up within herself. She took a deep breath and slowly exhaled concentrating on only her breath, just like in yoga class. The house looked immaculate, but she took one final look around just to be sure. Slightly self conscious, Rachel straightened her wings and pulled down her tutu for the hundredth time (it had seemed like a good idea at the time, but now she was feeling like the tutu was a little too revealing with white tights beneath), walked to the door and opened it.

'Where's our little birthday fairy?'

'Hi Sandra, come on in.' Rachel smiled warmly and embraced her mother-in-law.

The lead up to Georgie's third birthday party had been extremely stressful for Rachel. She had initially, with Georgie's approval, decided on a pink and gold theme. It was going to be so tasteful and understated. And, yes, it wasn't really hard to get a not-quite-three year old to agree when you showed them pretty pink balloons with glittery gold ribbons. But that was sort of the point – Georgie would have been happy with anything so long as it was pretty. And the other mothers had all gone to such lengths for their children's birthdays, she really had to put in a lot of work to make sure the theme was different and elegant and refined, while still actually being appropriate for a three year old.

All the women pretended to be friends, but they actually silently (and sometimes not so silently) judged each other, picking apart every parenting decision. They each, at times, felt the self conscious sting of not reaching the bar that the others had set; and they each had felt the self righteous superiority when someone else didn't live up to the inordinately high standards they all were striving for.

Two weeks out Georgie had suddenly decided she cared a lot about the theme. She declared that it must be a mermaid theme. It was imperative that Georgie look like Ariel from the Little Mermaid. Rachel had silently cursed herself for showing Georgie that movie and making such a big deal about how it had been her favourite one as a child. But, as always, Rachel had agreed, as part of her ongoing campaign to be the perfect mother. It was Georgie's day after all. And at least she hadn't requested a Frozen party. They'd been to enough of those to last a lifetime. And they had escalated to the point where now there was simply no way to top little Ava Lowe's Frozen themed third birthday. And if Rachel had to hear a group of three year olds screaming *Let it Go* for two hours straight again, she might actually lose it.

So mermaid theme it was. Until the week beforehand when Georgie had a change of heart and told all of her friends that it would be a fairy princess party. Mike had said that Rachel should just say no. She'd already gone to so much effort for the mermaid theme. And spent so much money. But Sarah Lowe (Ava's bitch of a mother, who was undoubtedly perfect) had accosted Rachel in the supermarket and told her about the gorgeous fairy outfit that she had specifically bought for Ava to wear to the party. There was no way Rachel could stick with the mermaid theme after that.

With a week's notice, Rachel didn't have a lot of time to arrange things for the party. There was certainly not enough time to get onto EBay and order things from China. But thankfully she could use a lot of the pink and gold decorations from the original theme. She could tweak a few of the games that she had planned. And she had gotten some fantastic ideas from the hours upon hours she had spent on Pinterest (thankfully she was pretty talented when it came to arts and crafts). Everything else she was able to pick up from a boutique kids party shop – she just wouldn't tell Mike how much it all cost.

The stress of the party had sent Rachel into a bit of a tailspin. She wanted it to be perfect for Georgie. This was, after all, the first birthday party that Georgie would really understand. And she really wanted to prove herself as a mum (though she wasn't really sure who she was proving herself to). And she really, *really*, more than anything, wanted to avoid being a laughing stock amongst all those bitchy judgey mothers. She didn't want to end up like Lucy Gilbert who had made the huge mistake of treating her daughter's party as though the kids having fun was the only thing that mattered. She'd had Bianca's birthday in a park, with no theme to speak of. Decorations had been limited to regular balloons (not even helium) and she had asked everyone to bring a plate of food to share. That just wasn't the done thing amongst the super mums in their circle – even if it did seem like a practical and *way* less stressful way to organise a birthday party. Poor Lucy had copped snide remarks from all angles and was pretty much a laughing stock from then on. Since the party, the super mums often spoke in hushed, earnest tones of how they felt sorry for poor Bianca, whose mother was obviously not coping well with motherhood and life in general. A few of the mothers (at the urging of Sarah Lowe, instigator) had offered to step in to make food for Bianca and her younger brother, Harry, since someone had seen Lucy feeding Harry pre-packaged baby food. It all seemed a bit over the top to Rachel; and she knew that in some circles (some of the mothers of the kids in Georgie's swim class, for example) it was considered completely normal to be relaxed and just focus on making life easy while doing the best thing for the children. But that wasn't at all deemed appropriate amongst the super mums. Maybe Lucy should have picked the women that she spent time with a little more wisely.

Rachel couldn't imagine how she could get on the wrong side of the super mums quite as disastrously as Lucy had. But there was no knowing what someone might catch you doing and take offense to. Rachel had been lucky enough to avoid being bullied throughout her schooling years, but now, as a grown woman, she certainly needed to tread very carefully to avoid becoming a victim to these bullies.

Mike had asked Rachel if she thought that she was putting a bit too much pressure on herself with the party. Surely a child's third birthday party didn't require such effort. Surely she didn't need to feel so stressed about it all. Georgie would love it no matter what they did. Rachel had responded saying that it's what all the other mothers did. It was what was expected. She couldn't possibly dial it back without becoming a laughing stock amongst all the other mums. Mike thought that she was exaggerating; he thought that the pressure to be perfect was coming from within. But Rachel knew what they'd all be saying behind her back if she didn't have colour coordinated decorations and themed party games.

A few more guests were beginning to arrive and Rachel was feeling a bit calmer about the whole thing. Everything looked amazing. Georgie looked amazing in her white tulle dress, with pink fairy wings and matching pink satin ballet slippers. Surely there was nothing for Sarah Lowe and her squad of super mums to find fault with. Surely.

Rachel was secretly thankful that Jax, from Georgie's children's yoga class, wasn't attending. He had a severe peanut allergy, which would have added a lot more effort to the food preparation. And let's face it, an emergency requiring an ambulance was not the kind of thing that would impress the super mums. There had been enough work in getting food ready for the party, without that kind of stress hanging over her head. Rachel had spent weeks preparing food for the event. Some items she had frozen ahead of time but most had to be made fresh in the days beforehand. To ensure that everything went perfectly to plan, Rachel had done at least two practice runs of each food item. Mike had told her that it was excessive but he was still pretty pleased by the amount of cake that he was able to eat. (Not that Rachel was allowing much of that. She really didn't want his weight blowing out again. A few years back, before they were married, Mike had gotten fat. Rachel loved him no matter what, but she couldn't tolerate an unhealthy household. So she had forced him to start exercising with her and she had cut out all junk food from his diet – or at least so she thought. He had actually still been eating potato chips and burgers at lunch and had thrown out the salads and carrot sticks that she had packed for him. So when the opportunity came to sample an array of cakes and give feedback about which frosting was better and which cake was lighter, he wasn't going to look a gift horse in the mouth.)

Once all the guests had arrived, they started the first activity – making flower head garlands. Rachel had been to the flower markets at dawn to buy masses of dahlias, freesias, lilies and roses (and had spent an hour de-thorning the roses – pricked fingers would obviously not do at all). Luckily it wasn't such a hot day, so the flowers hadn't wilted by the time the party started. The flower garlands had been an amazing success. Mums and children alike were all sporting flower crowns. Some of the dads even had flowers tucked behind their ears and drooping out of their shirt pockets. Rachel had braided some of the girls' hair and had woven flowers through the braids. The kids had seemed ecstatic when Rachel had instructed Mike to move a mirror out to the terrace so that they could all admire their floral handiwork.

Rachel dashed back into the kitchen to grab some more fruit fairy wands to put out. She had threaded fruit onto wooden skewers and topped with star shaped pieces of watermelon that she had painstakingly cut. To her delight, the kids loved them. This whole thing was going so well. This may even top Ava's perfect Frozen party.

As Rachel rummaged through the fridge for more supplies to restock everything that the kids had been devouring, she heard a couple of women talking in the dining room.

'...only has one child and doesn't work.'

'I know what you mean. Her life must be so easy. No wonder she has the time to pull off a party like this.'

'And maintain that ass. Wearing *that* tutu with *those* tights wasn't really necessary. She clearly just wanted everyone to get an eyeful.'

Rachel felt her cheeks burn with indignation. That last, particularly bitchy comment had been from Wendy. She thought that they were friends. She thought that they were defiant against the super mums together – not in the Lucy-Gilbert-not-trying kind of way, but in the kind of way where they still went along with everything, but rolled their eyes a little in private. She had tried so hard to impress these horrible women; to not be the next Lucy Gilbert. Apparently you could try too hard; be too impressive. Why had she cared so much? Why *did* she care so much?

'I feel sorry for her. She obviously doesn't have much going on in her life if she's got time to do all of this.'

'No, I feel sorry for Georgie. What kind of example is she getting from a stay at home mum?'

Rachel's heart sank. Were they right? Was she setting a bad example for her daughter? She wasn't striving for anything in life – apart from a happy child and a clean house (and to impress the super mums, which she was apparently failing at). Was her daughter going to be embarrassed of her when she was older? Was Georgie going to, red faced, tell her friends that Rachel was *just* a stay at home mum? Was her lack of purpose impacting her daughter's views on women's roles and gender equality? Should she get a job? Would her being successful – like Michelle – be more beneficial to Georgie than being at home, and available, for her? In that moment, Rachel wished she was a little more like Michelle. More driven. More successful. More important. She just wished that she was doing something that would mean that Georgie would respect her when she was a bit older. And she wished that she was doing something important, to shut those horrible super mums up. And she wished that she was doing something for herself.

Rachel thought bitterly that no one would ever talk about Michelle like that. And if Michelle overheard those mean women saying stuff like that about her – in her own home, no less – Michelle would tell those cows where to shove it. Michelle wouldn't even care if those nasty women didn't like her. But instead, Rachel was hiding in the kitchen, red faced, blinking back tears, hoping that they didn't notice that she had heard them talking about her, feeling terrible and doubting herself as a mother.

The fridge began beeping, the door had been ajar for too long. Rachel heard the women go quiet and she slammed the door shut and retreated to the bathroom. No matter how much fun Georgie had today, this would be Rachel's main memory of her daughter's first proper party. And she cursed those women – and herself – for that.

CHAPTER FIFTEEN

For John the following week passed slowly. He worried about Alex's safety. And agonised over his own role in the events – what he should have done. What he would do if he had his time over again. Justification of his own actions. What extent he was to blame for the situation; if he hadn't gone to Alex's apartment, none of it would have happened. Was he reading too much into this? Did he just witness a normal fight, between a normal married couple, where there was a little bit of jealousy, and had he just leapt to conclusions?

He wrestled with the question of whether he should speak to Michelle or Fiona about what he had witnessed. Maybe they would know more about Alex and Daniel's relationship. Maybe they would have some way to lift the weight of this problem from his shoulders. He eventually decided to subtly bring the subject up with Michelle over coffee, and maybe – just maybe – he would tell her what had happened.

'So, I caught up with Alex the other day.' John tried to sound as casual as possible.

'I'm glad. You really could do with expanding your circle of friends. I can't be the only person in Sydney that you know.' Michelle laughed.

'Mmm...' John gave a half-hearted smile. 'You don't think it's a bit weird, me hanging out with a married woman?'

'No. Not unless it was.' Michelle cocked her head to one side. 'Was it?'

'No. Just wanted another opinion. Have you met Alex's husband?'

'Ye-ah.' Michelle pronounced the word slowly, unsure where he was going with this. She would usually have no hesitation at saying exactly what she thought, but last time that had backfired a bit – Rachel and Kate had both leapt to Daniel's defence after having met the guy. She still had a bad feeling about him, but she was far less inclined to share her thoughts on the subject. Maybe she should mind her own business. That wasn't exactly her style though.

'And what do you think?'

'I only met him really briefly at a bar. He was really drunk. Why? What do you think?'

John ignored her questions. 'And what's their relationship like?'

'That's a weird question. How would I know what their relationship is like? What are you getting at?'

'Just wanted to know what you thought of him, is all. It's nothing.'

CHAPTER SIXTEEN

'Oh, the places you'll go!

Congratulations!

Today is your day.

You're off to Great Places!

You're off and away!'

As she read Dr Seuss to Georgie, a small knot formed in Rachel's stomach. Her mouth felt dry and her throat tightened slightly. Rachel continued reading without skipping a beat.

'You have brains in your head.

You have feet in your shoes.

You can steer yourself

Any direction you choose.'

I didn't go places.

Her reading was enthusiastic. As always. The volume of her voice built and dropped, emphasising the words of the story.

I didn't go places.

As she read aloud, the feeling in Rachel's stomach grew. The feeling of regret churned her stomach.

'And will you succeed?'

I didn't go places. I didn't succeed.

'Yes! You will, indeed!

(98 and 3/4 per cent guaranteed.)
KID, YOU'LL MOVE MOUNTAINS!'
I didn't go places. I didn't move mountains.

What the super mums had said about her at Georgie's birthday party had really gotten under Rachel's skin. She couldn't help but think about what she had and hadn't done in her life. And wonder about whether she was doing the right thing now.

Rachel wasn't in a 'slump' or 'the waiting place.' Dr Seuss hadn't written about her particular predicament. He hadn't mentioned sacrificing some of your dreams in order to fulfil your other dreams. Why can't we have it all? Was giving up her career to have Georgie the right decision? Yes. Without a doubt. But that didn't ease the pang of regret, jealousy and wondering. She wished that she had travelled when she was young. She wished that she had lived a little. She wished she'd gone places.

Rachel was happy with her life. But she had regrets. She really could have done so much more with her career before settling down. And she questioned what her future held. What would she do when Georgie went to school? What about when Georgie was in high school? Sure, Rachel would be able to find something to fill her time. Maybe. But would it be fulfilling? Would she feel challenged and satisfied? Would she still be happy with her life? Would her daughter be proud of her, admire her, look up to her? What kind of role model would she be for her daughter if she wasn't happy with her lot? Would Georgie – studying medicine or law or psychology – respect a mother who had never done anything with her career? And what would happen to Rachel when Georgie was no longer at home? Rachel's life revolved around her baby girl.

It felt as though every other part of herself had faded into insignificance when she had become a mum. She envied the purpose that Michelle's life had – the motivation, the ability to juggle work commitments and deadlines, the glamorous life of flying around the country for work, the ability – with time and finances – to jet off to Paris for a marathon. Rachel wouldn't trade her daughter for anything, but sometimes – just sometimes – she wished that she had done more; that she was more.

If nothing else, Rachel felt with absolute certainty that her daughter would never experience this predicament. Georgie would never feel regret about not having travelled or done something with her career or fulfilled her full potential. Rachel gazed into Georgie's bright blue eyes. *Oh, the places you'll go.*

CHAPTER SEVENTEEN

Finally the week's wait was up. Alex sent John a text message on the Monday morning asking him to meet her after work at a bar in the city.

When he arrived, John found Alex in a corner booth nestled in the back of the bar. It was surprisingly quiet, making it an easy place to chat.

'How are you?' John surveyed Alex looking for bruises or signs of injury, but saw nothing. It didn't set his mind at ease though.

'I'm fine.' Alex paused. 'Look, I know it probably seemed weird, or something, the other day with Daniel. He just over reacted. He gets jealous, that's all.'

'Over reacted? I thought he was going to hit you.' John paused, looked Alex in the eyes, and said quietly, 'Does he hit you?'

Alex's eyes widened. 'No. Never.' She was shocked that someone could think such a thing of Daniel.

'Alex,' John began in a sombre tone, 'I saw your reaction to him. You looked like you were expecting him to throw a punch.'

'Well, I'm not sure why it would look that way, because I definitely wasn't.'

Alex began to wonder why she had looked that way. It was true that Daniel had never hit her. He was jealous and acted crazy sometimes, but he would never hit her. Never. Even though she was adamant that was true, why was it that she could imagine it so clearly? Why could she, in her mind, see his fist moving toward her face, in slow motion, and feel the fear and panic and shock pulsing through her veins as he launched toward her. It had never happened. So why could she picture it just as though it had?

Alex couldn't seem to admit to herself that she expected Daniel to hit her. He had never actually done it before. Sure, there had been times that he'd pushed her or grabbed her so hard it had left bruises in the shape of his finger prints. But all of that was just him being a little rough. He had never meant to hurt her. And getting a little forceful was very different to hitting someone. At least that's what she continually told herself. It was easy enough to make excuses for him; to reason away his actions. He loved her so much, he couldn't help himself. But deep down she knew that it was only a matter of time. His jealous rage was an unstoppable force. And he had pushed Alex around for so long that he thought of her more as his property than as a person.

His anger, jealousy and callous words had chipped away at her; he had taken away so much of who she was, she felt as though her own sense of self had been erased; she had become Daniel's other half, as though she – Alex, as a whole – no longer existed. He had taken away the things that she loved, he had told her she was ugly and worthless for so long, that she was sure it was true, and he had drained the joy from her life. And despite that – or more accurately, because of that – she felt incredibly alone, yet she couldn't imagine subsisting alone without Daniel, the man who made her feel alone.

'So why is he so jealous?' Before Alex could answer, John continued. 'You know that his reaction was not normal, don't you? You said that it might have seemed weird, but weird is not a word that anyone would use to describe the way Daniel was acting. He was angry. He appeared to be violently angry. That's not weird. It's scary. I was worried for your safety.'

'Haven't you ever had a girlfriend who was jealous?'

'Of course, everyone has. But that's completely beside the point –'

Alex interrupted, 'And what did this girlfriend do? Yell? Get angry?'

John sighed, exasperated, and rolled his eyes a little. 'Yes, yes. She started following me. Hiding in bushes. And yelled and screamed about all the places I'd been and the girls that I'd talked to. But that's not the-'

'And did she ever get physically violent?'

'No.'

'I think you get my point.'

There was a long silence.

'Did you just say you had a girlfriend who *hid in bushes?*'

John put his face in his hands and rubbed his eyes. 'Argh, yeah. Megan. She wasn't actually my girlfriend at the time. We were only together briefly – just a few dates, really. Then I called it, and she started following me. I started seeing someone else and she kept accosting me – at work even –

and accusing me of cheating. *But we had broken up.* She was a fucking lunatic.'

'Oh my God.' Alex was lost for words.

'So maybe you see *my* point. You're saying that your husband's behaviour is normal because he's no more aggressive than the craziest person I know.' John added, a little more gently, 'Don't you see how that's concerning?'

'Well, I didn't realise that I was comparing Daniel to a certifiably insane person.'

'I'm really worried, Alex.'

'I think you're being a bit melodramatic.'

'No, Alex, I don't think I am at all.'

After their conversation, John decided against speaking to Michelle about Daniel. Alex had been so adamant that everything was okay. He didn't believe her, but, in the end, resigned himself to the thought that there was nothing that he could do about the situation if Alex was unwilling to admit that there was a problem.

CHAPTER EIGHTEEN

As Kate was getting ready for her date with John, she felt nervous but wasn't sure why exactly. Over the past few years she'd been on more dates than she cared to recall. The first few after her breakup with Peter had been stomach-knot-inducing, leaving her a stuttering bundle of sweaty palms and jittering legs. But it hadn't taken long before she was all confidence. And she had never looked back. Until now. Now she was as nervous as she had been on her first post-Peter date. She had checked her phone every five minutes hoping for a message from John since he had asked her out, and the night of the date she had tried on half a dozen outfits, messed up her makeup twice (her hands were not cooperating, making eyeliner impossible to use) and couldn't stop looking at the clock – willing herself more time to get ready.

She had been surprised when John had called. The guys she dated didn't usually call – texting was usually the *done* thing. And she hadn't really expected he would be interested after her disgraceful performance at the engagement party. But more than that, she had mostly been surprised by her own reaction – she was excited. Really excited.

John was going to be in Brisbane for Christmas. It was decided that two days before Christmas they'd head to a new restaurant that Kate had picked. She always had a list of restaurants that she wanted to try but couldn't afford, and would suggest them when she went on dates so that she got to sample a few of the finer things. But she made it a rule that there would be no fancy restaurants with any guys that she thought might turn out to be losers – there was nothing worse than feeling like you took advantage – or worse, like you owe them something – if you have to turn them down for a second date.

This particular restaurant had a view of the river and had just been opened by some celebrity chef who was supposed to be amazing. Just to see the decor was apparently worth the small fortune it cost to eat there. Getting a reservation, particularly at this time of year, would have been tricky, but John had managed it somehow. Maybe he'd just got lucky.

While she waited for John to pick her up, Kate began to regret her choice of restaurant. She wished she had picked something more casual. She was nervous enough without adding the fear of an unpronounceable menu and a snooty waiter to the mix. And why was he picking her up? It seemed so strange and formal, like something they do in movies. It only ever seemed appropriate if you had to go far. There really wasn't any reason they couldn't just meet at the restaurant. And it also meant that they wouldn't be drinking – she couldn't exactly drink if he had to stay sober in order to drive – and drinking on a first date always helped the conversation flow a little better. Picking her up was another thing to add to the list of slightly off-kilter things that John did. And Kate wasn't sure whether it was endearing or annoying, but either way, it got under her skin.

In the two weeks between John calling and their date, Kate had questioned why she'd actually said yes. She didn't want a boyfriend. She didn't want anything serious. She loved flirting and going to fancy restaurants and having meaningless sex with men, but she couldn't do that with Fiona's brother. So why was she going on a date with him? She knew she liked him a little too much, and that just spelled trouble. But, against her better judgement, she was going on the date. It was too late to back out now, anyway.

When John rang her doorbell and her mother answered, Kate felt like a teenage girl in an American movie being picked up for prom. Kate interrupted the conversation that John and her mother were having, wanting the awkward moment to be over as soon as possible.

'Hey, I'm ready. Let's go.' Kate turned back to look over her shoulder at her mother as she opened the front door. 'Bye Mum. Love you.'

'You look nice.' John closed the door behind them.

'Thanks.' Kate smiled but was unimpressed – she had been aiming for a little more than *nice*. You don't spend three hours getting ready to look *nice*. The logical part of her thought that she should cut the guy some slack – she'd never worried about that kind of thing before – she dressed up to feel good about herself, not for compliments from guys. And, so what if he was in desperate need of a thesaurus? A compliment was a compliment.

They walked down the driveway and got into the car in silence.

'So, whose car is this?'

'Huh?'

'You don't live here. Whose car are you driving?'

'It's my parents'.'

Kate admired the soft cream leather seats. She could easily become accustomed to this kind of car.

'Have you been to this restaurant before?'

'No, it's pretty new but I've been wanting to try it. Have you been to any of his restaurants in Sydney?' *God, this is so awkward!*

'Yeah, I've been to that one in the Rocks. I forget what it's called – the one that's always on TV.'

'Oh, cool.' Kate sounded bored. 'Was it good?'

'Really good!' John was a little too enthusiastic in an attempt to make the conversation flow a bit better. He wasn't successful. They sat in an awkward silence for the remainder of the drive.

Kate felt annoyed with herself for caring so much about this date – all that anticipation and it was turning out to be a complete flop. If she could just relax, maybe it would go a bit better, but for some reason she just couldn't.

'Do you remember when you and Fi Fi used to sneak out and drink with those idiots who lived across the road?'

'Oh my God, yes!' Kate instantly relaxed as she let an enthusiastic laugh escape her lips. 'Those guys *were* idiots! What was the name of the guy that lived there? Adam, wasn't it? Does he – or I guess his parents – still live there?'

'No, they moved years ago.'

'I can't believe Fi told you about that. It's actually a little embarrassing that we used to hang out with those losers. We just thought they were cool because they were older and had cars and could buy alcohol.'

'Fi Fi didn't have to tell me. I used to watch you guys sneak out.'

'You were spying on us?' Kate pulled a face in mock indignation and then laughed.

'I always wished that I could go with the two of you.' John gave a sheepish smile. 'I had a huge crush on you.' There was a brief silence. 'Now, that's embarrassing.'

Kate was thrown a little off guard. Guys lined up to flirt with her now. But back then, she had been a bit of an ugly duckling. No one ever had a crush on her. At least, not that she knew of. She felt a little awkward again, but kind of in a good way.

As they arrived at the restaurant, Kate again wished she had picked somewhere more casual – somewhere far less expensive. What did it say about her, on their first date, picking a restaurant that she clearly couldn't afford to eat at? She worried that it seemed like she was just taking him for a ride. Or that she was used to guys paying for everything – like she was *that* kind of girl.

Walking through the door, Kate momentarily forgot her worries about the choice of restaurant – she was so awestruck. From the door, you could see an open window that ran the length of the restaurant, opening the kitchen to the diners. The chefs all looked immaculate in their whites, and seemed calm in their bustling activity. In an open area near the entrance, hung a huge very modern chandelier, which was so low Kate wondered if anyone had ever hit their head on it. On the far wall was an enormous vertical herb garden. It was as though they had taken a perfectly groomed garden and turned it on its side. It was a mystery how they managed to have the plants grow sideways and indoors without them dying or the soil falling to the ground. Each table was covered in a fresh crisp white linen table cloth, and the centre adorned with a strip of real grass, that was planted into a sunken garden embedded in the table. The table cloths appeared to have holes cut out to fit the gardens perfectly. Every seat in the restaurant faced the floor-to-ceiling glass walls, overlooking the river. The decor had managed to strike an amazing balance between the edgy on-trend and the fine dining atmosphere.

The maître de showed them to their table, and they both sat in silence gazing around the room.

'This place is amazing.' Kate sipped at her water, while wondering just how expensive this was going to get. She had briefly looked at a sample menu online (the menu was seasonal and changed daily based on the best produce available at the market), but it didn't list prices. 'Is this much like the restaurant you went to in Sydney?'

'Not at all. It was really spectacular as well, but totally different. It had paper lanterns everywhere. Kind of hard to describe, but it was really cool. Next time you're in Sydney, we should go there.' John wondered if that was coming on too strong. Should he have said anything about them seeing each other again so early-on on their first date? He really should be trying to play it cool, but he just was never good at that.

'I'd love that.' Kate was suddenly feeling a little coy. She picked up her menu and began to study it; John followed suit.

'Do you know what you're going to have?' John asked after several minutes.

'No. I've heard the degustation is good, but...' Kate trailed off. She didn't want to say what she was thinking –

degustation was too ridiculously wanky. She loved fancy food, but that just seemed to take it too far; she never knew what she was eating, the meal took hours and hours and when she got something she loved, the portion was far too small for her liking. And in the end, she always ended up wanting to stop at McDonalds on the way home. 'Do you know what you want?'

'Degustation isn't really my thing. I was thinking the pork.'

They both looked back at their menus, the stilted awkwardness returning.

'Did you really have a crush on me in high school?' She didn't mean to say it, but the words just seemed to jump out of Kate's mouth. She looked down at the grass in the middle of the table, not wanting to make eye contact. The grass was long and thin; there were pieces of all different lengths, with a few tiny white flowers at the tip of some of the strands.

After what seemed like an age, John finally spoke. 'Yes. I had a massive crush on you. I can't believe you didn't notice.'

'But why?'

'I don't know. Why does anyone ever like anyone? I liked you.' Realising that his answer might sound mildly insulting, John added, 'You were – are – funny and nice. And fun. You never took yourself too seriously. And you're gorgeous.'

Kate looked up from the grass. 'Oh.' She looked back down, not knowing what to say. 'I wonder why this grass has flowers. It's very pretty.'

'That's not grass. It's chives.'

'Oh.' Kate felt a little silly at repeating herself – just saying the one syllable, as though she didn't know how to engage in a real conversation. 'Do you know much about gardening?'

'Not really. I like to cook, so I know herbs. I've never been particularly successful in growing them though. I live in an apartment now, so...' John shrugged.

Seeing an opportunity to steer away from the awkwardness, Kate jumped. 'So you cook, hey? That's pretty cool. What's your favourite thing to cook?' Now Kate was feeling a bit more like herself – a bit more in the swing of the dating thing.

'Mostly Italian.'

'I love Italian food!'

'Me too. Have you been to Italy?'

A small wave of self pity hit Kate. 'No. I'd love to go though. Have you?'

'Yeah, that's where I got into cooking. I took a class on a whim, and this little old nonna taught me how to make pasta from scratch. It was one of the most delicious things I've ever eaten – and I had actually cooked it.' John noticed the drop in Kate's mood as he spoke. 'Why don't you plan a trip? You'd really love it. Italy has great fashion – or at least, to a complete novice like me, it seems to. And the food is incredible.'

'I have no way to afford a holiday. I spend more than I earn as it is, and that's while living with my mother. If I ever get off my butt and move out, I'm going to be dirt poor.' Kate felt glum but didn't want her mood to ruin the date. 'Anyway, we should decide what we're going to order. The waiter is hovering.'

The rest of the evening continued as it had begun – bouncing from clumsy conversation to wonderful flirting to sweet self-conscious silences. As they finished their desserts, neither Kate nor John really knew if the evening had been a success or a total failure. Walking side by side to the car,

John, a little too casually to seem casual, ran his hand from the middle of Kate's forearm to her fingertips and slipped her hand inside his. Kate was surprised by the sweet gesture and more than a little shocked that it made her stomach do flips and had her feeling tongue tied.

During the car ride back to Kate's place, they sat in silence. Kate was unsure how the date was going to end – would John want to come in? Would he try to kiss her? Holding hands was sweet, but there was no going back from a kiss – they couldn't just be friends after that, if that's even what they were to each other. John certainly wouldn't be merely Fi's little brother anymore. But – who was she kidding – after seeing him in Sydney, she no longer thought of him as *just* her friend's brother.

The car pulled into Kate's street and she realised that her heart was pounding. She was nervous. It felt as though whatever happened in the next few moments would dictate – and possibly even define – their relationship. And despite that – and despite the longing that she felt to have him kiss her – she really didn't know what she wanted from him. She told herself to just wait and see. Let him make the moves and she would work out what she wanted later. She would never usually hesitate to make the first move herself, but this was just different. This time she actually cared – really cared – about the outcome. And about what he thought of her. Did he *want* to kiss her? And while she waited, Kate had difficulty keeping her legs still; a storm of nerves raged in her stomach.

The car was parked in the driveway and she should be reaching for the door and saying her goodbyes, but she didn't. She just sat in silence for what seemed like an eternity. And then John reached for his own door. Kate chastised herself for hesitating – for making the situation uncomfortable and for seeming desperate and being obvious. What was she thinking?

John appeared at her door, opened it for her and held out his hand to her. She laid her hand in his and in one graceful movement he helped her from the car. Their hands stayed touching – ever so gently – until they reached the front door.

Finally Kate's nerves abated briefly. 'Thank you. I had a really nice night.'

John leaned toward her, his free hand gently, but firmly, found her lower back and his lips pressed against hers. Kate relaxed into him, her anxiety released; she felt nothing but him – and them, together – in that moment. Nothing else mattered.

John pulled away. 'I had a really nice night too.' He kissed her again – gently and for a fraction of a second only; and then turned and walked away.

Kate had a feeling of contentment envelope her. A sense of stillness and peace came over her after her insides had been so alive with jittery anticipation. No thoughts of what she wanted or the ramifications of that kiss haunted her. She knew that later she would be plagued by questions about what it all meant and what exactly it was that she wanted from this. But in that moment, those questions didn't need answers; she didn't care about the future; she didn't care about anything other than how unbelievably heavenly that kiss had been. All she could think of was how much she just wanted to keep kissing John. And all she felt was bliss.

CHAPTER NINETEEN

The two months following Michelle's discussion with Andrew passed incredibly slowly for her. She couldn't stop thinking about the time that she was potentially wasting by waiting for Andrew. And she kept wondering whether she really thought that Andrew was the one or if he was just a conveniently timed sperm donor.

She wished that she had someone to talk to about her conundrum. Kate wouldn't understand wanting children or the potential problems that work might pose if she decided to do it alone; Alex was still in Paris – not that she would really understand Michelle's predicament either – the girl was happily married and didn't even have a job; and she was almost certain that Rachel wouldn't approve of knowingly bringing a child into the world to live in a single parent household. And there was no way she could talk to her other friends about it – she knew with absolute certainty that Jess would have ulterior motives, given that they were business partners; John was a guy and just couldn't understand the ticking time bomb that was attached to her ovaries; and Louise showed nothing but contempt for children and the people who bore them. Michelle decided to talk to Rachel. Even if she was judgey about it, at least Michelle would have heard another person's perspective, which had to be better than going through the same pros and cons list in her head over and over again.

Michelle would be back in town to visit her family over Christmas, so was planning on catching up with Kate and Rachel then anyway.

'So, I wanted to get your advice on something. Actually, not so much your advice, I guess I just need a sounding board.'

They sat on the terrace at Rachel's home, sipping ice tea in a vain attempt to cool down from the typical searing hot Australian summer. Rachel was re-tying her daughter's shoe laces, but looked up, hearing the gravity of the advice being sought in Michelle's nervous tone. Rachel nodded but remained silent.

'I think I want a baby.'

A smile spread across Rachel's face. 'I didn't know you and Andrew were so serious. I'm so happy for you!' Rachel gushed.

Michelle turned to watch Georgie, who had sprung into action, continuing on with her masterpiece by spreading paint across a stretched canvas that was sitting on a child sized easel. The smears of different coloured paint melded together in places to make large brownish patches.

'That's the part I'm not sure about.'

'Which part?' Rachel was still smiling broadly and watching her daughter make a huge mess of the Christmas present she was making for her grandparents.

'Andrew.'

There was a long pause. 'Oh.' Rachel took a long gulp of her drink. 'Well, it's very normal to want a baby. We're not getting any younger.' Rachel laughed, but stopped mid-laugh, as she didn't want to be seen as dismissive. 'Have you talked to Andrew about having children?'

'Yes. We talked about a month ago. He wanted me to give him a couple of months to think about it.'

'It sounds like you need time to think about it too.'

They both continued to watch Georgie paint, which was intermittently interrupted by singing, trips to the garden to pull grass and – as far as Michelle could tell – incoherent babbling about someone named Daisy (or possibly someone who was lazy). Michelle wondered if this was typical child behaviour or if this particular child had ADHD. She hoped the latter – the reality of looking after a small person who had such a short attention span seemed horrendous to her.

'I had been thinking about just doing it by myself. You know – the whole sperm donor thing. And then I met Andrew. I still want to have a baby. And I want to be with Andrew. But I don't know yet if I want to have a baby with Andrew.'

'And you don't want to wait a little bit, to find out if you do want to have a baby with Andrew?'

'I'd love to wait a little while longer, so I could know for sure. But, in the mean time, my eggs are withering away.' Michelle shrugged. 'And how does someone know for sure, anyway?'

They continued to watch Georgie, who seemed to have completely forgotten about the painting and had moved on to brushing and styling a doll's hair.

'I don't think people really do know for sure. I think it's a leap of faith for most people. They decide they want a baby, they think they love each other – or at least that they like each other enough to make a realistic go of it – and the timing's right.'

Michelle was surprised at how pragmatic Rachel was being. It seemed out of character for her to show any crack in the veneer of her seemingly perfect life and marriage. Could Rachel really have had uncertainty about her relationship before she got pregnant? Did Rachel even potentially not love her husband first? And, most shocking of all, did Rachel just practically admit that to Michelle?

'So you're saying that I should just do it?'

'Definitely not. I'm saying that no one ever knows for sure. But if you have a baby with Andrew, it's for life – the baby *and* your relationship with Andrew. If you split up sometime down the track, you'll still be a big part of each other's lives.'

'Mummy.' Georgie discarded her dolls and climbed onto her mother's lap. Her small arms looped around Rachel's neck, and Rachel pulled Georgie towards her and enveloped her in a hug.

'Yes, darling.'

Georgie mumbled something into Rachel's ear, and snuck a furtive look at Michelle, before coyly burying her face into Rachel's shoulder. Rachel stood, while maintaining a grip on her daughter, who instinctively wrapped her legs around her mother's waist.

The smallness of Rachel's figure was highlighted by the size of her daughter clinging to her. Georgie's legs, covered in cherub like fat rolls, hugged her mother's middle, feet hanging down, reaching past Rachel's butt and slapping against the back of her thighs as Georgie squirmed. Michelle wondered how they had gotten so old, that Rachel had a child that big.

It seemed absurd to think of her tiny friend being responsible for this enormous small person. She imagined Rachel in a few years' time trying to discipline a ten year old that was taller than her. It seemed even crazier to think that Michelle wanted this for herself. But she did.

'Georgie wants to give you something.' Rachel turned her face towards Georgie, speaking into the back of her head, as she was still pressing her face into Rachel's shoulder, 'Go on. Don't be shy.' Rachel slid Georgie down to the ground.

Georgie's face remained angled toward the ground; she cast her eyes upward at Michelle and gave a small but sweet smile. Tentatively, she reached a hand toward Michelle, opened her fist and held her palm upwards to Michelle. Michelle peered down and saw a small flower in Georgie's hand.

'For me?' Michelle plucked the flower from Georgie's hand. 'Thank you.' She wasn't able to properly hide the condescending tone from her voice, not that Georgie noticed, though. Michelle didn't have the patience for this sort of thing. Maybe it seemed cute when the child was your own, but Michelle was trying to have an extremely important grown-up conversation and this interruption was just a little bit irritating.

Georgie, with her plump little hands, grabbed Michelle's arm, pulling Michelle toward her. As she leaned down close, Georgie laid a small kiss on Michelle's cheek, and then darted off toward the garden. Michelle's lips involuntarily spread into a smile, immediately forgetting her previous annoyance and simply basking in the adorableness of the moment.

'She's so cute.'

'Mmmm. She's not usually like that with strangers. She gets a bit shy.' Rachel patted her face down with a handkerchief, in an attempt to dry the beads of perspiration that were running down her face. 'Have you thought about what you will do if, in a month's time, Andrew says he wants to have a baby with you?'

'I don't know. I figure there are two options – we have a baby or we break up and I have a baby with a test-tube father.'

Rachel frowned at Michelle.

'Obviously there are more options, but that's really the fork in the road,' Michelle quickly added.

'Do you really think having a baby alone is a good idea?'

'It's not a fantastic idea, but it's not the worst idea I've ever had. I want a baby and if that's how I need to make it happen, then that's the path I'll go down.'

'Have you thought through how you're going to explain that to your child when they're old enough to understand? Or how they'll feel about not having a father?' Rachel's tone was gentle.

'A lot of kids grow up without fathers. I don't think it's such a big deal.'

'But those kids had fathers in the beginning. You're talking about bringing a child into the world knowing that they'll never have a father.'

'Hang on – they may have a father. I might meet someone at some stage. It's not like it's a foregone conclusion that I'll be alone for the rest of my life.'

'Have you considered how you will care for a child on your own? You certainly won't be able to work the hours that you currently work. And with you living in Sydney and your parents living here, are you going to have a strong enough support network to do this thing alone?'

'I work more than sixty hours a week. Every week. I haven't taken a holiday in years. My job takes an inordinate amount of hard work and sacrifice. I'm used to working my butt off without a support network. Looking after a child cannot be any more challenging than what I'm used to. I can do it alone.' There wasn't even a tiny chink in the armour of Michelle's indignant self confidence.

A laugh escaped Rachel's lips before she could stop it. She quickly recovered, pursing her lips together to prevent any further laughter, and shook her head slowly. 'I don't doubt that you can do it alone. But I don't think you'll want to.' Rachel let her lips form a sympathetic smile. 'I wouldn't go comparing your work to being a parent. There's just no comparison. It's just different. And like nothing you've ever experienced before. Your work is challenging and satisfying; being a parent challenges you physically and emotionally, but rarely challenges you mentally. It can be extremely isolating and lonely, and that's with an extremely supportive and loving partner; doing it without a partner could mean weeks without adult conversation. In some ways it's harder than anything you've ever done before.' Rachel raised her hand to silence Michelle. 'And that's not debatable, every mother feels that way because it's a continuous physical and emotional, sleep deprived investment. But it's the most rewarding thing you'll ever do. And sometimes it's easy. And sometimes it's horrible.'

Michelle nodded vaguely. She'd heard all of this before, but didn't quite believe that Rachel's "job" was anywhere near as difficult or demanding as her own. But mothers always harped on like this, so, she supposed, there must be *something* to it.

'Another thing you'll need to consider is what you'll do with the baby when you go back to work. I imagine you'll need to either sell out of your business or take a very short maternity leave.'

'Yes, I've considered this. I think that I can realistically take six months off. I can probably work from home a bit in that first six months. Then I think I would have to get back to business as usual. I don't think I could handle doing nothing for longer than six months anyway.'

Rachel just smiled at her friend's naivety. There was no point in debating the *doing nothing* notion. Michelle would only ever understand from experience not explanation. 'You know that business as usual is going to be impossible to achieve without support, don't you?'

'I don't see –'

Rachel interrupted, 'For you, business as usual is working more than twelve hours a day, travelling a lot, and working weekends. To do any of those things, you would need someone to look after your baby.'

'That's what day care is for,' Michelle said flippantly.

'No, child care centres don't take the children overnight while you go away for work, they're not open weekends, and they usually only operate twelve hours per day. You could get a nanny, but they're not going to work those kind of hours either. And then what happens if the nanny gets sick?'

'I'd work something out.' Michelle's words were dismissive but she began to feel a small sense of panic rising in her stomach. How did people have careers and babies? They have partners and parents helping them, that's how.

'Look, I don't mean to rain on your parade. I understand what it's like to want a baby more than anything.' Rachel paused, her words caught in her throat and a glassy sheen momentarily clouded her eyes. She cleared her throat, blinked hard a few times and continued, 'But I'd hate for you to walk into motherhood alone and blind to just how hard it can be.'

CHAPTER TWENTY

After her first date with John, Kate had been like a giddy school girl. She had debated whether she should call him or wait for him to call her. She had analysed every second of their date – had he been telling the truth when he said he'd had a crush on her in high school? Were the awkward parts actually far worse than what she remembered? Was he even interested? Had he only kissed her because she had hesitated for so long in getting out of the car? Her angst had been finally alleviated two days after their date, on Christmas day, when he had texted her. He had wished her a merry Christmas and said he'd like to see her again before he flew back to Sydney and *apologised for taking so long* to contact her after their date – which was absurd – two days was nothing, though it had in fact felt like a lifetime to Kate on this particular occasion. Kate had always hated those games, but accepted that it was a necessary part of dating.

They saw each other on Boxing Day, for what turned out to be the best date Kate had ever been on. Still disconcerted by the intensity of her own feelings, Kate allowed her mind to linger on the memory of their kiss throughout most of their second date. She'd been a little distracted by these thoughts but found their conversation so engaging, that she had managed to stay focused.

It was a far more casual date than their first – dining at a bar that served Mexican street food. The place was trendy but not so much so to make John feel uncomfortable. Drinking icy cold beers and eating soft shell tacos somehow seemed much more appropriate than fine dining in the swelteringly hot weather.

Even in the stifling, sticky heat, Kate had longed to touch John. She had sat a little too close to him. Her long tan legs – bare in her cut-off denim shorts – had been pressed against his, making her sweat even more. Her thighs had stuck to the bench seat and to each other. It was the kind of heat that is typical of a Brisbane summer; the kind that no one ever gets accustomed to, even if you have lived through these oppressively hot, humid seasons your whole life.

Kate's skin was covered in a sheen of sweat. For most people, such heat would make them look like they were melting – their makeup dripping down their faces, discomfort from the muggy, still air etched onto their faces. But for Kate, particularly in that moment as she was bursting with happy anticipation and delicious memories of that kiss, the heat made her dewy skin look like it was glowing. Even at that early time in their relationship, the first hints of love had been beginning to work their magic on her. Kate looked beautiful, more so than she had ever done before.

Kate and John talked about their Christmas days; about their families and strange family dynamics; they laughed and talked about their shared memories of being teenagers. When they finished their meals, they ordered more beers and kept talking. It was only when the staff started dropping not so subtle hints for them to leave (turning the lights up to full intensity and stacking chairs around them), that they grudgingly stood and left the bar.

It had been an amazing date. And the evening had ended in a similar way to their first date, with a brief but all consuming kiss that had left Kate wanting more. And with a promise from John that he'd be back in town very soon.

CHAPTER TWENTY-ONE

Kate adjusted her eye mask and checked her reflection in the mirror. She looked good. After two amazing dates with John, her excitement about the masquerade ball had dwindled. When her friend Adam had initially suggested the ball for New Year's, she had been all for it. Now, it seemed a little less appealing. But she'd already paid for her ticket, John wasn't in town and there was no way she could afford to go down to Sydney again – last time had cost her a fortune, even without having to pay for flights.

She did look incredible though. She wore a full length emerald green backless silk dress that clung to her curves in all the right places. Adam worked in a department store and helped her borrow clothes. She would pay for them, wear them (making sure she didn't spill anything on them – she had an amazing dry cleaner who could fix up most spills if it came to that, but she did try really hard not to), and she would return them, when Adam was working, for a full refund onto her credit card. It was wrong. She knew it was wrong. And they didn't do it *too* often, but who were they really hurting? And sometimes you just want to look good in something you haven't worn a thousand times. And Kate could not afford to do that on her budget, especially not a dress like this one.

Kate had a lot of friends. People tended to like her. And she'd managed to accumulate some very helpful friends over the years. She had a girlfriend who was a makeup artist, who let Kate use her staff discount and take unopened testers and samples from the store. Kate went drinking with a hairdresser (an ex of Adam's, whom she never mentioned in Adam's company) who did her hair pretty cheap. He worked at the kind of salon where haircuts cost more than a week's salary for Kate. Sometimes she did some hair modelling for the salon, but mostly Kate would just go to his house and they'd drink wine and he'd do her hair for fifty bucks. And of course, Kate knew a lot of bar tenders, who would give her a few free drinks on the sly or at the very least fill the shot measures to the point of overflowing before slopping the booze into the overpriced cocktails. She was missing someone to provide her with cheap or free spray tans, but hopefully she'd make a few new friends before the night was out. All in all, Kate's network meant that she was able to live in a style that she certainly couldn't afford. Even still, her credit card was maxed, she was spending every cent that she earned, all while living with her mother and paying only a token amount of board.

Kate had toyed with the idea of somehow extorting money out of Nose Hair, but didn't want to push her luck. Keeping her (shit) job wasn't too much skin off his hair sprouting nose. But money. That could just be enough to tip him over the edge. She had felt a little guilty, but, honestly, that cheating scumbag was the one in the wrong. Sure, she'd chucked a sickie. Who hasn't done that before? He couldn't actually prove that she hadn't been sick. She was pretty sure he couldn't fire her for it. But having that little titbit of juicy gossip about him and that trashbag Kylie had completely alleviated all pressure on her. Problem solved. Except it didn't solve the problem of hating her job.

That would be her new year's resolution: she was going to get a new job. Like John had said, there must be something in fashion with the same shitty pay as her current job. She couldn't handle dealing with Tony Nose Hair and that stupid slutty bitch whore, Kylie, anymore. They were disgusting, horrible people. And spending all day with them was crap.

And she wanted to travel. She *needed* to see the world. This year would be her year. She was going to do it. She was going to go somewhere. Anywhere. Kate longed to spend a year abroad, like Sally the Irish chick who had screwed up Kate's job. But that was pretty unlikely to happen, unless Kate miraculously won the lottery (which she never entered because tickets were too expensive). So, yes, her resolution would be to leave Australia this year. Just one little holiday. It was going to happen. No matter what.

****

Rachel sat at the outdoor table absentmindedly watching sand spill through the timer.

'It's a country starting with L. It's in Europe.'
'Lithuania?'
'Nope but you're close.'
'Close geographically?'

'Time's up,' Rachel said cheerily. She had forgotten that she was supposed to be in charge of the timer and hadn't really been paying that much attention. Not that it mattered much – she and Mike were winning by a pretty big margin.

'Okay, so resolutions. Anyone got any?' Paul said as he walked in carrying a bottle of wine and three beers.

'We're making the switch from white to wholemeal – everything.' Cassandra pulled a mock pained expression. 'I know what you're all going to say – none of you have touched white bread since the nineties, but it's my kryptonite. I literally can't control myself. Fresh, hot bread with butter and vegemite – ohhhh... I need to stop thinking about it.'

Cassandra was Rachel's older sister. The two were extremely close and looked very much alike, prompting the perpetual question: *Are you twins?* In personality, they were nothing alike. Cassandra detested all things healthy. She was a cavalier kind of mother, who believed in doing whatever worked for the family and – as she would put it – didn't buy into any of that super mum crap. She worked part time for financial reasons and didn't really care too much about her job – it was a means to an end for her.

For all the healthy eating, intensive hours at the gym and with her personal trainer, Rachel and her sister were roughly the same size with very similar figures.

'Cass, I don't know who you think you're kidding. There's no way you're going to stop eating bread,' Paul, Cassandra's husband, said as he topped up her glass of wine.

'Firstly, I didn't say I was going to stop eating bread altogether. And secondly, it's a resolution – no one actually does it. It's just something we say, do for a couple of days if we're lucky and then forget.'

'Well, I fully intend to stick to mine. I'm banning weight related derogatory comments from our household.' Kelly gave a hopeful smile.

Kelly was one of Rachel's closest friends. She bounced from fad diet to fad diet. She was constantly critiquing her physique and comparing herself to Rachel. Kelly had recently broken down in tears and told Rachel about an incident with her five year old daughter, Frankie.

Her cheeks wet with tears and between mouthfuls of chocolate cake (which was decidedly not recommended in the Paleo diet), Kelly had said, 'We were at Axl's birthday party yesterday and Frankie was offered cake. She said no. I was so proud of her. And then she said that she couldn't eat it because she's watching her weight.' Kelly had paused and then sobbed, 'Apparently she's too fat.' Kelly shovelled a huge chunk of cake into her mouth and said woefully, 'I shouldn't be eating this, but I just can't think about calories right now.' Kelly looked up from her cake and met Rachel's gaze. 'She's five. FIVE. And she's worried about being fat. And I was proud of her. What kind of mother am I? What have I done?' Kelly had sobbed, while cutting herself another piece of cake.

Rachel had hugged Kelly. Once the tears had subsided, Rachel discreetly confiscated Kelly's fork.

'It's going to be okay, sweetie, but you should talk to Frankie about this. She needs to know that she shouldn't worry about her weight or food. And you need to think about how you're going to set a better example for Frankie.'

Rachel had personally been quite conscious of this with

Georgie. Not that Rachel had a bad relationship with food like Kelly did. Rachel exercised a lot but that was never about weight. And she ate healthily, but that was because she felt better about herself when she did. Rachel was certainly a fantastic example without really trying. But just being a good example wasn't enough. Georgie was a big girl. And Rachel worried that someone might say something to her, that she might somehow – even at three – glean an understanding that being a bigger girl wasn't generally considered to be a particularly good thing. She was three, for goodness' sake. Her chubby cheeks and the little fat rolls above her knees were gorgeous. But people were cruel and Rachel didn't want her beautiful little girl finding that out when she was still so young.

'Rach, do you have any resolutions?' Mike flopped down in the seat next to her.

'I think that I'd like to learn a language. Mandarin maybe. It will be good for Georgie too. We can learn together.'

Rachel had some other resolutions that she didn't want to share with the group. Firstly, she wanted her and Mike to have more sex. They seemed to be growing apart lately. He was just so busy with work and she was busy with Georgie and training. Aiming for twice a week would be a good goal. Though she certainly couldn't share that with the group and definitely not with Mike. If he thought she was 'scheduling' sex, he would be particularly unimpressed. She found him so attractive, but finding the time was just hard. She really needed to *make* the time.

Secondly, and most importantly, she wanted to do something that Georgie (when a little older) would respect her for. Start a business, get a job, write a book. Something. She hadn't a clue exactly what as yet, but that was okay. Rachel had a plan to brainstorm ideas and do some research. A full plan would be in place by April; implementation of the plan was set for June. Of course, it would depend on what her plan ended up being, as to how long the implementation process would take. It was perfect timing for Rachel to start something new, actually, what with Georgie starting kindergarten next year. Whatever it was, it would have to fit in to kindy hours. Rachel was definitely not planning on putting her daughter into childcare. She still needed time to be there for Georgie and to be as good a parent as ever. It shouldn't in any way diminish the quality Georgie's life. This resolution was for Georgie's benefit, after all.

****

Michelle stood on the private terrace by the harbour, waiters circling with trays of delicious canapés and drinks. She watched the fireworks exploding above her, sending streaks of colour through the dark night sky. Andrew's arm was wrapped around her waist and she had a glass of French champagne in her hand. Life couldn't be better.

That thought was interrupted by a small ache in her pelvis. Her ovaries didn't agree. Life could be better. It could be a lot better.

A waiter waved a tray of spoons containing individual tasting portions of Atlantic salmon tartare with crème fraiche, topped with Beluga caviar. She shook her head. The fireworks had finished and she hadn't noticed; she was still staring blankly at the sky.

'Michelle's business is doing extraordinarily well, I'm told.' Steven turned to Michelle. 'You know, I saw a write up about you in relation to the Business Woman of the Year Awards. Quite impressive.'

Michelle had worked her ass off, as had her assistant, Helen, for three fucking years for that award. *Three years.* Three years of positioning the firm, making sure she had the perfect resume, making sure all the right people knew who she was. And she didn't even win. Sure, she won the state award, but that wasn't what she'd set out to do. She wanted to win the whole fucking thing. It had been devastating. But everyone had kept telling her how fantastic it was. Andrew, in particular, had been incredibly impressed, though she wasn't quite sure why he felt that being runner up was so bloody fantastic. Either way, it had bolstered the business immensely. She'd gotten a heap of amazing free publicity and the firm was that much closer to being a household name. All in all – despite technically being a loser – the outcome was pretty good, she would grudgingly admit.

'Thank you. It's an honour to just have made the finalist list last year. And to have won the state based award was a real coup for our firm. A lot of work goes into the application process, actually.'

'As well as all the hard work that goes into being a business woman deserving of such an award in the first place.' Andrew was incredibly proud of Michelle's accomplishments. He felt it really was a big deal, and he never let her forget it.

'No doubt.' Steven smiled at Michelle in a drunken way

that boarded on a leer. 'So what have you got in your sights this year? I'm sure you've got big plans.'

A baby. That was what she wanted. That was her big plan for the year. That was her resolution.

****

Alex sat on a stool at the bar. Why did she come? Daniel had made it pretty clear that he didn't want her there. She should have stayed back at the apartment. But instead, she was in this insanely trendy bar, with the coolest, most beautiful people she'd ever seen. (How did French women look so effortlessly chic all the time?) And she didn't understand a single word that anyone was saying.

Some friend of Daniel's had told him that this was the place to be for New Year's. Daniel had quite strongly suggested to Alex that he go alone. She wasn't a night owl. She'd feel tired. And she didn't speak any French. It would be boring. She hated parties. They all seemed like good reasons, but Alex had felt a renewed sense of fun lately. She really felt like she had something to offer the world. Reconnecting with her school friends had her feeling better about herself and wanting to put herself out there a bit more. But sitting in that Parisian bar, watching Daniel flirt with a beautiful French woman, she regretted it. She'd made a mistake. She shouldn't have come. She should just be back at the apartment, reading her book.

'Daniel,' Alex spoke loudly to be heard above the music. 'Daniel.' Still no response. 'Daniel!'

He turned around. He looked annoyed at the interruption to his conversation.

'I'm going to go.' Alex's voice was somewhere between irritated and dejected.

'Okay.'

Alex looked at Daniel, waiting for an offer to walk her back to the apartment. They were in a strange city, after all. But Daniel had already turned back to the gorgeous French woman. Alex hovered.

Daniel glanced back toward her, his eyes narrowed with aggravation. 'See ya.' He resumed his conversation with Frenchie, turning his back to Alex.

Crestfallen, Alex picked up her bag and coat and walked out of the bar. The burst of icy, fresh air when she exited didn't help her gloomy mood. Daniel would definitely pay more attention to her if she looked like Frenchie. She was incredible. Her skin was bronzed, her hair light brown. She looked as though she'd never coloured her hair or worn an ounce of makeup in her life. Not much different from Alex really, except Frenchie looked like she was naturally perfect. She didn't need hair colour or makeup. Her clothes looked designer, but thrown together in an effortless sort of way. Alex wondered again how French women all seemed to be able to pull that off.

Alex adjusted her scarf and pulled her coat tighter around her middle. It was cold. Really cold. Why was she walking home by herself in the cold? She began to march faster, trying to keep warm. Fucking French women. Alex exhaled loudly and watched as a cloud of vapour was expelled from her mouth.

This was the last time. The very last time. She was never going to let some pretty girl hold Daniel's attention again. Next New Year's *she* was going to be the one he was looking at. She would be the one that he flirted with and smiled at. This year she was going to lose weight. She was going to do whatever it took. Count calories. Exercise. See a dietician. Stick her fingers down her throat, if that's what it took. She was going to get thin. And Daniel was going to love her.

CHAPTER TWENTY-TWO

In the days and weeks between their Boxing Day date and their next encounter, Kate and John were in contact constantly – texting throughout the day, and having long phone conversation in the evenings. They flirted, they talked about their career aspirations – and lack thereof for Kate (though Kate intentionally neglected to mention blackmailing her boss to keep her job – it wasn't her proudest moment and she didn't really want John to know that about her), they talked about Sydney and Brisbane, the pros and cons of living in each, their dreams for the future, the places they had travelled to and wanted to travel to, their shared love of Italian food and John's love of cooking and sometimes they talked about nothing at all. Kate got to know John in a way that she'd only ever experienced with Peter – although she did question whether she had ever really known Peter at all. Kate felt like she knew John – and he knew her – so intimately that it was as though they'd been together for years. And that closeness was paired with the giddy love-struck sensation of a couple who've only just met.

When the pair were finally reunited, Kate expected their

date to culminate in the kind of passion that they'd shared verbally – emotionally – over the previous few weeks. But it didn't.

John had told her that he had a date planned for them. It was a surprise. In typical John fashion, he had awkwardly bungled the conversation about the date.

'You should dress nicely,' John paused and realised the implications of his words. 'I mean –'

'Seriously? You don't think I usually dress nicely?'

'You always look amazing. I just meant that you shouldn't wear jeans. I suppose – dress up would be the right –'

Kate laughed heartily. 'I'm just fucking with you. I knew what you meant.'

Kate agonised over what she would wear and eventually decided on a gorgeous midnight blue dress that her friend Adam helped her 'borrow' from his work (she hadn't ever mentioned this borrowing arrangement to John, who probably wouldn't approve). The dress had a high neckline and the hemline finished just below the knees, with a scooped back that came to about two inches below where her bra would have sat (had she been wearing one), which gave a strikingly sexy edge to an otherwise demure dress.

John stood talking with Kate's mother in the living room. As Kate descended the stairs, she saw John stop mid-sentence and stare at her. A small smile played across his lips, his eyes almost comically wide. Behind John's back, Pauline wriggled her eyebrows and gave her daughter the thumbs up. Kate always dressed well, but for once she wasn't looking like such a tart. And, in Pauline's opinion, this bloke was one of the best Kate had ever brought home. He was smart and nice. And he actually seemed to genuinely like Kate – not just want to get into her knickers. Pauline hoped that this was going to work; that her daughter wasn't going to screw this up; and that maybe – just maybe – she was going to get to have her sewing room back and – fingers crossed – a grandbaby sometime soon. Kate had always said she didn't want kids, but Pauline knew that she'd change her mind once she met the right fella.

'Am I dressed nicely enough?'

'Yes.' John's eyes were still wide, and the small smile he'd been wearing spread to an all-out grin. 'You look incredible.'

As they drove toward the city, Kate wondered what the surprise was; where they were going. She hoped that at some point it would involve a hotel and some sex. It had felt like a long time since she'd last gotten laid. And the anticipation with John was killing her.

They pulled into the car park attached to the art gallery. Kate wondered again where they were going. Surely, not *actually* to the art gallery. Was it even open at night time? She supposed she didn't mind art galleries. But it wasn't *really* her thing. It didn't seem like the amazing date she had been anticipating. They walked through the car park, into the lift and, yes, toward the gallery entrance. Kate felt a little guilty about being so disappointed. She just had expected... more. She thought that John had gotten to know her so well, but maybe she was wrong.

Her thoughts of disenchantment were interrupted when she saw the poster outside the entrance with the word *Chanel* emblazoned across the top of a black and white picture of Audrey Hepburn in a classic Chanel dress.

'I hope that you hadn't guessed the surprise. I figured you probably knew that the Chanel exhibit was opening officially tomorrow, but tonight is a preview. There's some people giving some talks about... something... dresses, I guess, and there are drinks and canapés.'

Kate wrinkled her nose and grinned for a split second before throwing her arms around John's neck and kissing him long and hard on the lips.

John gave a coy smile. 'I'm glad you like it. I thought you would, but honestly, I'm not really sure I understand an art gallery having an exhibit on clothes. I guess it's art...'

Kate laughed and kissed him again. 'This is amazing.'

They went inside and Kate felt thankful that she had had Adam hook her up with this dress. Everyone there was dressed so well. They all seemed to be seriously into fashion. And there were a few celebrities (if you could really call them that – there was the cute weather girl from that breakfast show and that woman who was somehow involved in horse racing – the one who was always presenting the *fashions on the field* things).

'I thought that you'd enjoy looking at the dresses. Plus it's a pretty good opportunity to network. Maybe make some contacts that might be able to set you up with a job in fashion.'

Kate felt a glowing warmth growing inside her. John was so sweet, so thoughtful. He knew her so well. She hated her job (and realistically needed to abandon ship before Nose Hair decided the threat of being ousted as a cheating scumbag wasn't all that bad – or before he got outed by someone else and she no longer had any leverage). And she would have loved to get a job in fashion. This was all just so perfect.

A handsome woman in her sixties, wearing a perfectly tailored black and white blazer over a white dress walked toward them. She embraced John, kissing him on the cheek before turning to Kate. 'Hello, Kate, I assume? I'm Vivian. It's lovely to meet you.'

'Nice to meet you too,' Kate said hesitantly. Who was this woman? How did she know her name? How did she know John? And where did she get her botox done? It was incredible – you couldn't even tell that she had anything done to her face, save for the fact that her skin looked like it belonged to a twenty-five year old.

'Vivian is a friend of my mother's. She actually was the one who got us the tickets for tonight.'

Vivian smiled warmly (all the lines around her eyes appearing so naturally and then disappearing to beautiful, flawless skin when she stopped smiling). 'Yes, John tells me that you're interested in fashion. That you're hoping to get into the industry.'

Kate felt momentarily panicked. *Was* she hoping to get into the industry? Going to this kind of party was amazing. But this woman was so well dressed, well spoken, well educated, had money. Did Kate really fit in here? Could she really hold her own amongst these kinds of people? Did she really know enough about fashion to work with these sorts of people? She imagined this woman lunching with John's mother, the two of them dressed in Chanel dresses, ordering three hundred dollar bottles of wine. Then she imagined her own mother – never having owned designer anything in her life, drinking wine from the box, swearing, yelling at her about getting *'tarted up'*. Kate imagined what this woman would think of her mother; what Vivian would think of her if they knew about her arrangement to 'borrow' dresses from Adam's work. Was this woman going to ask her questions about Chanel? Kate wouldn't know the answers. Knowing about fashion – particularly Chanel, when you're at a Chanel exhibit – seemed like a pretty big prerequisite to working in fashion. Kate just wasn't ready for this kind of conversation.

'I do really enjoy fashion, but I wouldn't say I know much about it. And no, I'm not looking to get into the industry.'

John furrowed his eyebrows at Kate's response but shrugged it off and got the three of them some drinks.

The moment Kate set her eyes on a dress that Marilyn Monroe had worn, in a glass cabinet, dazzling under the spotlights, Kate forgot her insecurities; she was awestruck. This was perfect – the evening, the dress, the moment, John – nothing could bring this down.

Kate leant over to John. 'Thank you.' Without any regard for proper manners or Vivian, who was standing with them, Kate kissed John passionately. 'This is amazing.'

It was so amazing, in fact, that the lack of sex involved in the date – although made painfully more obvious by how incredible the date was – didn't mar the evening at all.

****

The very next day, John and Kate went on their fourth date. John was only in town for the one night, so they had to make the most of their precious time together. Kate's idea of making the most of their time together would have been spending the night in a hotel after the Chanel exhibit and lying in bed all day, together, with a room service breakfast. Given that they had each gone to separate beds – not in a hotel – after the previous night's date, that wasn't really a realistic expectation on Kate's part. However, she did live in hope that whatever they were doing was going to involve alone time, in a bed; though Kate wouldn't have minded if it were in the back of a car – or anywhere at all, to be honest. John however had other ideas.

'I know you said you love Italian food. And I love to cook it. So, I thought that maybe you'd enjoy cooking it with me.'

Kate's heart started racing at the prospect of the two of them being alone together. She felt her face flush a little. Maybe this was a ruse to get her alone at his house (well, his parents' house, but she was sure that he would have arranged for them to be out). Maybe they were actually going to cook and the fun would happen after lunch. Before seemed like a better option to her, but he was obviously a bit of a slow mover. He was a gentleman (more so than anyone she'd ever encountered before) and he probably wouldn't want to jump right into things. As her mind raced through the options and a story of how the day would go played out in her head, her cheeks developed into a darker shade of pink.

'There's this amazing Italian restaurant. The food is just like you would imagine an Italian nonna cooking – not fancy, just delicious. They do these cooking classes...'

The words snapped Kate straight out of her fantasy about the day ahead and back to reality. No, they weren't going to John's parents' house. No, they weren't going to be alone. And no, no, no, they weren't going to be having sex. Not today.

The date went well, despite Kate's initial surly mood due to the lack of alone time. John was right – the food was delicious and the class was fun. It wasn't long before Kate was laughing and covering John with her flour-coated handprints.

Even though things weren't playing out the way she had hoped, Kate loved spending time with John. They had fun. He made her feel happy – and a little giddy – in a way that she wasn't sure she'd ever felt before. And for John, their dates were incredible; with every passing moment, John saw more to Kate – more to love (though he felt he had already loved her since they were kids) – a woman who was passionate about her love for her friends and family; a woman who came across as the most self-confident – sometimes bordering on arrogant – person, but who underneath it all was plagued with insecurities about her vocation in life; a woman who didn't take herself too seriously, who danced like an idiot, who laughed heartily when pasta sauce splashed all over her face. This was a woman he could imagine spending the rest of his life with.

Just as he had in their previous three dates, John drove Kate home, walked her to her door and kissed her in a way that left her unable to sleep for thoughts of him and his lips. Kate wanted him, but she didn't dare make a move – he obviously had some sort of reservations and, lacking her usual confidence in this department, she feared his rejection. John was flying back to Sydney that afternoon, leaving Kate's shaky self-confidence to analyse his actions.

'I've just never had this problem before. I'm not sure what to do.' Kate had explained the situation to Michelle over the phone, and they had performed a post-mortem of each of the dates.

'He's obviously interested. He wouldn't speak to you for three hours every night if he weren't.'

'Tell me exactly what he's said to you about me. Word for word.'

'He honestly hasn't said much at all.'

'Urgh! That's not a good sign.'

'He's a very private person. And it's not like he tells me much about himself.' Michelle added jokingly, 'He's got you for that.'

'So he hasn't said anything at all.'

'He said that he'd seen you. And that he really liked you.'

'When? When did he say he really liked me? Maybe something happened on our last date. I mean – waiting two dates seems kinda normal. Maybe even three. But four? I mean, we've known each other forever.' Kate was speaking slightly too fast and her voice was slightly too high – she sounded panicked.

'Calm down. I'm sure it's not anything that you've done. He might just be a slow mover. Maybe he's just a bit weirded out about location – you live with your mum and he stays with his parents when he's in town.'

Kate gave that some thought. Maybe that was it. A hotel was obviously the answer. But maybe he thought that was too forward. Maybe he preferred a more organic kind of lead up to sex, not a contrived hotel rendezvous.

Michelle's voice changed to a serious, low tone – the kind that was reserved for only the most juicy gossip. 'But, you should probably know, he's been hanging out with Alex. A lot.'

'What? What do you mean?' Kate was genuinely confused as to where Michelle was going with this.

'Well, I don't know if I'm reading too much into this. They've been hanging out a bit. You know John doesn't really know anyone in Sydney. And that's great – they both need to get out and make new friends.' A note of concern crept into Michelle's voice. 'But I'm actually worried that Alex has a crush on him.'

Michelle was sincerely concerned for Alex. Although she had posed the conversation as though it was some sort of scandalous gossip, she actually thought that Alex might be setting herself up to have her self-confidence obliterated. At some point, someone was going to find it laughable that John would be interested in Alex. That added to having a husband who called her a pig, might just send Alex over the edge. Michelle felt relief at finally being able to unburden herself of her worries.

'She's married. That's crazy.'

'Because no one has ever cheated on their husband before.' Michelle's voice dripped with sarcasm. 'Plus her husband is a total dick.'

Kate pulled a face at her phone. 'He's really not. I'm certain you just caught him at a bad time. And he's actually really hot.'

'Whatever.' Michelle was dismissive. They would have to agree to disagree about Alex's husband. 'All I know is that she's been acting really weird. And spending an insane amount of time with John. I'm not saying that you have something to be worried about – I'm sure she'd never act on it and I honestly think that John is really into you. But I just think you should know, in case something – I don't know – just in case you need to know.'

Kate brushed it off, but she did feel a little worried. She didn't think for a minute that John would be interested in Alex, but Kate really didn't want Alex getting hurt. Or jealous. Kate recalled the way Alex had acted while they were in Sydney. Maybe there was something to what Michelle was saying. Maybe Alex had been jealous.

CHAPTER TWENTY-THREE

Michelle had agonised over what she wanted with Andrew. Her conversation with Rachel hadn't clarified anything for her – it had just left her with even more questions and doubts about whether she really could do it alone. She still felt completely confused. What did she want? And did she really want it with Andrew or was that just particularly convenient timing? The two months were finally up and she still was no closer to an answer. Michelle eventually decided that she would just wait to see what Andrew said. Maybe what he said would make the question moot anyway – maybe he would just leave her. That thought began to stress her out. She really did love him. And she didn't want to be alone again. She'd been lonely for too long.

She began to wonder whether she should bring it up at all. If she didn't, then she wouldn't have to hear the excuses followed by the breakup. If she didn't say anything, then maybe they could just maintain the status quo. But Michelle wasn't that kind of woman. As much as she hated being alone, and hated the thought of losing Andrew, she couldn't be with someone who didn't want to be with her. And coasting along in this relationship by avoiding a breakup conversation wasn't going to cut it for her.

Michelle came home from work early to cook a roast. It was the only fancy meal that she knew how to cook. As she threw the tray with the roast in the oven, she once again felt an appreciation for the fact that she'd met a guy who could cook for her. And that the green grocer now sold pre-cut vegetables for roasting. God, who had the time to do this every day?

The smell of the roast was permeating the house. Michelle set the table, lit candles and opened a bottle of red to let it breathe, but decided to have a glass to calm her nerves.

'You're home from work early.' Andrew planted a kiss on Michelle's lips. He noted the table setting and candles. 'Something smells great. What's the occasion?'

'No occasion. I just thought we could have a nice dinner and a talk.' Michelle was trying hard to sound casual but wasn't quite able to pull it off.

Andrew raised his eyebrows. 'Hmm... I think it's been about two months since we last had a chat, so yes, we're probably due one.'

Michelle was caught off guard. Andrew remembered – so much so that it was the first thing he thought of. And not only did he remember, but he remembered the timing. This was either a very good or very bad sign. But then again, Michelle wasn't quite sure what she wanted – so what result would actually be a good one? Michelle felt a sense of frustration at her own indecision. This was not like her. Obviously Andrew saying he wanted a baby was the result she wanted. That way the ball was in her court and it would be her decision to make.

Michelle poured Andrew a glass of wine and sat back in

her chair, stretching her arms above her head and letting one hand drop back to the base of her neck, the other relaxed to the table and cradled her glass of wine. After a few moments, Michelle realised that without thinking she had adopted dominating body language, the kind she had studied and perfected when she first started her business (being a young woman starting a business from scratch in a fiercely competitive industry, Michelle had needed every trick in book) – but this wasn't a business meeting. She couldn't command the outcome that she wanted by controlling the situation and dominating the room to force Andrew into submission. She needed to just let Andrew say what he wanted and accept it.

'I've thought a lot about our conversation.' Andrew paused, took a sip of wine, and then looked at Michelle intently.

'And?'

'And... I'm sorry, I don't want kids right now. We're just too new. And I'm just not ready. I really need to be focused on building up my firm right now. You know I'm still in the stages of needing to do an enormous amount of BD. I wouldn't have any time to spend with a child. Plus all my money needs to go into the business right now. I just can't afford a child now. Based on my business plans – and being realistic about growth in this economy – I think that having children is something I can really seriously consider in about seven or eight years.'

'Seven or eight years.' Michelle took a large gulp of wine.

'Michelle, I know that's not what you wanted to hear. But I think you should be thinking about your business too. I would have thought that it would be the same for you.' Andrew registered the look on her face but continued despite it. 'I know your business is far more established and I'm really still building my client base. But nevertheless, I would have thought that you would need to focus on maintaining your market position here in Sydney and pursuing your growth strategy in Melbourne. What with the economy the way it is, you can't rest on your laurels. You're going to need to be aggressive to just maintain your market share.'

Michelle knew that what Andrew was saying was right. But she didn't have six or seven years to wait. She would be in her forties by the time she had a baby. That was taking too much of a gamble on her eggs still being good by then. No, she couldn't do it. And having a baby was just too important to her. She absolutely hated admitting it – it made her sound like Rachel, for God's sake – but having a child was more important than her business. And more important than Andrew.

Michelle drained her glass and refilled it without making eye contact with Andrew. She took a large sip from her fresh glass and looked up at him. 'I think that this means the end for us.' Her words caught in her throat just a little. She swallowed, trying to remove the lump that had formed.

'Michelle, I love you. You just need to look at this logically and have a little bit of patience.'

'I don't have seven or eight years to wait. I'm not getting any younger. My eggs aren't getting any younger.'

'You'll be forty. It's really not that old these days.'

'No, I'm turning thirty-five this year. I'll be well and truly in my forties. And that's when you want to start *thinking* about children. It could be years on top of that to actually get pregnant, assuming I can at that age. Do you know what a woman's age does to the statistics – the risk of miscarriage, complications, multiple births, Down syndrome?'

'Michelle, I've made my decision. This isn't a negotiation.'

'I know. And I've made my decision.' And it hurt. A lot.

****

Michelle didn't have time to wallow in the grief of her breakup. Between marathon training, the business acquisition that she was in the middle of and now the logistics of actually getting pregnant, Michelle didn't have any spare time. It was probably a good thing, because in actual fact she was devastated. But it was her decision. If forgoing her relationship with Andrew was going to get her a baby, she was willing to do it. It was hard. It hurt. But that's just how much she wanted a baby. She would walk to the ends of the earth if she had to, to make it happen. Her body and soul ached for a baby.

She was thankful that she and Andrew had never fully committed to moving in together – there really wasn't anything that was *theirs*. He'd only moved a few of his things into her place, put the rest in storage and rented out his apartment, so it was mostly just clothes that he had to move. And his ridiculously oversized television. She was doubly thankful that he'd moved into her place. She really had far too much on to be bothered with kicking tenants out and moving herself.

Over the years, Michelle had done research on donor

sperm, including importing it from the States, and IVF versus artificial insemination. But her research had been merely theoretical. She hadn't actually talked to any experts, so now she had the task of finding the best clinic and best doctor in Sydney and getting an appointment. With only a few months left of training before the marathon, she wasn't planning on trying to get pregnant immediately. She would simply make enquiries and book an appointment for just after she returned from Paris. That would also give her a bit of time to get her head around such a big leap.

CHAPTER TWENTY-FOUR

Over the short time that Kate and John had spent together, Kate had eaten more and drank less than she had in years. A shared love of pasta was responsible for the few kilos that she had put on. And going out drinking with her friends just seemed a little... pointless, when she could spend hours at home on the phone to John. She had practically given up smoking all together – John hated it, and, having only ever been a social smoker, without so much alcohol in her life, she just didn't seem to need cigarettes. Kate was looking – and feeling – the best she had in years. Her face, previously marred by hollowed out cheeks and skin drab from lack of sleep, was plump and renewed – she was actually looking her age. Kate had gone from a gorgeous-as-long-as-you-don't-look-too-close kind of girl, to actually being beautiful. Nourishment and happiness were solely responsible for the change.

To Kate the lack of sex on their first four dates was an enormous worry; a cloud that loomed over their relationship. The number of dates didn't seem quite so bad, but the length of time they'd been 'seeing' each other (but not actually *seeing* each other because they lived in different cities) made the wait seem huge. She still toyed with the idea that it meant John wasn't really interested in her, but deep down she knew that he wouldn't spend so much time with her – and on the phone to her – if that were the case. She also had a theory that he had something weird going on in his pants – a deformity or a major sizing issue – that he was embarrassed about.

She had grilled Michelle for information, asking if there were any exes that Michelle knew of – anyone that he might have slept with. But Michelle had no more insight into John's sex life than what Kate did. As embarrassing as it was, Kate decided to ask Fiona. Surely she would know *something*. But again Kate was underwhelmed with the response. Fiona had heard girlfriends mentioned, but no one serious enough to bring home to the family. And she was completely clueless about any one night stands.

Kate was immensely frustrated but was having so much fun otherwise with John that she was hesitant to push the point.

The lack of sex also had another interesting effect on their relationship – Kate couldn't get enough of John. She wasn't used to being kept at a distance physically, and it left her wanting him. At times she felt deranged with frustration. She couldn't concentrate; she couldn't think clearly, all she knew was that she wanted John. Badly.

Kate was not willing to wait any longer. She wanted him and was determined to get what she wanted. She wasn't used to needing to make the first move, but figured that – given how long they'd waited already – she shouldn't be too subtle about it. So she booked a hotel room that she couldn't afford, with a plan to seduce John. She wasn't going to take no for an answer.

'I've got a surprise for you.' Kate announced during one of their daily phone calls. Kate was in her preferred place for conversations with John – lying in a warm bath. For this particular discussion, she was multitasking – shaving her legs, with the phone on speaker next to her.

'Really?' John sounded suspicious. 'What is it?'

'It wouldn't be a surprise if I told you.' Kate's voice was teasing. 'Don't make any plans for Saturday night, okay?'

By the time Saturday came around, Kate was nervous. What if he turned her down? She entertained the thought, but didn't really – seriously – consider it a possibility. Sure, it was very strange that he hadn't made his move yet, but no straight, single man had ever said no to her. And this particular straight, single man was her boyfriend. Surely he wouldn't. And yet, despite that, she still felt nervous about the proposition. But her nerves were more about their enjoyment of the evening, rather than whether it would actually occur. They had waited too long. There was too much anticipation. Would they over think it, making it a fizzer?

Kate always kept herself well groomed and ready to be seen in her underwear – shaved, waxed and tanned at all times. But on this particular occasion she had paid extra attention to every little detail. Standing in her bedroom in front of the full-length mirror in her underwear, she looked as though she had stepped straight off the catwalk of a Victoria Secret show. She shimmied into a white figure-hugging dress, but soon realised that the dress was so tight that the detail of the lace in her underwear was completely visible. Three outfits later, she decided on dark blue denim skinny jeans, a sheer black blouse, black ankle boots and a cropped black leather jacket, which she probably wouldn't need. The black lace of her bra was on show through her top but, unlike the white dress she had tried on, the hint of lace gave a racy edge to the outfit while still looking demure.

Kate was a little late in picking John up from the airport, but he now had come to expect her tardiness, so had dawdled getting off the plane. He threw his small bag in the trunk and climbed into Kate's late model Toyota Corolla, pushing a litter of empty Diet Coke bottles and shoes from the seat onto the floor. They kissed briefly but with the passion that can only be found between very new couples and teenagers.

'So, where are we going?' John tried to sound casual.

'I told you – it's a surprise.'

'I've got a surprise for you too.'

Kate turned her head to John, her eyes lit up with excitement. 'Really? What is it?'

John opened his eyes wide. 'Kate!' His eyes darted from her to the road. 'Maybe we should talk about this when you're not driving.' He laughed, 'I'd like to live long enough to find out what your surprise is.'

Kate wrinkled her nose at John and turned back to face the road.

Kate pulled the car into the hotel driveway. 'Surprise.' Her voice didn't quite convey the enthusiasm that she had intended. She sounded a little flat – her nerves were getting the better of her. This felt like a big step for their relationship. She asked herself again for the thousandth time why they had left it so long. Why she was the one making the first move.

'A hotel?' John's tone matched Kate's – a little bleak, void of enthusiasm.

Kate was taken aback by his tone. Could it be that he didn't want to sleep with her? What were they doing together then? She felt confused, offended, angry. 'I thought that it would be nice to stay somewhere nice. We've waited so long...' Kate checked herself. Maybe she was reading the situation incorrectly. Maybe they just needed to relax. Talk about something else. Take the pressure off. 'So, ummm... What's my surprise?'

'I found you a job.' John inwardly cursed himself. That came out wrong. 'It's not definite, but I know the owner, so it's practically a sure thing. The job's as a manager at a clothing store. A boutique on James Street. The pay's pretty terrible, but -' John shrugged, 'I think it will be great. You would manage the staff and could decide what stock to -'

Kate wasn't listening to John, she interrupted him. 'What?' All of Kate's insecurities about their relationship and her lack of career came bubbling to the surface. 'You got me a job? Because I'm not capable of getting a job on my own?' Her eyes flashed with rage. 'Is my job not good enough for you?'

A part of Kate knew she was being unreasonable. But she was overwhelmed with the idea that her boyfriend thought he had the right to decide what her job was. And that he didn't seem to want to sleep with her. And that he thought that she would quit her job at a moment's notice for something with terrible pay, just because he deemed it appropriate. And the thought of going to work each day and trying to keep up with people like Vivian, John's posh family friend she met at the art gallery, was absolutely nerve-racking.

'That's not at all what – my friend just told me she was looking to hire someone and I thought –'

'You can tell your friend that I'm not interested.'

'Kate –'

'No.' Kate closed her eyes and took a deep breath. She tried to calm herself but instead felt anger and indignation wash over her. 'I think you should get out.'

'Kate.' John was shocked.

'Get. Out.' Kate's voice was calm, but the pain bubbled under the surface.

Kate drove around the corner, pulled over and screamed while punching her car horn. What the fuck had she just done? She loved him. Actual love. And she'd just thrown a tantrum over him trying to get her a new job. She knew it had nothing to do with the job – she was just feeling insecure about them not sleeping together, about him not seeming enthusiastic about sleeping together.

With the realisation that she'd just acted like a crazy person, she reached into her handbag to grab her phone. She needed to apologise. And she needed to do it now. As she fumbled around in her bag, she heard the click of the passenger door opening.

'I'm sorry I upset you. I'm so sorry. I won't mention anything to do with your work ever again. I just want you to be happy.' John paused, with a pleading look in his eyes he added, 'I love you.'

A smile burst onto Kate's face. 'I love you too.' She awkwardly but eagerly crawled partway into the passenger seat, grabbed his face and kissed him hard.

CHAPTER TWENTY-FIVE

Kate was lying in the bath, flipping through a magazine and daydreaming about last night's hotel romp with John, when her phone rang. She scrambled to reach it, sloshing water all over the bathroom floor.

'Hi!'

'Hey Kate, it's just me, Alex.'

'Ah, yep, I know. Your number's in my phone,' Kate said cheerfully. 'How are you?'

'Oh, me – yeah, I'm good. Michelle said you wanted to speak to me. Something about John's ex… or something?'

'That!' Kate closed her eyes and exhaled loudly. 'I was just having a little moment of craziness.'

'You couldn't be crazier than his ex though.'

Kate barely registered Alex's word. 'No, I was just so caught up in the fact that we hadn't slept together, but…' Kate gave a deep, satisfied sigh, 'That's not a problem now though. We had an incredible night last night. Stayed in a hotel. It was just absolutely perfect.'

'Oh.' Alex could feel her spirits sinking. Maybe she did have a little crush on John. Knowing that Kate had slept with him had her stomach churning furiously. She could feel her cheeks getting red, and an anxiety rising within her chest with every breath she took.

'What did you say about his ex? I love a good crazy ex story,' Kate said dreamily, still thinking about the previous evening.

'She followed him – stalked him – and caused a massive scene at his work, saying that he was cheating on her.' Alex's words were dismissive. She wanted out of this conversation now, so she could go find that block of chocolate that she'd hidden in the back of the pantry and wallow in her jealousy. Diet be damned.

'Oh that is crazy. John would never cheat. And to cause a scene at his work... completely shameful. Some women just have no dignity.'

'Hmmm... I guess the craziness got the better of her when she realised he was sleeping with someone else.' Alex's voice was dry. She was contemplating her own craziness and jealousy. Just like John's ex, she wasn't in a relationship with him. And just like John's ex, she felt unhinged at the thought of him with someone else. But unlike the ex, Alex had never even been with John. That probably made her even crazier than the crazy ex.

'What?' Kate sat straight up in the bathtub. 'You mean he was actually cheating?' She spat the words out with a fury that her friend had never heard in her voice before.

Without thinking, that selfish part of Alex that wanted John all to herself spoke, 'Yeah, he was cheating on her.'

Kate's mouth was ajar. She had no words. She loved John. He was handsome and fun and a total gentleman and he made her heart skip a beat whenever she looked at him. But now... now she knew the truth – he was a cheating scumbag just like Peter. She felt a familiar fury burning in her guts, while her heart shattered into a million pieces. Were any of those things she knew about John even true? Was he going to rip her heart out, just like Peter did? Once a cheater, always a cheater. There was no getting around it. Men who couldn't keep it in their pants just couldn't be trusted. She knew from the very beginning that she shouldn't get into a relationship. That's how you get hurt. What had she been thinking? She tried to steel herself. She wasn't going to let this upset her, but she still sobbed in the bath, between moments of tooth grinding rage.

An hour later when John called, she sent the call straight to voicemail. She was a strong, independent woman. There was no way she was going through hell again because of some cheating fucking man. She was done.

CHAPTER TWENTY-SIX

Alex sipped her coffee and waited for John. Their weekly ritual of coffee on a Monday morning was sometimes interrupted by John's trips up to Brisbane to see Kate. Alex hated the weeks that she didn't see him. She never really knew how lonely – friendless – she had been until she started spending so much time with John. And now she couldn't imagine it any other way. The companionship was a beautiful thing. And having him as her little secret made it feel special – as though a small part of him just belonged to her – it felt a little naughty, although she wasn't technically doing anything wrong.

Daniel didn't know about John. Their one meeting had gone so badly, she never mentioned John to Daniel ever again. Not that Alex expected Daniel would feel any differently about John had their first meeting been under better circumstances. No, Daniel seemed to like Alex's solitude too much. He wasn't thrilled at her reconnecting with Michelle, Rachel and Kate really either. But that was just Daniel. It wasn't something that Alex cared to think too much about – if she did, she might have actually realised that Daniel was extremely controlling. A fact that she seemed oblivious to. And having no close friends to point it out certainly assisted in keeping her in the dark.

'Sorry I'm late.' John sat and waved over the waitress to take his order.

John was often late. The coffee shop was around the corner from his work. He would come to meet Alex whenever he could make a break for the door without being sidelined by a colleague with a question – or more likely a problem; meaning that Alex was very much accustomed to settling in with a coffee, watching the world go by and waiting for John's late arrival.

'How was your weekend with Kate? Is she ecstatic about the job?' It had been a week since Alex's conversation with Kate. She wasn't sure what the fallout had been. She was certain she could claim innocence – she'd gotten the wrong end of the stick. Or maybe Kate had. Alex had practiced what her response would be if John asked. She wasn't a very good liar, but she was pretty sure she'd be able to pull it off.

They often talked about Kate. Too much for Alex's liking. Sometimes Alex loved to hear him talk about Kate; sometimes she felt incredibly happy for the loved-up bubble of bliss that her two friends lived in; and sometimes Alex imagined John was talking about her when he had that goofy smile on his face. And sometimes she hated it; sometimes it felt like her little secret – that tiny little part of him that belonged to her – wasn't hers at all. On those days, she tried to wear her brightest smile, while she felt her insides wither like an old bouquet of flowers in the heat of summer.

'No, she wasn't ecstatic.' John spoke slowly. 'Have you

spoken to her lately? She hasn't answered my calls or replied to my texts in a week.'

Alex felt a little flicker of victory spark inside her. He was hers. She didn't have to share anymore. A small smile played just beneath the surface of her lips, but she caught it with a deep inhale of air into her lungs. 'Because of the job?' Alex tried to pull her best that-just-doesn't-make-any-sense look. Lying really wasn't her thing.

'I don't... think so. I honestly really just have no idea.'

John sounded miserable. Alex wondered when she became this person. When did she become the kind of person who wanted anything but happiness for her friends? John was hurting and she was pleased. Why? Because she wanted him all to herself. And to make the whole situation a million times worse, she was the one who'd caused it all. She was a bad, bad person. Why was she doing this? She was married. Sure, if she was honest with herself, she had a little crush on him. But nothing would ever come of it, and, really, she didn't want it to. More than anything else, she wanted him to be her friend. Why would she begrudge John – and Kate – the happiness that everyone wants? Why was she so jealous?

'Don't worry. I'm sure she'll call you. She likes you. Just give it a little bit. She'll call. And it will all be okay.' *Liar!* 'There's nothing worse than a guy overstepping the boundaries.' *Why are you lying?* 'Give her some space. It will all work out.' Alex was aghast – why did she say that? She knew it wasn't true. She knew that Kate wouldn't call.

CHAPTER TWENTY-SEVEN

'There are so many hot guys here.'

Michelle looked around the room. She didn't see anyone she would consider hot. She grimaced at Kate. This was going to be a long night.

Some underweight *boy* (who was surely at least ten years their junior) in skinny jeans and a tight t-shirt had sat on a milk crate next to their table and struck up a conversation with Kate. He seemed to be talking passionately about his own clothes.

'Michelle, I've got to go to the loo. Can you *please* talk to Hamish while I'm gone? I really don't want him to leave.' Kate pressed her hands together as though praying and looked up at Michelle with pleading eyes.

'Okay.' Michelle didn't sound chipper about the prospect.

'So Hamish, what do you do?'

'I'm a fashion designer.'

Michelle was surprised and a little impressed. He would definitely have a lot of shared interests with Kate. Maybe this guy wasn't such a waste of time after all. 'So what kind of clothing do you design?'

'T-shirts.'

'Oh really? Did you design the one you're wearing?'

'Nope.'

Having a conversation with this guy was like trying to get blood from a stone. 'So which stores stock your shirts? Would I have seen them around?'

'Just an online store. They take submissions from designers and print them onto t-shirts.'

'Wow. And you make money from that? That's amazing.'

'No, I don't really make any *money* from it.' He said it as though money was not the point.

'Oh.' Michelle wondered how this guy seriously called himself a designer.

Hamish looked at his phone, stood up and walked off.

'See you later. Nice to meet you, wanker,' Michelle called out in a facetiously friendly tone after he was already out of earshot.

Kate looked crestfallen when she returned from the bathroom. 'Where did Hamish go?'

'He left. I couldn't stop him. He saw someone walk past with pink shoelaces and he was like a cat chasing a laser pointer.' Michelle saw the look on Kate's face and raised her eyebrows. 'That guy was a total tosser.'

'I liked him.'

'No, you really didn't.' Michelle looked her friend in the eyes and held her gaze. 'What happened to this philosophy that you don't need a guy? It wasn't that long ago that you were lecturing us all about how you don't need a boyfriend and that you were so happy alone. And now you're trawling the dregs of some crappy hipster bar.'

'That was then.' Kate took a swig of her drink. 'I didn't need anyone when I was happy.'

'Talking to these losers isn't going to make you feel better. And you're not going to do anything other than sleep with any of these guys – they're far too beneath you for a relationship.' Michelle grabbed Kate's hand. 'If you miss him, call him.'

'Once a cheater, always a cheater. Besides which, he hasn't even bothered trying to call *me*.'

'You know I'm not getting involved in this cheating crap. He didn't cheat on *you*.' Kate had made Michelle promise not to talk to John about their relationship. Unlike her divorce, she didn't want every single person she'd ever met to throw their two cents in. True to her word, Michelle had abstained from talking to John, but continued to defend him to Kate, in the brief moments that Kate would allow John to be part of the conversation. 'So maybe you just need to call him. Talk to him about it.'

Kate exhaled loudly through her nose. 'Enough about that cheater. Sleeping with one of these *losers* will give me an ego boost, which is exactly what I need right now.'

'The Kate I know doesn't need a guy to boost her ego. The Kate I know already knows that she's amazing and doesn't need another person to make her feel that way.' Michelle was losing patience. 'The Kate I know is smart enough to know that a woman doesn't have to be amazing in any meaningful sense in order to get laid. Cut the ego boost crap.'

'No man is an island.'

'Don't give me that trite shit.' Michelle seemed to be at the end of her tether.

'If you need to go home, just go. I don't really need a wing man anyway.'

'You begged me to fly up here. You said you needed a wing man. You actually used those words. I'm here. I'm your wing man. But I'm not excited to assist in self-destructive behaviour. I'll help you talk to guys – I'm trying to be supportive – but please, for the love of God, can you pick one that isn't such a fucking douche.'

'Thank you for coming. I really do appreciate it.'

'Of course I came. I was worried you were on the brink of a spectacular, Britney circa 2007 style meltdown.'

Kate flashed a tight smile. 'I'm okay.'

'Good, because you'd look fucking terrible with a shaved head.'

Kate gave an unenthusiastic chuckle. 'Why don't I go get us some drinks?'

'Just a diet coke for me, thanks.'

Kate registered that Michelle hadn't been drinking all night. Kate wasn't being entirely self-involved when she had begged Michelle to visit – in part she had been a little worried about Michelle too. Michelle had seemingly taken her break up with Andrew really well. But Kate wasn't completely convinced. Yes, Kate was a little late to the party in providing a shoulder for her friend – she had been so wrapped up in John to really give Michelle the attention that she deserved. But, no one moves on from a break up with a live-in boyfriend that easily. Even if you're not totally invested in the relationship, you've just had someone say that they don't want to be with you – for whatever reason – it's a blow to your self-esteem; it's someone saying that you're not good enough for them, and that's enough to feel a little down about yourself. But Michelle was adamant that she was fine. It had been a couple of months, and Michelle still seemed weird and Kate thought a night out as two single ladies would do a world of good. But Michelle wasn't even looking at any of the guys. And wasn't drinking.

'You always drink. What's going on?'

'I leave for Paris next week.'

'Lucky you.' Kate didn't mean to sound so bitter.

'Well, I need to be prepared. You can't drink like I normally do and run forty-two kilometres.'

'It's still like two weeks away, isn't it? C'mon.' Kate wrinkled her nose. 'You know you want to.'

Michelle had planned to avoid alcohol entirely – she wanted to be as healthy as possible by the time she was inseminated, which would be in four weeks, just after she returned from Paris. But this was definitely not information she wanted to share. She was far too nervous about the whole thing to have anyone calling her to ask if she was pregnant yet. Or worse – giving her a reason to doubt her plan. 'No, I'm fine. Anyway, two weeks isn't that long when you're in training for a marathon.'

'I always drink and it never affects my running.'

'Yep. And when was the last time you ran a marathon?'

'Ummm... never. I love running, but why the fuck would I pay money to go for a run? Running's free, Michelle. I have way more important things to spend my money on. Like drinks.'

When Kate returned with their drinks, she also had a guy in tow. 'This is Etienne.'

'Nice to meet you.' Michelle sounded bored. 'Etienne? Are you French?'

'No, why?' Etienne replied with an Australian accent. 'Is it the dimples?'

'No, no reason.' Michelle pulled a face at Kate. Was this guy serious? She steeled herself to make an effort with this guy. For Kate's sake. 'So, what do you do?' This was Michelle's classic initial question. To her, a response to this question could tell her whether a man was deserving of the next ten minutes of her time or not. A person's success, drive and ambition were important to Michelle, but also their ability to spin. Marketing ran in her veins, and being able to sell yourself – and to engage in small talk that captivates – was important to her.

'I'm a writer.' Etienne said loftily, while raising his eyebrows, waiting for a suitably impressed response.

'Who do you write for?' Michelle immediately assumed that he meant he was a journalist.

'I write for myself.'

'Like a blog?'

Etienne screwed up his face, unimpressed at the thought of something so passé as a blog. 'I write poetry. Poetry doesn't belong in a blog.'

'Oh.' Michelle was dumbstruck. She had no idea how to respond to this. 'So, um, you write for yourself, as in...'

'I don't believe in allowing anyone else to read my poetry. That's the first step to selling out. Writing is a huge part of who I am as a person and I don't think I should share with all of you –' Etienne made a sweeping gesture with his hand, '-

vultures, just so that you can peck away at my soul. I write to fuel my own desires; to nourish my soul.'

'Ahhh – okay.' Michelle gave herself a minute to recover. Was Kate listening to this? She surely wasn't interested in this guy. But as Michelle looked over, Kate seemed to be nodding along to the beat of his bullshit – although she didn't actually appear to be paying attention. 'So that's your hobby. What do you do to, you know, nourish the rest of you?'

Etienne looked outraged. 'It's not a hobby. It's my passion. Did you not hear me say that it *is* my soul?'

At that point Michelle decided that she couldn't carry on this conversation, no matter how hot Kate thought Etienne was. As Michelle turned and fled to the bathroom, she heard Etienne say something about a dystopian futuristic dreamscape. Luckily for all involved, her back was turned by that time, so Etienne didn't see her roll her eyes nor did he hear the loud groan that involuntarily escaped her lips. When she returned from the bathroom, Etienne was gone.

'Can we please get out of here? Some guy just told me he's into parkour. We're too old to be here.' Michelle looked around. 'Where'd the poet go?'

Kate looked glum. 'He told me my vagina was a resplendent ghetto playground for lost and beautiful souls. I just couldn't listen to him talk any longer.'

'Thank God! I was worried that there was something wrong with your hearing. Wait. You showed him your vagina?'

CHAPTER TWENTY-EIGHT

Michelle felt bile burning the back of her throat. Her stomach was churning. She swallowed hard, willing her breakfast to stay where it was. This was new for her. She was so nervous that she was going to throw up. This was a huge step, but it's what she wanted, so why should she be so nervous? And yet, she was.

She sat in a waiting room that was filled with black and white photographs of babies printed onto canvases. A naked newborn sleeping, its wrinkled face looking beautifully fragile; an angelic cherub smiling up at a Labrador, with the dog's large tongue curled, mid-lick; tiny fingers grasping a father's finger. These photos were made to tug at the heart, and they worked.

Michelle had had so many consultations, signed forms, made decisions about sperm (which was the second hardest decision she'd ever had to make – the first being to start trying to get pregnant); and after all of that, today was the day. She was as healthy as she'd ever been in her life. Training for the marathon meant that she was fit; she hadn't had alcohol in months (two weeks in Paris and she hadn't had any wine – that alone was proof that this was the most serious she had ever been about anything in her life); she ate salad every day. This was it. She was prepared. Soon there would be a baby growing in her belly. With that thought, she felt the bile rising from her stomach again. *Keep your shit together, Michelle!*

Michelle's name was called and she walked – a little unsteady on her feet – into the doctor's office. The wall was littered with hundreds of photographs of babies, thank you cards and birth announcements – proof that this process worked.

She chatted to the doctor while she lay on the hard, narrow bed. Michelle didn't know how she managed to make small talk when all she could think about was the fact that her life was going to change forever. Her voice, in fact, was not as steady as she imagined and she was noticeably distracted, responding with affirmative noises at inappropriate times.

As she left the clinic, Michelle felt giddy with excitement. Or was it nerves? On her way home she stopped at the store to pick up some pregnancy tests. The doctor had told her to wait – it would take a little while before a test would actually read positive; nevertheless Michelle wanted to be prepared. And, truth be told, she knew that she would take the test early and often out of pure excitement.

A week later, well before the doctor had advised her to, Michelle took a pregnancy test. It didn't take long before the test became a standard part of her morning routine. Each morning, she would climb out of bed, sit on the toilet and hold a plastic stick between her legs. She would lay the stick on the vanity next to the sink and let it work its magic while she had a shower. The first few days she had bounced out of bed, excited to take the test. And she then felt a wave of disappointment when the single line would appear to indicate *not pregnant*. Each time, she consoled herself with the knowledge that it was actually far too early to get a positive result. After those first few days, she no longer felt excitement at taking the test; it was just another part of her morning routine, like eating breakfast. She would still feel the sinking feeling of disappointment when there was only one line.

One day she forgot about checking the test after her shower. She ate her breakfast and remembered that she hadn't looked at the stick yet. Shrugging, she imagined that it would just be negative again. She continued to get ready for work. Checked her emails, did the dishes, read the morning news on her phone. Michelle just glanced down at the pregnancy test as she brushed her teeth. She expected it to be negative. But there it was, as plain as anything – two lines. Two lines.

CHAPTER TWENTY-NINE

'Who's Jake? I don't think I've heard you mention him.'

'Rachel, Jake is her *ex*-boyfriend.'

'Mum,' Kate sighed. 'He's obviously not my ex anymore.'

'Mrs Harris –'

'Pauline. You make me feel old.'

'Pauline, you don't really sound like you like this idea very much.'

Kate turned to Rachel. 'Stop stirring shit. Mum has been pressuring me to move out.' Kate gestured towards her mother. 'She's getting what she wanted.'

'No, this is not what I wanted. I want you to find somewhere to live. I never said I wanted you to shack up with some bloke.' Pauline grimaced. 'This is just a rebound. You're still hung up on what's-his-name.'

'John,' Rachel said helpfully.

Kate rolled her eyes. 'John's not relevant to this conversation.'

Rachel narrowed her eyes, sceptical. 'So, tell me, why did you and this Jake guy break up?'

'I don't really remember.' Kate looked back at the box she was packing, avoiding eye contact.

'That's a load of bull dung, missy.' Pauline turned to Rachel. 'He was an idiot. He treated her like she was an object.'

'Mum! Seriously, are you going to help us pack or are you going to talk all day. You're distracting us.'

'This is my house, I'll do what I want,' Pauline said as she started pulling clothes from the wardrobe. 'Why do you own so many bloody clothes?' Pauline sounded exasperated. 'Anyway, they broke up because he was an idiot. He thought she was only good for one thing.' She wiggled her eyebrows and looked at Rachel knowingly. 'You know what I mean. Didn't want to hear what she had to say. Just wanted her to look good and show her off to his friends.' She continued gently folding clothes and packing them in a bag. 'Who moves in with someone after a week, anyway?' Pauline seemed to be talking to herself now. 'He just happened to be in the right place at the right time. Not really a sound basis for a relationship. No wonder it didn't last. And it won't last this time either.' She turned back to Kate, pointing her index finger and speaking louder this time, 'You should have higher standards. And stop acting like such a bloody floosy.'

'And how did you two get back together?' Rachel's real question was why, and that was implied.

'We just ran into each other in a bar and got to talking –'

Pauline interrupted with an overly loud groan, and rolled her eyes.

Kate raised an eyebrow, annoyance written all over her face. 'We got to talking and we just hit it off really well. We honestly couldn't remember why we broke up in the first place.'

Pauline opened her mouth to say something, but Kate held up her hand to silence her mother. 'And, yes, as my mother said, it is particularly convenient. I need to move out of here -' Kate shot her mother a cold look – 'and he wants to get back together.'

'And, Kate, tell us why this idiot wants to get back together with you.' Pauline's voice was dripping with attitude. Before Kate could respond, Pauline continued talking. 'Because look at her –' She gestured toward Kate – 'she's gorgeous. And he's got all the personality of a lump of bloody coal. As Kate would say, he's very *image conscious*. That's a bloody euphemism, if ever I've heard one. He wants to be getting around with a beautiful girl on his arm, and you missy, fit that bill. He doesn't care about anything else.'

Rachel wished this awkward exchange would end. She was happy to be getting the inside scoop on Kate's relationship with Jake, but didn't love being in the midst of this mother-daughter dispute.

Pauline hadn't finished. 'Honestly Kate, you should be dating a man who worships the ground you walk on. Someone who wants to hear what you've got to say. Despite the way you act sometimes, you're a smart cookie. You need a bloke who can appreciate that.'

'He does worship the ground I walk on, Mum.'

'Thinking you're a hot piece of ass and worshiping the ground you walk on are not the same thing.' Pauline swung her arm around with her outburst, dropping a dress mid-fold. 'And I thought you were a feminist.'

'I am a feminist. But I'm also a realist. I don't earn very much money. And he can afford to pay for things. I need to move out of here, so...' Kate shrugged. 'And he loves me. And love is the most important thing, isn't it?'

'Love *is* the most important thing. But he doesn't love you. He loves the way you look. And you sure as bloody heck don't love him. So I don't think love is particularly bloody relevant to this conversation.'

'What am I supposed to do?' Kate was practically yelling. 'I don't want to be alone. And Jake wants me. I have to move out of here. I don't really know if it's the right thing to do, but I don't feel like I have many other options.'

Pauline's voice was gentler, 'Honey, I'm sorry if I made you feel as though you have to move out. You can stay for as long as you want.'

'Kate, you're the one who told me you don't need a man to be complete. And I think you're right. You definitely don't need a man that you don't love.' Rachel felt that she had to add something to the conversation. Pauline seemed to be right, but she'd gone about this the wrong way and had probably done more harm than good.

'You're right. I'm pathetic.' Kate sounded bitter and angry. Her words were an accusation.

'No, you're not pathetic. That's not what I meant.'

'She actually is pathetic.'

Rachel glared at Pauline. Why would she say that to her daughter?

Pauline continued, 'I can't think of anything more pathetic than moving in with some fella that you don't even like just because he says he loves you and you're lonely. What a loser, hey?' Pauline nudged Kate with her elbow, and chuckled. 'My daughter isn't a pathetic loser. So, maybe stop bloody acting like one.'

CHAPTER THIRTY

Michelle hadn't really expected that it would happen on the first attempt. She felt almost a little surprised. She was pregnant. Pregnant. It was exactly what she had wanted. What she had been trying for. But somehow it was still a little bit of a shock.

Michelle began to think about the life growing inside her. In less than nine months time, this thing would be a living, breathing, human. A baby. And she would be a mother. Someone would call her Mummy. Nine months and she would be completely responsible for the life of another human being. Really, she was already responsible for another life – whatever she ate, drank, did, already had the potential to dictate the fate of her baby. That responsibility felt like a heavy weight – not a burden, she was elated, she wanted this so much – but the gravity of this situation was making an unmistakeable imprint on her breathing. She was excited beyond words, and yet terrified. Her life had just changed forever. This was real. It was frightening. And she was all alone. She hadn't really comprehended before what doing this alone meant. Even now, she didn't truly understand. But it was beginning to dawn on her – she had no one to share her excitement with. She had no one to talk giddily with about baby names, nursery layout and how absolutely crap she was feeling. She had never felt so lonely. Or so exhausted. Or hungry. Despite all that, it was the greatest feeling she had ever experienced. She was going to be a mother. She was going to have a baby.

Michelle called the doctor's office and made an appointment for the following week – it was the soonest she could get in to see Dr Carroll. Next week felt like an eternity away.

She stood in front of her mirror, side on, lifted her shirt and assessed her tummy. It looked the same, of course, but she imagined that it didn't. She expanded her belly to form a little pot and rubbed it, smiling to herself. She wanted to call someone, anyone, to share her good news. But it was so early, she knew the risks, and didn't really want to complicate things by having someone else know just yet.

Eight days she had to wait to see the doctor. Eight days. And a lot can change in eight days.

CHAPTER THIRTY-ONE

'That's a great dress.' Jake's friend, Troy, looked Kate up and down, appreciating her slender waist and curves. His eyes lingered a little too long on her breasts.

'Thank you.' By the time Kate spoke, Troy had already turned his attention back to Jake. The two men launched into an in depth discussion about football – or maybe they meant soccer – she wasn't entirely sure.

Kate patiently waited for a break in the conversation, but before one happened, Jake turned to her, 'Babe, can you grab us a couple of beers.' Jake didn't wait for a response, he simply turned back to Troy and continued talking about some sports team.

The ball was raising money for a charity. Apparently no one really cared which one – Kate had asked three different people and had been given three vague and totally different answers.

She had felt quite excited at the prospect of the ball. Getting dressed-up in a new gown, drinking and partying: it sounded like an amazing night. But so far, everyone had been boring, most were middle-aged, no one was dancing and no one had been remotely inclined to have a proper conversation with her. Jake's friends only seemed interested in ogling her. And Jake was giving the impression that she was there as his personal bartender.

Kate sighed to herself, as her thoughts returned to John, as they had done, again and again, since last Christmas. John had never made her feel this way. He had always made her feel as though *she* was important; he had listened to everything she had said; he had laughed at her jokes, asked her questions about what she wanted. It was heart breaking, soul destroying, maddening, infuriating, crushing that he hadn't been everything that she thought he was – that he had turned out to be just another lying cheat.

Jake had bought Kate a new dress for the occasion. It was a white Grecian style dress, with a high split to her upper thigh. Most of the skin on her back was exposed and the white fabric looked gorgeous against her brown skin. She had felt like Julia Roberts in Pretty Woman going shopping with someone else's credit card, but now she was feeling more like a true to life whore, not the romanticised movie version – having a man pay for things for her, so that she could stand next to him, looking pretty and sleep with him when they got home.

Kate wondered if this is how Alex felt. Kate had been so jealous of Alex; her beautiful apartment, her little Mercedes, the travel – oh, the travel – but being a kept woman didn't sit well with Kate. She wanted her partner to *be* a partner – equals; she wanted to feel valued, not just because of the way she looked; and she wanted to feel loved – really loved, not just the way you love a pair of shoes. Then again, Alex was married to Daniel. Surely he wouldn't have married someone who he thought of as an object. He seemed so sweet though – this probably was nothing like the way Alex felt.

Kate sauntered off to get beers for Jake and Troy, but was scanning the room for someone more interesting to talk to.

From across the room, a man seemed to be trying to catch her eye. They locked eyes, he waved and started walking towards her. He was feigning knowing her, so that they could talk, most likely. But she had no one to talk to, so maybe she'd throw the guy a bone – who knows, maybe he was interesting. Or interested.

'Kate, right?'

Shit! He does actually know me. Where have we met before? He looks really familiar.

'Tom. John's friend.' He smiled, not offended that she didn't remember him.

Tom was actually John's best friend. They had been close most of their lives, growing up next door to each other, and their families had remained close, even now, years after Tom's family had moved away. Kate had actually met Tom innumerable times while they were growing up, and again at Fiona's engagement party. But Kate had had a little too much to drink already, and had never been that great at remembering faces to begin with.

'Oh, sorry, that's right. How are you?'

'Great. And how are you? Not that I really need to ask – I hear so much about you from John.'

He didn't seem to know that Kate and John had broken up. It was an awkward situation, but Kate wanted to know exactly what John had been saying about her, so she didn't really want to jump in with the news of their breakup. 'Really? What's he been saying about me?'

'You know he's so in love with you. He's always droning on about how smart and nice you are. And hot, but that part's obvious.' Tom gave her a good natured wink.

'He said that? That he's in love with me?'

Tom began to look a little uncomfortable. 'Um, well... I don't remember his exact words,' Tom mumbled.

Kate felt a pang of regret. Why did things have to be this way? She missed John so much. Thinking about John, and contrasting Jake to John, really made her realise how much of a dick Jake was. He wasn't loving at all. She had really only gotten back together with him because she was so lonely. But now that seemed like a stupid reason. It was better to be alone, than to feel like you don't matter.

Kate had to remind herself that she didn't miss the *real* John. She just missed the way he seemed to be. The *real* John was a cheat. Even though that didn't feel at all like the truth. It was the truth.

Tom and Kate continued to chat for a half hour before Jake's unwelcome sobriety reminded him of her absence and he had to take matters into his own hands.

Jake spotted Kate and came up behind her. He grabbed her ass and squeezed.

'So that's where you are. I was worried that you'd gotten lost.'

Tom looked at Jake's hand on Kate's rear and raised his eyebrows.

'Argh, Tom, this is Jake.' Kate tried to subtly pull away from Jake.

'I'm the boyfriend.' Jake, without any tact, took a metaphoric piss on Kate. Turning to her, he said, 'So, I'll just get my own drink, shall I?'

'Yeah, that'd be great.' Kate felt no need to apologise. She wasn't his personal waitress.

Without another word, Jake turned, walking off toward the bar.

Tom stood looking at Kate waiting for an explanation.

'John and I actually broke up a couple of months ago. I didn't say anything – I just thought it might be a bit awkward.' Kate laughed a little nervously. 'This is definitely far less awkward.'

'Well the replacement seems charming.'

'He's not that bad. He's just a little... rough around the edges.' Kate didn't believe that at all. 'We're going to the Maldives.' Kate piped up, happily, in an attempt to change the topic. But all that she managed to do was give the impression that she believed a man paying for a holiday for her made up for that man being a complete dick.

Jake had suggested a holiday and Kate had jumped at the chance. She wanted so badly to travel. Those gorgeous beaches and that crystal clear blue water she'd seen in pictures seemed idyllic. She imagined lying by their private infinity pool in her bikini, snorkelling off a boat, drinking cocktails, going for runs each morning on the beach. She had already bought two new pairs of bikinis and an amazing oversized hat, like the ones that ladies wore in ads for tonic water (she wasn't quite sure how she was going to fit it into a suitcase though). Sometimes when she thought about the holiday, it almost seemed worth sacrificing her self-worth for. Her mother would be so disappointed.

'Sounds great.' Tom was unenthusiastic. He was amazed that Kate was actually such a... gold digger. The expression on his face said it all.

Kate recognised the look on his face. He thought Jake a fuckwit and her almost as bad for being with him. 'He's really alright.' She reiterated, lost for what else to say.

'Hmmm... In my experience, if the best thing you can say about a person is that they're alright, you don't really like them enough to be dating them.' Tom was a little drunk and annoyed at Kate for not being forthright about her and John. And pissed off on behalf of his mate, who clearly got dumped for some rich dickhead. 'I suppose there's always the exception of when that *alright* person is taking you on expensive overseas holidays.' Tom didn't care if he was being rude.

Kate's mouth dropped open a little. Who did this guy think he was? He had no right to talk to her like that.

'Fuck you. That has nothing to do with why I'm with Jake.'

She was angry, but even through her clenched teeth and indignant rage, she could see that maybe Tom had a point. She'd always known that Jake wasn't really *the one* or any of that other shit that people go on about. But that was okay. She just didn't want to be alone. And she needed somewhere to live. But after only a week of living with Jake, she wasn't so sure that this was such a great idea. Living with her mum had been a lot easier. If she was really honest, the promise of an overseas holiday really helped. Didn't she deserve to go somewhere? Didn't she deserve some overseas travel? It's not like it was asking much. Alex travelled all the time. Even Michelle got to go away for work heaps. And she had been to Paris for the marathon. Paris for a fucking marathon. As though Paris wasn't a big deal at all – just pop over there to go for a fucking run. When would it be Kate's turn? But that really wasn't reason enough to be with a guy that she wasn't in love with. She was reluctant to admit it, but maybe this Tom guy had a point. Maybe her mum had a point. God, what the fuck was she thinking? She needed to break up with this idiot. She wondered if she could wait until after the holiday. She knew it was wrong, but she really, really wanted to go. But it was so bad. That would make her just as bad as what Tom seemed to think she was. Then again, who gives a fuck what some random guy thinks of her. She really wanted to go somewhere. Anywhere, really. And the Maldives seemed so heavenly. But what kind of whore uses a guy for a free holiday? Plus she'd need to spend the whole time with Jake. He wasn't that bad though. And she really, really wanted to go. Fuck.

CHAPTER THIRTY-TWO

Michelle day dreamed about her baby. Would it look like her? Would it have her eyes? Was it a boy or girl? On her lunch break one day, she wandered into the baby section of a department store. She looked at socks that seemed implausibly small; a white, lace dress and imagined dressing her baby girl up like a little doll; it was a girl, she could just feel it. A mother with a cherub-like child in a pram walked past Michelle, and she grinned joyfully at the chubby baby. She hoped her little girl would have chubby cheeks and dimples like that. It didn't matter though. Whatever she looked like, she would be perfect.

Michelle began writing lists of what she would need to do and to think about. There were so many decisions to be made. What would she need to get organised in order to take time off work? She would need to get one of the other partners up to speed on all of her clients. She would immediately need to get child care sorted – there were enormous waiting lists for all of the great centres. And she needed a nanny – an au pair. But that couldn't really be organised until much later. She should think about what language she wanted the au pair to speak though. That would narrow her search a little; she did want her child learning a second language as young as possible. She would also need to make a full list of what she would need to buy – pram, clothes, cot, bassinet, car seat. Shit! Car seat! Would a car seat even fit in her car? It only had two doors. Would she need to buy a new car? Why had she bought a sports car? It was so impractical.

And then she felt a dull ache in her abdomen. She brushed it off, thinking it was just period pain. A few seconds later it dawned on her – she shouldn't have period pain. Panic set in immediately. She rushed to the toilet. There was blood.

Michelle stared, deadpan, at her blood stained underwear. Was it possible that the baby was okay? Surely it was possible. She pleaded to a God she didn't believe in. Please let my baby girl be okay. Please. Please. But Michelle knew it was unlikely that little speck of life that had been growing within her was still there. She knew. Pleading – begging, bargaining – was not going to help her. Her tiny little, dimpled, baby doll was gone before she had ever really existed.

Michelle's analytical mind told her that this was normal. She knew the risks were high this early on. She should have expected this. She would just try again. There was never any real expectation that she would definitely fall pregnant the first time. She had been extremely lucky that it had worked the first time. At least now she knew she wasn't barren. Yes, lucky. It seemed a very weird word to be using given the circumstances. She didn't feel lucky.

She couldn't quite convince herself to stick to these rational thoughts. Her throat felt tight and her eyes stung with unshed tears as she went about her day. She continued on with her life as though everything was normal – as though her heart wasn't breaking. No matter how much she told herself to think about this with her head not her heart – to get back up, dust herself off and get back on that insemination horse – no matter how hard she tried, she just couldn't stick to the rational thoughts. And it hurt. A lot. When she found out she was pregnant, she had no one to share her news with. And now, she had no one to share her pain with.

'I understand that it's quite upsetting for you. Unfortunately about one in five pregnancies end in miscarriage. But those rates are based on women who know they're pregnant. Realistically, it's estimated to be more like one in three. We just have to try again. This is actually a very good sign. You've successfully been inseminated.'

'Hmm...' No part of Michelle felt like this was a good thing. Knowing she was pregnant so early was a mistake. The risks were too high that early on.

Michelle felt overwhelmed by a sense of loss that she couldn't articulate. Her baby girl was gone. But it wasn't as simple as that. Her reason for walking away from Andrew was gone. And, worse, the nameless, silent, unspoken joy that had offset the doubt in her methodically calculated plan was gone. And the doubt had come rushing back, coupled with dread and fear and loss and heartbreak, filling the gaping void in her womb.

She went about her days as she always had, but she didn't quite feel like all of her was there, paying attention. It was as though her head was clouded with a fog, but she had to go about her day as if that fog – that anguish – didn't exist. Her mind told her that it didn't make sense; that a tiny speck of life had been within her and now it wasn't – and that tiny speck wasn't a big deal. But no matter how much she tried to convince herself, that heavy feeling that threatened to drag her to the ground never eased.

****

Since the miscarriage, Michelle had undergone two more rounds of donor insemination with no success. *The miscarriage.* At first, Michelle would say she had lost a baby. But repeating that to doctors, nurses, pathologists each time she was asked the standard list of questions that seemed mandatory amongst medical professionals was hard; every time she said the words a lump would form in her throat; her voice sounded strange, even to herself; she soon decided to use the word miscarriage. It didn't convey the gravity of the situation. And that's what she needed. She needed it to feel clinical. She needed it to be business. She needed the loss to not be hers, to just be some sort of vague, medical term that was just a word; not something that she lived and breathed and constantly tried to push from her mind.

Three rounds of donor insemination and her nerves felt frayed. She'd known people who had tried to fall pregnant, albeit naturally – with sex and a real penis, something that seemed a distant memory to her – and some of those women had tried for years unsuccessfully. How did they cope with this? The wild excitement at the thought that this really would be the time, only to be met with the crushing disappointment when it didn't work? How did they live with the constant hope that was inevitably crushed? How did they deal with the nerves? The anticipation? The loss? The compulsion to be the healthiest version of you that you could be (particularly no alcohol)? The constant failure? Failure was not something that had ever sat well with Michelle. And in this situation trying harder, studying more, pushing yourself further, weren't options. There was nothing more she could do to make this work. She was used to being in control; to being able to methodically devise a plan, execute her plan and achieve the outcome that she wanted. Failure was a rarity. And when it did occur, she had a contingency plan; a way to deal with the failure and still get the desired outcome, or at least a version of it. But not with this. With this, she had to leave it up to her body and fate. She couldn't will her body to do this. There was absolutely nothing more that she could do to make this happen. Her body seemed to be working against her. This is what her body was made to do. And it wasn't doing it. Her body wasn't just failing at falling pregnant – it was failing at being a woman. She was powerless. And it was wildly frustrating, and more than a little devastating.

The doctor had warned Michelle that it may take some time. The success rates were less than ten percent. They had discovered that something wasn't quite right with Michelle's ovulation, so she had started on fertility hormones. But Michelle wasn't able to rein in her discontent, so Dr Carroll had suggested she consider IVF. It was far more invasive. And more expensive. But the success rates were more than eighty percent. Michelle cursed Dr Carroll for not suggesting IVF initially. She was told to expect it to be hard on her; to expect an emotional turbulence unlike anything she'd ever experienced before; but Michelle didn't care. She wanted this. She would walk through fire to make this happen. She would not be defeated by her own body.

But now here she was, three rounds of artificial insemination down, one pregnancy, one miscarriage; and, realistically, her journey had only just begun. From the online forums that she had been frequenting, she had learned that this was an ordeal that could go on for years without success. And without getting any easier. Was she really prepared for that? She wanted a baby. Undoubtedly. But did she want to go through all of this by herself, only to have it not work? She supposed that there was only one way to find out if it would work. And that was a hard, potentially very long, road. Now that she'd started walking down that road, she wasn't sure if she had the strength to do this. Maybe Rachel had been right. Maybe this whole idea – of doing this alone – was crazy. Maybe it was going to be harder than she could imagine. So far, it had been. It shouldn't have been, but the hormones were wreaking havoc on her mind, emotions, body. And the loss of her baby (she had tried to convince herself to think of it only as a speck of something that might have turned into a baby, but she was never really able to do that) still made her feel hollow. She didn't imagine that the speck was actually a person – she had imagined what it might have been, that was all – but she missed it. She missed that brief but undeniable feeling that she had had when she had felt and imagined a life growing inside her. She missed the connection – the strongest connection to anything that she had ever experienced – that she felt towards the speck. And this was hard. Really hard. And she wanted a baby. And she wanted to give up. And she wanted to hug someone. And to confide in someone. And to be told that it would all turn out alright. This was the difference between Michelle's situation and that of so many of the faceless voices online: so many of them had partners for support. She wanted all these things, but more than anything, she wanted to feel that feeling again – the feeling of life growing inside her.

CHAPTER THIRTY-THREE

Kate wasn't proud of herself. She knew it was wrong. But she had done it anyway. At the time, and even now, it was difficult to admit to herself that she was doing something so horrible. So instead of accepting the truth, she had continued to try to convince herself that Jake really was a good guy and that she did really, genuinely like him. But a cold shudder would run through her every time he had taken her shopping (which was a lot). She suspected that he loved the swooning adoration bestowed upon him from sales assistants and the envious sidelong glances thrown their way from other customers when he bought her extremely expensive things; she imagined that it made him feel like a big man. It made her feel like a terrible person – she had accepted expensive gifts from someone she didn't love... or particularly like at all. It hadn't felt quite right when he was buying her things. But she deserved to have nice things for once in her life though, didn't she?

The decision to stay with Jake so that she could still go to the Maldives hadn't been a conscious one. She hadn't deliberated and come up with a calculated plan in which she would get as much as she could from him by way of clothes, shoes, handbags, dinners, and holidays and then ditch him. Rather, she had thought about ending it with him and then convinced herself that she really did like him; then he had acted like a dick and she had nearly packed up her things again, but then had convinced herself to give him another week – maybe they could turn things around. She honestly hadn't been sure at the time if she was just setting her standards too high after John – she couldn't realistically hold Jake to the same standards as John. Jake wasn't that kind of guy. And their relationship just hadn't been like that. She hadn't loved Jake. And she really had loved John (and – probably, heartbreakingly – still did). But at least Jake couldn't *really* hurt her – that was the benefit of being with someone you don't really care about. So she had thrown herself full force into this rebound relationship. And going to the Maldives was just a bonus.

Jake had bought Kate a whole new wardrobe for their trip. Although he had said – while leering at her – that he expected she wouldn't be wearing much at all on their holiday. That had left a bit of a bad taste in her mouth. She didn't have a problem with meaningless sex. And she supposed it wasn't meaningless when you were in a relationship. But maybe that was the part that didn't feel quite right – it was meaningless to her but it shouldn't have been. Maybe her problem had been that she was still hung up on John. Kate wasn't sure, but she had tried to push it from her mind. The less she thought about it, the better the sex had been.

As expected, the trip had been spectacular, with the exception of the Jake factor. He had just been a pain in her ass.

And Kate couldn't help herself – she had spent most of the trip imagining how different it might have been had she been there with John.

During the flight, Kate had been bursting with excitement. She had read so much about what there was to do there – which admittedly wasn't much – and looked a photos and restaurant reviews. She had planned out the books she would read, the magazines to take, the outfits she would wear. It was going to be fantastic. And she spent the flight telling Jake trivia about the Maldives, the meals she wanted to order at the resort's restaurant, the sunset cruise that the resort offered that sounded breathtaking, and the treatments she wanted to have done at the day spa. Jake was less enthused, mostly due to Kate's excitement. At first he had been bemused by her enthusiasm, but that had waned quickly. Apparently being excited about a holiday wasn't very cool. That had been the beginning of the two of them rubbing each other the wrong way.

The villa that they had stayed in was set on stilts above the water, with a private infinity pool on a deck overlooking the water. A huge window opened out from the bathroom to the private deck, meaning that you could lie in the enormous two person bathtub and look out over the tranquil turquoise water. The entire place had been flawless. Kate couldn't have imagined anything so beautiful. As they had been shown to the villa, Kate had let out an excited squeal and had jumped – fully clothed and in front of the resort staff member who'd shown them to their room – into the infinity pool. That seemed to be the final straw in dorky enthusiasm for Jake – he had told her to stop being so immature and to get a grip.

Kate hadn't let Jake put a dampener on her mood. She changed into her favourite new swimsuit – a black strapless one piece with two large cut out sections that wrapped around her left side. She had planned on heading to reception to borrow a snorkel and exploring the waters around their villa but Jake had had other ideas.

'Hmmm... Does the top come off that thing? I thought you might want to do a bit of topless sunbaking. Or maybe you could take the whole thing off. We have a private deck for a reason.'

Kate had immediately responded by lecturing him on the dangers of sunbaking. She wasn't entirely being honest – she was always sun smart... to a degree. She did actually love lying in the sun, but he didn't need to know that.

The rest of their trip had continued much as it had started – with them both irritating each other, and Kate trying to avoid Jake as much as possible.

As much as their relationship had been doomed from the start, their trip to the Maldives had been the death knell for them as a couple. As soon as their flight had landed back in Australia, Kate had texted her mum asking if she could move back in with her. Three days in to their ten day holiday Kate had decided she was going to dump him when they got home. She hadn't wanted to seem like the kind of bitch who uses a guy for a free holiday or to make the rest of their trip incredibly awkward, so had planned on telling him a few days after they got back; maybe a week or two if she could stand him for that long. But after their flight back there was no way she was going to spend a second longer than she had to with him.

CHAPTER THIRTY-FOUR

From the street, Alex could hear music, laughter and shrieking. She steeled herself, walked through the front door of the maid of honour's house and was greeted by an overwhelming sight. There were women everywhere – dancing, talking, drinking – and the noise they were making was deafening. Most had plastic tiaras on their heads and some were sporting pink feather boas. And, dear God, the penis paraphernalia.

Kate ran up to Alex, hugged her and shoved a tiara on her head. 'Hope you've got your dancing shoes on. Tonight is going to get messy!'

One of the bridesmaids (clearly identifiable as such, due to the pink sash she wore diagonally across her torso with the word *bridesmaid* emblazoned across it in glittery writing) stood on the coffee table and whistled for attention. 'Ladies,' she paused while the talking died down, 'tonight we celebrate our beautiful friend, Fi. This is her last night out as Miss Fiona Masters, so let's make it a good one!' The room erupted in cheers. 'We have a game that we'll be playing tonight.' A few women groaned, which was met with a lot of laughter. 'Anna's going to be coming around with some cards. Each card has a dare written on it. Once you complete the dare, come to Anna or me for another card. The person with the most cards at the end of the night wins. The game begins once we arrive at the first bar.'

Anna (also wearing a *bridesmaid* sash) began to walk around the room with a pink, glittery bag. 'It's a lucky dip, ladies. No swapping.'

Alex dug into the bag and grabbed a laminated card that had a lanyard attached.

'What did you get?'

'Get a man to buy shots for you and the bride.' Relief was written all over Alex's face. 'This shouldn't be too hard. What's yours?'

'Kiss a red head.' Kate chuckled and winked at Alex. 'I like this game.'

****

As they walked into the first bar, the women were all in fits of laughter comparing the dares they had been given.

Fiona's sister was the first to complete her dare. She stood on a chair and sang the National Anthem to the entire bar, earning herself much applause, some wolf whistles and a drink courtesy of the bar tender.

Michelle's competitive nature got the better of her. Her first dare was the next to be done with a quick flash of her knickers to a bald man. Thankfully she was wearing a skirt and could pull her underwear up and the waistband down a little to complete the task without too much embarrassment.

Rachel, Kate and Alex sipped on their drinks and laughed as they watched various women in their group make fools of themselves. Michelle was the main offender and quickly accumulated a sizable sum of lanyards around her neck.

'Who's supposed to be kissing a red head? There's one over here.' Anna seemed to have memorised all of the dares that she had handed out.

'That's me. I hope he's cute.' Kate was immediately grabbed by Anna and one of the other bridesmaids. Kate laughed as the women steered her towards the red head.

As soon as Kate caught sight of the man they were heading towards, she stopped dead in her tracks, nearly tripping the other two women. Her face froze mid-laugh and slowly morphed into an expression of shock.

'What's wrong?'

'That's my ex-husband.' Kate regained her composure, turned and fled back to her friends before Peter was able to see her.

'I just saw Peter. He was the red head I was supposed to kiss.'

'Oh, no! Are you okay?' Rachel wrapped her arms around Kate. 'You didn't kiss him though, did you?'

'Of course I didn't fucking kiss him.' Kate was indignant and pulled out of Rachel's embrace.

Michelle, meanwhile, was trying to convince a man on the dance floor to remove his shirt, when she noticed the commotion amongst her friends and made her way back to them.

'Is everything alright?'

'Peter's here.'

'Oh, honey, did you talk to him?'

'No. I haven't spoken to him since we got divorced. I'm definitely not going to talk to him when I'm wearing a pink tiara.'

'You know what you need? A drink. I'll just be a sec.'

Michelle returned quickly with a tray of shots. They each downed two shots of tequila before the conversation could continue.

'So, do you know what Peter's been doing?'

'I used to stalk him on Facebook. But, really, I was getting too obsessive, so I stopped.'

Michelle pulled out her phone and did a quick search. 'Looks like he's married to someone named Jessica.'

'Oh! That's her, isn't it? The one he cheated with?' Rachel grabbed Kate's hand and squeezed.

'He married her.' Kate threw back another shot and stared dismally at the empty shot glass for several minutes. 'I always thought he was cheating because we didn't work. But does this mean it was the other way around? Was she the cause of all the problems in our marriage?'

Kate's shoulders were slumped, her voice doleful, her eyes glistened with unshed tears. Her marriage to Peter and its subsequent demise usually felt like a lifetime ago – like a parallel world where another version of herself had resided, that she remembered fragments of as though it was a dream; but not in that moment. In that moment, the tortuous agony that he had inflicted on her – the grief and sorrow that she had suffered by his hand – came flooding back. In that moment, she was reliving the pain all over again. In that moment, she felt exactly as she had when she'd read the message from Jessica, when she'd confronted him on her birthday and he'd said the words that would forever be etched into her memory *I don't love you anymore.* The look on his face had been the hardest part. There was no love in that look. There was no regret. No pity. His features told of relief – like a man who'd been holding up a dam wall with all his might for so long, he let it go and the water crashed into everything in its path causing a wave of destruction, but he didn't care, because he didn't have to use all his strength to hold that wall anymore. He was relieved that he'd been caught. He wasn't sorry. He didn't care that he'd hurt her. Even if she had forgiven him, even if she'd wanted to reconcile, he didn't want to. It was over. And he was happy.

In that moment in the bar, Kate again relived that pain. Added to this was knowing that he'd left her for someone else. She had always assumed it was her that he was running from, not Jessica that he was running to. Was that better or was it worse? She wasn't sure.

'I know this is hard. But does it even matter? Either way, you're better off without him.' Michelle's tone was forceful, with only the slightest hint of sympathy.

'She does have a point. You're a much better version of you without him.' Alex beamed at Kate, her eyes full of admiration.

'That is true. I am fabulous now.' Kate flashed a big smile. 'I'm going to the bathroom.' With that she walked off.

Michelle turned to Rachel, 'I have never seen her like this

before. She's usually so confident. I can't believe she's this rattled over a guy.'

Rachel grimaced and shook her head slightly. 'You were in Sydney when they broke up. She took it really hard. But, honestly, I don't think that there's any other way to take a breakup like that. I mean, her husband – her high school sweetheart – was cheating on her and left her. No matter how confident a person you are, no one would really be okay.' Rachel was surprised at Michelle's lack of empathy. Maybe there was a reason she'd always been single.

Alex was silent throughout the exchange. She couldn't imagine anyone cheating on a girl like Kate. Sure, she wasn't quite as glamorous back then, but she'd always been beautiful. 'I'm going to walk past him. I want to see what he looks like now and work out if he saw Kate.'

'He'll recognise you. I don't think it's a good idea.'

'He's not going to recognise me. He hasn't seen me since high school. And I'm not a very noticeable kind of person. And I won't get too close.' With that, Alex walked off before Rachel could protest any further.

Alex returned just as Kate was coming back from the bathroom.

'He's with a woman.' Alex turned to Michelle. 'Show me his Facebook page. I want to know if it's her.'

Michelle pulled out her phone again, quickly navigated to the right page and held her phone up to Alex.

'Yep. That's her.'

Kate groaned. 'Could this get any worse?'

'Yes, it could get way worse. For him.' Michelle had a mischievous glint in her eyes.

'I think that you should talk to him. He hasn't seen you in years. He should see what he's missing out on.' Alex raised her eyebrows and smiled at Kate. 'He should see that you're so much hotter than that *Jessica*.' Alex spat out her name as though forming the word in her mouth would somehow contaminate her.

'Okay.' Kate's face was serious and full of frank determination. She nodded to herself as she psyched herself up for the confrontation.

'Do you want me to come with you?' Rachel's voice was full of concern. She wasn't convinced that this was a particularly healthy thing to do.

'No.' Kate pulled the tiara from her head, the lanyard from around her neck and checked her reflection in a small mirror she pulled from her handbag.

'What are you going to say?'

'I'm just going to say hello. Coming up with any sort of burn will smack of desperation. Like I care about him or something.' Kate had a calculating look in her eye as she gave a tight smile. With that she walked off.

Michelle turned to Rachel. 'Don't worry about her. She knows exactly what she's doing.'

Kate walked confidently towards Peter. Her stride was long and steady in her enormous heels.

Peter looked up as she approached. He began to squirm and seemed to shrink backwards away from her. 'Kate.' He stammered her name.

'Hello Peter.' Kate gave an enormous smile. 'I saw you from across the room. Just thought I'd come over and say hello.'

The woman who was with Peter – presumably Jessica –

turned to him, completely ignoring Kate. 'Kate? As in your ex, Kate?'

Peter didn't know where to look. His gaze darted frantically from Jessica to Kate, around the room, and finally landed on his drink where he stared with a slightly crazed look in his eyes. 'Ah, yes, ah, that's her.' As he spoke his eyes shot up to Jessica several times but only managed to stay on her for a fraction of a second at a time.

'She doesn't look anything like how you described her.' Jessica's voice was shrill.

'Oh, honey, I don't think you should take his word as gospel.' Kate turned her head slightly and raised her eyebrows.

'I – ah –' Peter stammered, not sure what to say to either of them. 'Kate! Are you just here to stir up shit?'

'No, I'm just here for a bachelorette party.' She shrugged with a smile.

'God, Peter, grow a pair.' Jessica's voice had lost its shrill tone and was now just dripping with disdain.

'Yes. You wouldn't think that he'd be quite so shy around the only two women he's ever slept with.'

'I've slept with more than two women.'

'Oh, that's fantastic. So you cheated on me with someone other than her.' Kate gestured wildly toward Jessica. She was losing her cool and immediately realised she would have to rein it in a little if she wanted to maintain the upper hand. She pulled her hand back to her side, hoping that it looked natural and attempted to relax her facial features. Peter hadn't noticed any of it. He was far too busy staring at his drink.

'No. I didn't – I – Jessica was the only person I cheated on you with.' The words burst out of Peter's mouth before he had time to think about the implications of what he was saying.

'Wait, what are you saying? Then when did you have another lover? You cheated on me?' Jessica's voice hit an octave much higher than Kate had previously believed possible for an adult.

'That's not – I didn't say that. I just –'

'Well, when did you sleep with someone else?' Jessica glared at him and shouted, 'When?'

'I –'

Jessica cut him off before he could answer her. 'Is it Carla? You said there was nothing going on with her.'

Kate pressed her lips together to suppress a smile. 'I think I'll leave you two to it. Seems like you've got a lot to talk about.'

Kate burst into fits of laughter as she reached her friends.

'What happened?'

Kate managed to get out the words in short bursts between her hysterics. 'I know I shouldn't be laughing – I've been there – it really sucks to be Jessica right now. I think he's cheating *on her.*'

'Oh – my – god.' Michelle's words were slow and deliberate. She looked scandalised. And then burst out laughing.

'Once a cheater, always a cheater. What did she expect?' Rachel's lack of empathy was out of character, and her words were slightly slurred.

'I think she already knew he was cheating. He just accidentally confirmed it.'

'I think this calls for more drinks.'

****

As is always the way with any group of women, particularly beautiful women, their entrance was noticed by almost every man in the bar. They had had a lot to drink already. Rachel, who wasn't used to drinking much at all, was feeling the drinks. A lot. Her tongue felt too big for her mouth. She was sure that she was slurring her words. Her stilettos wobbled a little every time she shifted her weight on them. But she was too drunk to feel the pain she would normally be experiencing in her feet, which was a plus.

Within a minute of walking through the door, a man approached Rachel and Michelle. He'd quickly sized up the group and had easily determined that Rachel was by far the drunkest – the best target for his advances.

'Hello ladies. I'm Brad. Can I get you two a drink?'

'Hi. I'm Rachel and this is Michelle.' Rachel was trying hard to negotiate her swollen tongue around her mouth in order to speak without slurring. She wasn't at all successful.

'Thanks Brad. Our friends have already gone to get us drinks. Have a great night.' Michelle steered Rachel away from Brad with the expertise of someone who had encountered this exact situation a million times.

'I think that guy was hitting on us.' Rachel gazed at Michelle with wide eyes.

Michelle and Rachel both burst into fits of laughter.

'I don't know why we all lost touch. We have so much fun

together.' Rachel exclaimed as she wiggled herself onto a bar stool.

'Well, you had kids. And I moved away. And Alex moved away. We're all just in different places.'

'Kid not kids. I only have Georgie.' A look passed over Rachel's face that Michelle had never seen before, though Michelle didn't really take much notice.

'Oh, yes, only one now. I know you though. You would want the perfect little family.' A bitter tone crept into Michelle's words. She had been defeated by her failed IVF attempts. Her body had betrayed her. And just that morning she had decided to give up. She had spent the last two weeks jabbing herself with needles, feeling like a bloated, bruised and sore woman on the brink. She was due for egg retrieval on Monday, but staring down the barrel of another gut-wrenching doctor's appointment, she just couldn't face it. She just couldn't hear the doctor say that low number again. Three last time. Three eggs. That's it. Apparently she just didn't have the internal fortitude for this. Maybe she just needed a little break and she'd try again in six months. Michelle imagined that it all had been so easy for Rachel. Rachel surely hadn't been through IVF. Her perfect little eggs would obviously be doing their thing perfectly. 'You'll have another one and it'll be a boy. Because that would be perfect and you wouldn't settle for anything less.'

Fat tears began to slide down Rachel's face. Within seconds she was sobbing.

'Oh god! I'm sorry!' Michelle's bitterness instantly dissipated. She wasn't certain what she was apologising for, but she could easily guess. Michelle knew the pain of having trouble falling pregnant, though she had never expected that Rachel had experienced it. She knew she should have been more careful about what she said, but she bitterly thought to herself that Rachel was lucky to have a child. Two was just plain greedy.

'I can't have another one. I can't have a boy.' Rachel's speech was punctuated with sobs. Rachel was usually a very private person and had never told any friends this before. She tried unsuccessfully to rein in her sobs that were fuelled by alcohol and unexpressed sorrow.

'Oh, Rachel, I'm so sorry.' Michelle hugged Rachel, as if a tight hug would push the hurt back inside Rachel and the cork could be put back in the bottle, leaving Rachel's feelings ready to be dealt with another time by another person. But Michelle's hug did not have the desired effect. Rachel sank into her arms. The sobbing became more erratic, with gasps of breath taken at unpredictable intervals.

Michelle sat stiff and awkward. She continued to hug Rachel in silence, patting her back until the sobs settled to a rhythm and became softer.

Rachel, only just regaining her composure, decided that she couldn't leave this untold. So she launched, before the crying could claim her voice again.

'There were...' Rachel's voice cracked a little but she continued, 'complications when Georgie was born.' Rachel paused. Her face showed an internal struggle and she suddenly, completely and miraculously regained her composure. Her usual, perfectly composed expression regained claim to her face. 'I had to have a hysterectomy.' Her words felt heavy in her vodka glazed mouth. A weighty silence followed. There was no response to that statement. Hysterectomy. The long, thin, purple scar down Rachel's abdomen ached with the word. There was, of course, a much longer story behind that word. But the word alone told enough of a story, Rachel didn't need to elaborate. Her feelings of loss were written across her face. Loss of the ability to have the family she wanted, loss of the future that she was so sure had been in store for her, loss of her own sense of worth as a woman.

Michelle was struck by Rachel's vulnerability. It had never occurred to her that Rachel's life was anything but perfect, in a Stepford wife kind of way; anything other than exactly what Rachel had wanted and planned for.

After what felt like an eternity, Michelle responded with one word. 'Fuck.' There were no words that could offer Rachel any consolation and Michelle instantly knew there was no point in platitudes – the kind that had been offered to Rachel in hospital: *Well, at least you've got one…. You could always adopt.*

'Let's get some more drinks.' Rachel's voice was filled with frank determination. This would not ruin her.

****

Rachel and Mike had fallen pregnant easily. They had expected it to take a little while – they had so many friends who'd tried unsuccessfully for years; they had friends who'd gone through gruelling rounds of IVF; they had friends who had had multiple miscarriages. Rachel's heart broke whenever she heard these stories. And when they had decided that they wanted a baby, they had prepared themselves for a wait, for tracking ovulation and seizing windows of fertility. The doctor had told them to realistically allow for a year of trying to conceive before they sought additional assistance. Twelve whole months of constant sex sounded like a dream to Mike, but Rachel knew from friends how trying that could be. Sex to a schedule sounded like anything but fun. Not that they ever found out first hand, because within a few very short months Rachel was pregnant. She was overjoyed but had to be careful in the retelling of the story – the pain of trying unsuccessfully to conceive seemed a raw kind of pain that never abated. Even though she'd never personally experienced it, Rachel knew that, and she tried to be sensitive to the feelings of others. She never wanted to rub her good fortune in the faces of anyone who wasn't as blessed as she was.

Rachel had a dream pregnancy. The worst of it was a little morning sickness in the beginning, but that didn't last long. As with everything in her life, Rachel's positive attitude made even the negatives, like morning sickness, seem like happy miracles that should be celebrated. She was in complete awe of her body – it was creating another human being; it was working so hard at making a miracle, so of course she needed to cut it some slack – if her body needed her to vomit, so be it; if it needed her to avoid eggs (which made her stomach lurch every time she even thought about them), so be it; if her body needed her to eat chocolate everyday and put on far too much weight for her liking, so be it; and if her body gave her stretch marks, so be it. It was all in the name of forming something greater than herself. And it made her love her body even more. It was creating life. And that was incredible and awe inspiring.

As soon as they learned that they were having a little girl, Rachel had picked out a colour scheme and Mike painted the nursery. By the time she was seven months pregnant, the entire nursery was complete. The walls were off-white, with a pale apricot horizontal boarder at chest height around the room. Rachel had taught herself to crochet and had spent many painstaking hours making an apricot and gold blanket which was draped over the rocking chair. All of the baby clothes hung on tiny coat hangers in the wardrobe. The sheets were in the cot, even though Rachel knew they would need to be washed again to remove any dust before the baby came. The room was exactly the way Rachel wanted it. It was perfect. She would awkwardly lower herself to the floor and sit cross legged in the nursery, hands resting on her round belly, just absorbing how perfect the room was – how perfect her life was – and imagine the moment that she would meet this precious person that was now growing in her belly. She would imagine singing lullabies, playing peek-a-boo, reading her favourite children's books from when she was young. Yes, her life was about to become complete. She and Mike were undoubtedly the luckiest people around.

Just like any other first time mother, Rachel had been a little nervous about the impending birth. But she told herself over and over again that some short term pain would be nothing once she had her baby girl in her arms. She read all of the books and was as prepared as anyone could be. She had done yoga throughout her whole pregnancy, and had learnt about breathing and meditation as a form of pain relief. But she told herself that it didn't matter how much it hurt, it would all be worth it. And she was fortunate enough to be right.

For a full week Rachel had strong contractions at sporadic intervals each night. Mike would sit eagerly by, timing the contractions with an app on his phone. The first night it happened, they had excitedly called the hospital. An uninterested mid-wife had told them that this was probably not the real thing yet. She didn't sound like she was in enough pain. She should call back when the contractions were so painful that she couldn't talk. In the meantime, she was told to take some painkillers, stay home, get some sleep. Sleep. Hah!

Finally one night the contractions became steady. They came in waves and hit her hard. After six hours of steady contractions, the doctor informed Rachel that she still wasn't in active labour – she hadn't dilated enough. At that point Rachel's will broke a little and she asked for an epidural. She had planned on having a natural birth; an epidural wasn't a part of her birth plan. Pain relief wasn't part of her birth plan. Meditation was supposed to have been enough. But it just wasn't. She felt like a failure and she hadn't even become a mother yet.

'That's a good decision, hun. There's no medal for going drug free,' the mid-wife had told her.

The rest of the birth was a blur to Rachel. Mike was by her side the entire time – rubbing her back, holding her hand, wiping her face with a cool towel. He was her rock. He was the one who told her she could do it, when she didn't think she had it in her. He talked to her about the nursery to take her mind off the pain. He was amazing.

Eventually someone – she wasn't even sure who – placed

her baby girl on her chest. The baby's dark hair was matted with white gunk, her skin was red and caked in the white stuff and her pouting lips quickly found Rachel's breast. In an instant the pain, the loss of dignity – the whole world – just melted away. This tiny person was the only thing that mattered. The only thing that Rachel could believe existed at that moment.

After some time – it could have been hours or just minutes that Rachel had been staring at those tiny feet – she was moved from the birthing suite to the maternity ward. She and Mike were in a state of bliss. They took turns holding the precious bundle. They marvelled at what they had created and how tiny those fingers and toes were.

She was so thankful for how lucky they had been. No problems conceiving and an amazingly easy pregnancy. And the birth was certainly not that bad – it had already begun to fade into a blur that culminating in this little miracle. They were truly blessed – the luckiest people on earth to have each other and this beautiful little girl. She should have suspected that bad luck would catch up with them at some point. But that wasn't Rachel's style. She was always a positive person.

Rachel was lying in bed, holding her little miracle when a strange feeling passed over her. A wave of light-headedness hit her, her stomach seemed to flip flop. She didn't feel right. Not right at all. She asked Mike to take the baby because she was feeling dizzy or woozy or something that she couldn't quite put her finger on. Rachel didn't want to drop her delicate bundle. She supposed she was just tired. She hadn't slept yet. She did feel exhausted. Then she felt something wet beneath her. Her cheeks burned with embarrassment. She didn't think she could have lost any more dignity than she already had in the past twenty-four hours. Rachel quietly told Mike that she thought she had wet the bed and asked if he could call for a nurse.

By the time the nurse arrived Rachel was so dizzy she couldn't focus. The room seem to swim around her. She tried to look at the nurse but couldn't quite keep her eyelids open and her eyes fixed on the moving target.

'You should still have your catheter in,' the nurse barked at her as she pulled back the sheets to reveal a bloody mess. Rachel was vaguely aware of an alarm sounding, as though from a distance, a flurry of activity, people shouting, and then she blacked out.

Mike had to give permission for them to perform the hysterectomy because Rachel wasn't conscious to do it herself. Even though without the hysterectomy she would have surely lost her life, Mike still felt deeply responsible for Rachel's sense of loss and the depression that followed. He had no other choice but the guilt still weighed him down. This wasn't his fault but he couldn't help but feel that Rachel believed it was. Mike tried to grasp at the feelings that overcame Rachel. If he could just pinpoint the exact emotion, then maybe he could help. But the onslaught of a tsunami of emotions made that impossible; there was no distinction between each of these feelings; sometimes they melted into each other – pain and anguish becoming one; and sometimes they crashed into each other fighting to be the dominant one that pounded Rachel the hardest at that moment – guilt and joy combating each other.

The overwhelming happiness experienced by new parents

was forever overshadowed by a feeling of loss. Rachel, being an incredibly positive person, had never before experienced anything that could make a dent in her happy little world. And this experience hadn't made a dent in her happiness – it had obliterated it. At a point in time when she should have been overjoyed, Rachel was plagued with a despair that pulled her to lows that she previously hadn't known existed.

Rachel had always liked to present a polished veneer of her life to the world. The months following Georgie's birth had felt to Rachel as though they were – more than ever before – in need of a portrayal of a perfect life. Rachel should have been happy. Everyone else she knew seemed to be overwhelmed with joy on the birth of their babies. Everyone else she knew lied. Everyone else she knew hadn't had a hysterectomy. People kept asking Rachel 'aren't you just completely in love?' And Rachel's honest answer would have been *no*. No, she didn't feel in love. No, she didn't feel happy. No, she didn't feel any of that. All she felt was pain. Loss. Unhappiness. She felt numb when she looked at her baby. But she pretended.

Mike could see her unravelling. He could see the toll that pretending to be happy was taking on her. He could see her reluctance to leave the house or even shower. He tried to help her. But he didn't understand. He would never understand the loss. And he couldn't begin to comprehend how she didn't feel inundated by love for their beautiful baby girl. How could his wife look at the precious little person that they had created and still feel unhappy? How could she let anything mar the fact that they had created life? And not just any life – the life of the most beautiful, perfect little being to ever exist. Mike tried hard to be understanding, but he couldn't understand.

He tried to support Rachel, but sometimes he felt angry. He knew that she was hurting, but what kind of person could wallow in grief when the most joyous thing had happened to them. He never told her in the years that followed, but there were times when he hated her for ruining – or at the very least disfiguring – the happiest time of his life. He was a patient man. And a loving husband. But he could never understand.

And then one day Rachel's sheer determination returned. She finally accepted the counselling that had been offered to her by the hospital and she cast the blackness from her mind and focussed on her beautiful baby girl. Deep down Rachel still hurt badly, but she never showed that to anyone. Not even to Mike, her wonderful, supportive, loving husband. Revealing this to Michelle had been the most truthful she had ever been with herself or with another person.

****

As the alcohol flowed, dares were completed and more and more lanyards were accumulated by various women. Michelle and Anna had both amassed the majority of the lanyards. The two were neck-and-neck for the win and had gotten so competitive that the rest of the group were standing back and watching. The group was divided between women who were laughing along with – and maybe a little bit at – Michelle and Anna; and the women who were shaking their heads, amazed and embarrassed that grown women would be acting like trashy teenagers.

Michelle's current task was to serenade a bald man with a

moustache. She had been stuck on this one for a little while – she just couldn't find a man who fit the bill.

Anna had also come up against a hard one – she had to find a man to do a tequila slammer off the beautiful bride – he had to lick the salt from Fi's neck, drink the shot and suck the lemon from her mouth. As soon as Anna had unveiled her seemingly easy dare – what guy wouldn't agree to do that? – Fiona had mysteriously disappeared. No one seemed to be able to find her anywhere.

Kate finally found Fi hiding in a stall in the bathroom. Kate recognised Fi's sequinned stilettos in the stall next to her own.

'Fi! Is that you in there? Everyone's been looking for you!'

'Please tell me Anna's not in here.'

'No, you're safe for now. I totally don't blame you for hiding.'

'Why do bachelorette parties always seem to deteriorate into this Girls Gone Wild shit? I don't want some guy I don't know trying to slip in the tongue while sucking a lemon out of my mouth.'

'Hey, there's a trashy fun bar just down the street. It just plays awesome nineties pop. Why don't we go have a dance and give Anna some time to cool her jets?'

'Yes! Let's do it.'

Kate peered out of the bathroom door to check that the coast was clear, and the two women ran from the bar in fits of giggles.

Fi pulled off her *bride-to-be* sash and tiara. 'Uh, I'm so glad to be free of that trashy thing,' she said as she shoved them into a bin on the street.

Kate pulled off her own tiara and the lanyards she'd accumulated and followed suit.

As the two women walked into the bar, Britney was pumping through the speakers.

'Classic! It's so bad, it's good.' Fi was grinning.

'Let's dance.'

They navigated their way through the crowd to the dance floor. They danced and took turns going to the bar to buy drinks. Each time Kate would go, she returned with their usual drinks *and* shots. It wasn't long before they were both feeling the effects of far too much alcohol.

A stranger started to grind up against Fi. She clumsily pushed him away without looking and stumbled. Kate caught her arm and helped her regain her balance.

'Do you want to sit down?' Kate shouted over the music.

'I need a bathroom.' Fi's face was pale, her makeup smudged around the edges, her eyes not quite focusing.

Kate, also quite drunk, but much better at handling her alcohol, steered Fiona toward he bathroom. Fi fell into a stall and locked the door behind her.

'Fi, I'm right here. Just shout out if you need me.' Kate called over the sound of Fiona vomiting.

A few minutes later, the retching sounds stopped.

Fiona emitted a long cry.

'Fi, unlock the door.' After some time of no response, Kate repeated herself, more sternly. 'Fiona. Unlock the door. Now.'

Thirty seconds later the latch turned. Fiona was still kneeling on the ground; the stall reeked of alcohol fuelled vomit. Fiona was crying silently and staring into the toilet bowl.

'Oh, hun. Are you done? Let's get you cleaned up and get you home.'

'My phone.' Fiona hiccupped silently and gestured toward the toilet.

Kate steeled herself, swallowed, then peered over her friend's head. There in the bowl, amongst the vomit was Fiona's phone.

'Okay. You're going to need to get a new phone. It's not the end of the world.'

Fiona leaned forward with her hand outstretched; Kate intercepted her by grabbing her elbow.

'I think it's okay to leave it there. It's not going to work, so no point in putting your hand into that –' Kate pulled a disgusted face – 'for nothing.'

Kate grabbed her friend's arms and hoisted her into a standing position, flushed the toilet and steered her friend to the sinks. Fiona caught a glimpse of her own reflection in the mirror but was too drunk to react. Kate wet a paper hand towel and began wiping at her friend's face and hair. She pulled a hair band from her purse and secured Fiona's hair, which was matted with vomit, into a pony tail. Kate then handed a small pack of mints to Fiona, who stared blankly at the pack, not really able to focus on what was in her hand. Kate took the packet out of Fiona's hand, removed two mints and pushed them into Fiona's mouth.

'There. Let's get you in a cab.'

Kate helped Fiona through the mass of bodies dancing to Michael Jackson. As they walked out the door of the bar, the fresh air hit their faces, aiding in sobering up Kate – though the view of the toilet bowl had already partially done the job.

Unfortunately, the fresh air had no discernible impact on Fiona. They walked – and in Fiona's case, stumbled – down the street to a taxi rank. The queue was mercifully short. During their four minute wait to get to the front of the queue Fiona began to feel the impact that the alcohol was having on her stomach again. She leant over a nearby rubbish bin and started dry heaving.

When their cab arrived, Kate grabbed Fi's hand, whispered, 'Act sober,' and opened the taxi door.

'No way, sweet 'art. She's not getting in my cab.'

From the look on the driver's face, Kate knew there was no point in arguing. They moved away from the line and she sat Fiona on an electrical box. Kate contemplated calling her mother, but didn't think anything would be worth the tirade of the When Are You Going to Grow Up lecture that she'd heard on repeat for the last year.

Kate pulled out her phone to call Michelle. She'd be able to work out some sort of plan. It went straight to voicemail. 'Michelle, I'm with Fi and she's really drunk. I'm trying to get her home but no cab driver's going to take her in the state she's in. Call me.'

Kate then tried Rachel and Alex in the hope that they'd both still be out, but she knew it wasn't likely given the hour and how drunk they'd both been.

'Fi, what's Isaac's number?'

Fiona looked at her blankly.

'What is your fiancé's phone number?'

The blank look didn't change.

'Fiona, please try to remember. I want to call him and ask him to come pick you up.'

Fiona's expression finally moved. She lurched forward and began throwing up again, this time she was on her hands and knees on the footpath, with her head over the gutter.

'Fuck.' She contemplated calling Fi's parents. She assumed they still had the same landline number from over a decade ago. It was very late, but she wasn't sure what else she could do with Fi. Then a thought occurred to her: John. John would have Isaac's phone number. This might be an awkward conversation, but she would just need to suck it up. Though Kate wasn't entirely sure why she cared, because, apart from Fi's wedding, she was unlikely to have to see John again.

Kate had suffered over the previous months thinking about John. But that pain was nothing compared to the pain of losing Peter, which she had relived earlier in the night. A part of her heart had turned to stone when Peter had left her. And that part would never be revived. She would never really love someone with her whole heart again. She would never really, fully trust anyone again. She would never love anyone in the same way. And she never wanted to feel that kind of hurt ever again. It was definitely a good thing that she and John had broken up. Definitely. She just had to keep reminding herself.

Kate took a deep breath and dialled.

'Hello.'

'Hi. It's Kate.'

'What's up? I assume you're drunk dialling.' John teased, easing the tension almost immediately, although he wanted desperately to ask what had happened – why had Kate ditched him without giving any reason. But he tried to play it cool.

'You wish. I'm with Fi.'

'That's right – it's Fi Fi's bachelorette party. Having fun?'

'Well, *Fi Fi* is currently throwing up in a gutter. So no, not really having fun at all. No cab driver is going to let her in their cab. I wanted to grab Isaac's number from you. Hopefully he can come and pick her up.'

'You've corrupted my big sister.'

'Hmmm.' Kate wasn't in the mood for this kind of banter. And although she knew he was joking, she didn't like him blaming her for the situation. Fiona was a big girl – she should know when enough is enough. And she should be better at handling her liquor.

'Okay. Okay. I'll text you his number.'

'Thanks.'

'By the way, I'm in town at the moment. So if you can't get a hold of him, I can come pick you up.' There was an awkward pause. 'I can come and pick Fiona up.'

'Thanks. But I'm sure Isaac will be happy to come and get her.'

As soon as she hung up the phone, a text came through with Isaac's contact details. She immediately dialled.

'Hello?'

'Hi, Isaac?'

'Ah, yeah, who is this?' Isaac sounded hesitant.

'This is Kate. Fiona's friend. I'm with her right now. She's really drunk. Are you able to come and pick her up?'

'Oh.' Isaac paused. 'I've kinda been drinking.' Another long pause. 'I don't want to sound like a dick, but... can't she just catch a taxi?'

'She's too sick.'

'Oh...'

'Don't worry about it. I'll get John to come pick her up.' Kate didn't try to mask the irritation in her voice.

Kate hesitated before dialling John again. She was reluctant to call him; she still didn't want to see him again. If she was completely honest, she knew that she would have trouble controlling herself. It was so hard to remember that he was a cheat. She kept remembering how her stomach would do flips when she saw him – when what she really should have been thinking about was how he would have stomped her heart into the ground when he inevitably cheated on her. But she knew she didn't have a lot of options right now. And John would come quickly, which would mean that this night would be over sooner, which, in that moment, was what she really wanted more than anything else.

As she waited for John to arrive, she cursed Fiona for drinking too much and being such a lightweight, and Michelle for not answering her phone, and Rachel and Alex, who she could only presume left early, and Isaac for not being available to pick up his inebriated fiancé.

In spite of herself, Kate checked her reflection in her compact mirror, reapplied lipstick, ran her hands through her hair in an attempt to make it look a little less dishevelled, and popped a couple of mints in her mouth. She was not looking forward to seeing John, but, nevertheless, she wanted to look her best. He should know what he was missing out on.

****

Michelle was feeling great – and terrible – she had won. Anna hadn't been able to find Fi, so after forty minutes of searching, they had called it: Michelle was the winner. It was stupid, but Michelle had needed the win. After completely giving up on the idea of IVF, she had felt despondent. She had given up a great relationship for something that wasn't going to happen. Lose, lose. Who knows, maybe she would start IVF again sometime, but she couldn't cope with the lows right now. There was just too much bitter disappointment each time it didn't stick. And she felt crazy from all the fertility hormones that were still pumping through her veins. And she was bloated and getting fat and feeling the worst – physically and mentally and emotionally – that she'd ever felt in her life. It was too much to go through alone. She had been defeated.

Finding out that Rachel's life was less than perfect had also left Michelle with a hollow feeling. She almost felt glad that she wasn't the only one pretending to be leading a flawless life, but her heart ached for Rachel. The pain of not being able to conceive hit a little too close to home for Michelle. She wouldn't wish that feeling on anyone.

The win was a futile victory. It meant nothing. It didn't change anything. It made her feel good for a few seconds and that was it. Why did she need to throw herself into this stupid competition?

She was drunk – messy – and talking to a handsome, bearded hipster who had helped her fulfil one of the dares.

'I won, you know.'

'I think everyone in this bar knows that,' Beard laughed.

'I won the marathon too.'

'Yeah? You won a marathon? You're an athlete?' Beard was

dubious. If that was true, he would be incredibly impressed. She did look *really* fit.

'Yep, the Paris marathon.' Michelle was gesticulating wildly, making her drink slop everywhere.

Beard grabbed her arm and took her drink from her hand, narrowly avoiding the drink from spilling all over him. He took a moment to admire his own reflexes. If that's what he could do drunk, imagine how ninja-like his reflexes would be sober. He should definitely think about training for that ninja reality TV show.

'Showed that dickhead. So arrogant. Thinks he's more important than me because he's a man. I started the fucking business. I'm one of the founding partners. Dickhead.'

Beard frowned. He didn't have a clue what any of that had to do with winning a marathon. He wasn't sure if he'd missed something while he was thinking about his ninja skills or if she just wasn't making sense. She was absurdly drunk, but so was he.

Michelle leaned across him to grab her drink that he'd set down on the bar next to him. Beard mistakenly thought that she was trying to kiss him. He leaned in, lips parted and kissed her. He wrapped an arm around her waist and pulled her close to him.

Michelle had no intention of kissing Beard, but kissed him back anyway. His kiss had a slightly sobering effect. She felt all the emotions that she'd been trying to block come rushing back. Breaking up with Andrew was the wrong decision. Why had she done it? She was so lonely. And all she wanted was a baby. Sixteen year olds fall pregnant with unwanted babies all the time. And here she was – wanting one so badly and having the means to really provide for a child – give it whatever it wanted – but she couldn't fall pregnant. And she missed her lost baby – the speck. Or maybe she missed the feeling of knowing that there was life growing inside her. She hated the hollow feeling in her chest that she got when she thought about the speck. The whole process of trying to get pregnant had been tough – worse than tough. She'd felt more crushing disappointment than she'd ever known before. And that was intermingled with so much hope. The highs she felt when she thought it had really happened – when, after a doctor's visit, she had been absolutely certain that it had taken that time. And then seeing one line. That one fucking lonely little line. The little line that would leave her sobbing on the bathroom floor for hours. Then she would pick herself up and continue as though her soul hadn't been destroyed by a fucking stick with one fucking line on it. Life was unfair. And she was alone. So she kissed Beard. A drunk, sloppy, passionate, desperate, lonely kiss. He moved his hand to her butt. This was not unusual for him. He liked to think of himself as a bit of a Casanova; in reality his looks, confidence, sole interest in one night stands and ability to disregard how drunk a woman was were the reason he did so well with the ladies; his charm had very little to do with it.

'Do you wanna come back to my hotel?'

'You're staying in a hotel?' Beard's interest heightened. She was obviously from out of town, meaning she wouldn't get too clingy. Even better. He generally liked woman, so hated when they got too invested and he had to be *that* guy – ditching them and hurting them.

'Yep, it's walking distance from here too.'

Beard leaned in and kissed her again. 'Sounds great,' he said softly. 'Let's go.'

The five minute walk sobered them both up just a little. Michelle wasn't a stranger to one night stands. But since she'd broken up with Andrew she hadn't even contemplated a man, so this would be the first time in quite a while. It felt good. Sure, she was doing it because she was lonely, but it was nice to feel attractive, to do something for herself that had nothing to do with work or, ironically, trying to get pregnant.

Michelle had to check the cardboard slip that contained her key for her room number. They stood in the lift with a middle aged couple, in awkward silence. The couple got off several floors below theirs, and Michelle and Beard continued to stand in silence, on opposite sides of the lift until the door closed behind the couple; Michelle laughed, breaking the silence and they began kissing again.

They arrived at the door to Michelle's room. It took three drunken attempts with the key card to open the door. As soon as the door was shut behind them, Beard started undressing himself. Once his pants were undone, he pulled Michelle's skirt up. It was clumsy and quick but Michelle felt warmed by the experience – a little less lonely. She rested her head on his shoulder and fell into a heavy sleep. The touch of another person while she slept was comforting, she forgot what she was missing in her life and just felt at peace in her drunken state.

When she woke in the morning, Beard was gone. Michelle still had the lanyards from last night around her neck. She looked at her phone. 12:30.

'Shit!' She was supposed to have checked out of the hotel

hours ago. Oh well, there was no point in rushing now. She was already late, what would another half an hour do?

Pulling the lanyards from around her neck and throwing them into the bathroom bin, she took off the clothes that Beard hadn't removed the night before. She hadn't even asked his name. *I'm such a whore.* She laughed out loud at that thought. Michelle didn't believe that at all. It was her life – her body – she was entitled to do whatever she wanted with it.

She took a shower, washed her hair, brushed her teeth and dressed. She wasn't feeling great. Way too much alcohol. She didn't feel like visiting her mother today, but she had promised. Not that she would have much time with her before needing to leave for the airport.

CHAPTER THIRTY-FIVE

A few days after the bachelorette party, Alex and John were both back in Sydney. The wedding was less than two months away and John needed help picking a tie to wear.

'Alex, I need a woman's perspective. Please.'

'I'm just not really very good at this stuff. Can't you ask Michelle?'

'She's so busy at work. She's in Melbourne for the next week at least – something to do with buying out a firm. She doesn't have time.'

'Please. Just come along and make sure the sales assistant doesn't convince me that I need to buy a purple velour suit or something.'

'Okay. Okay.'

They arranged to meet at a department store in the city after work. John wore the suit he planned to wear to the wedding and Alex dutifully stood by as he held up tie after tie against his chest.

'Did Fi tell you the colour scheme of the wedding?'

'I've tried to be very supportive of her in her wedding preparation.' John made a face as he pulled the end of the tie through to finish off a perfect half Windsor. 'But I can't say that I've actually taken on board any of the specific details in the preparation.'

'So, what you're saying is, you haven't listened to a word she's said.'

'Exactly.'

'If you're going to be wearing a boutonniere, I think we need to know. It would probably be white – or some variation of white – but you should probably check just in case it's not. You don't want the tie to clash.'

'Boutonniere?'

'A flower in your button hole.'

John groaned and rolled his eyes. 'Why do they have to make wedding stuff so complicated?'

'I think you should call Fi.'

'Okay.' John pulled his phone from his pocket and dialled.

John launched into an in depth conversation with Fiona and wandered off. Alex stood up from the armchair that she was sitting on, and began looking over the ties that were on display. While comparing two particularly nice blue ties, Alex felt someone approach her side and grab her arm. She looked up to see Daniel's face inches from her own and contorted with rage. Daniel pulled her silently by the arm through the store, never once loosening his grip on her. As they burst through the doors and the fresh air hit her in the face, Alex was shocked from her mute state.

'Daniel, please let go of me.' Alex pulled her arm, trying to free herself from his grip. 'You're hurting me.'

Daniel remained silent, and clutched her arm mercilessly. He raised his arm to hail a passing taxi, which stopped immediately. Daniel dragged Alex toward the cab, opened the door and shoved her inside. Daniel finally spoke, giving their home address to the driver, while Alex quietly sobbed.

John returned to the tie section after a lengthy conversation with Fiona, resulting in him being told to wear a dark blue – but not navy – tie. He couldn't see Alex anywhere, but assumed she hadn't gone far, as her handbag was still sitting on the armchair. He continued rifling through the ties, now with a narrower colour palate to focus on. After a while, he began to worry about where Alex had gone. He picked up her handbag and began to systematically work his way through the store, looking for her.

He found a shop assistant who had been helping them with ties earlier. 'Excuse me, I seem to have lost my friend. She was wearing jeans and a black top and –'

'I remember her.' The woman interrupted him. She wouldn't quickly forget a scene like the one she had witnessed earlier. Although much quieter than most of the arguments that she witnessed in the store, the look on the man's face was imprinted in her mind. 'She left with a man.'

'Oh. That seems really weird for her to leave without her bag. Are you sure it was my friend?'

'I'm absolutely certain.' The woman seemed to hesitate for a moment, pondering whether she should provide any further information. 'It seemed like they were having an argument.'

It must have been Daniel. John began to worry. No matter how much Alex reassured him that Daniel was a good guy, he wasn't convinced at all. But what could he do? He couldn't even call her – he had her phone. Maybe he should go to her apartment, but that might stir Daniel up even further. And, if he was honest with himself, he felt like that might cross some boundaries in his friendship with Alex. John decided that if he hadn't heard from Alex by the next day, he would talk to Michelle.

CHAPTER THIRTY-SIX

Kate was going to do it. She was going to call John. Yes, it had been months since they broke up, but seeing him after Fi's bachelorette party had brought all her feelings for him flooding back. Maybe Michelle had been right all along – maybe she just needed to talk to him. She hated anyone who cheated. But maybe she should give him a chance to explain. She was in love with him. And that feeling just wasn't going away.

It took Kate a few days to summon the courage to make the call. What if he'd moved on? What if there was an amazing explanation – what if he wasn't a cheating scumbag like Peter – and he'd completely moved on? He had seemed so casual when she'd called him. Not at all like someone pining. And he'd given up trying to contact her only a week after their hotel rendezvous.

The night of the bachelorette party had been crazy, but she wanted him to know that it wasn't alcohol – or at least not entirely alcohol – behind their last encounter. And she needed to know the truth about him.

John had come to pick up Fi and Kate. Just like when they had spoken on the phone, he had joked with her, immediately easing any tension. Kate had felt so relaxed; she had felt just as she had when they had been dating, making it even harder to bear being near him. She really missed him so much.

Fi had thankfully stopped vomiting for the car ride. She had quickly fallen asleep in the front seat, with the window down blasting fresh air onto her face. John and Kate had chatted easily – like old friends – for most of the drive, except for a few awkward pauses, when Kate thought too hard about how much she wanted him and missed him and then had chastised herself, reminding herself of how much Peter had hurt her.

When they arrived at Fiona's place, they woke Fi, but she had been far too drunk to do much more than keep her eyes open. John and Kate had carried her into her apartment, taking her shoes off, putting her in bed, with a glass of water and aspirin on the bedside table.

John had given Kate a lift back to her mother's house. But for that leg of the journey the conversation didn't flow as freely. The silence enveloped them; pregnant with all the unspoken questions and declarations of love. He'd pulled the car into the driveway and turned off the engine. Sitting in the car in her mother's drive way, Kate suddenly felt like she didn't know where to put her hands; when she smiled she felt as though she was showing too much teeth or it looked fake or something; and she questioned how she normally breathed – surely she was doing it too loudly or quickly and now that she'd thought about it so much, she didn't know how to breathe naturally, or talk naturally or doing anything that seemed natural at all.

Sitting there, awkwardly, Kate wondered if it was just her. Was this all in her head? Did he feel the same way? She missed him so very much. And maybe that whole once-a-cheater-always-a-cheater thing wasn't true. And he really just didn't seem like a cheater. Not at all. Not the John she knew. And she – stupidly – in the drunken heat of the moment, had decided on one clear way to find out if he still had feelings for her. She had leant across and kissed him. Except, as it turned out, it wasn't a clear way to find out how he felt. He had looked surprised and was momentarily speechless. Kate had opened the car door and run inside, before he could say anything. She had been overcome by panic. What if he had a new girlfriend? What if he was just like Peter? What if he broke her heart again? What if he said he wasn't interested? What if he felt sorry for her – the loser who chased a guy who was completely uninterested? She couldn't stick around to hear him say it, so she ran. It seemed sensible at the time. But now she didn't know what to do. She thought he might have called her. But he hadn't, which seemed like a very bad sign. Despite that, she needed to talk to him. It was up to her.

And so, nervously, she picked up her phone to call him. As she did, her phone started ringing. Jake. God! What did he want?

'Hi.' The irritation in Kate's voice was clear.

'Hey, how are you?'

For fuck's sake, doesn't he even have the decency to sound even a little unnerved talking to her after that fucking flight? Unashamedly confident until the bitter end. What a fucking arrogant knob.

'What do you want?'

'Polite.' Jake's voice was dripping with smug superiority.

'I don't have to be polite to you, you fucking cock sucker.'

'Way to stay classy.'

'Oh, I'm un-classy one? I don't exactly think that having some slut bag flight attendant suck your dick while your girlfriend is asleep is a very fucking classy thing to do.'

On their flight back to Australia, Kate had been fast asleep in her chair when she woke up to notice that Jake was no longer next to her. She figured he must be in the loo and decided to take the opportunity to stretch her legs without having to squeeze past him to get to the aisle. As she walked toward the bathroom, she had seen a flight attendant exiting the toilet and wiping her mouth, followed shortly after by a very satisfied looking Jake.

Kate had seen red. She had completely lost it and started shouting at both Jake and the flight attendant. Thankfully the flight attendant had wanted to keep the situation under wraps for obvious reasons, so Kate hadn't gotten into any serious trouble. There were some threats of landing the plane at the closest airport and having Kate arrested, but Kate had calmed down eventually after making an enormous scene. It wasn't her finest moment. She had wanted to breakup with Jake anyway, so it shouldn't have bothered her quite as much as it did. But it had been as though the pain was a shadow of how she had felt when she had found out that Peter – her husband, the love of her life – had been cheating on her. It was like the phantom pains that an amputee has. It hurt even though there was nothing there to hurt.

And now this smug son of a bitch was calling her. Why?

'You do know that un-classy isn't even a word.'

'Why the fuck are you calling me?'

'You still have keys to my apartment.'

'Get some more cut. Change your locks. I don't care.'

'I thought you might like to see me. Maybe have some angry makeup sex or something.'

Kate exhaled loudly, making an angry sounding groan, and hung up the phone. She wasn't going to waste any more time on that moron. And she wasn't going to dignify that with a response. Her mother had been right. Why had she ever thought getting back together with that tosser would be a good idea?

CHAPTER THIRTY-SEVEN

A ringing sound abruptly woke John from a deep sleep. He picked up his phone from the bedside table and tried to answer it. After what seemed like a full minute, he realised that it wasn't his phone ringing – it was Alex's phone. He stumbled around his room in a sleepy haze, trying to locate Alex's handbag. It rang out and immediately began ringing again. John then dug through the bag and finally found the phone.

'Hello.' His voice was raspy.

'What's your address?'

'What?' John tried to process what was happening. 'Alex?'

'What's your address? I'm coming over.'

'Alex, it's the –'

Alex interrupted before he could point out what she clearly knew – it was late. 'Be outside your building with my handbag in ten minutes.' Alex hung up before John could ask for an explanation.

John threw on some clothes and went downstairs. He felt a little annoyed. If she wanted her handbag back so badly, she should have called at a reasonable hour. It was after two in the morning. He had to get up for work in a few hours. He waited outside his building for a full fourteen minutes. It was very inconsiderate for her to make him wait. As he began to wake up and his brain began to function properly, he started to consider the possibility that maybe Alex was in trouble. As the minutes passed, he became more and more worried; feeling a little embarrassed at his previous annoyance.

Finally a taxi pulled up in front of him. Alex slowly got out of the cab. Her gait was rigid, as though every movement was sending shooting pain throughout her body. Without a word, she reached for her handbag, rummaged around inside and pulled out her wallet. She leaned back into the taxi through the already open door and handed the driver a fifty.

'Keep it,' she muttered and slammed the door.

As she turned to face him, John got a good look at her for the first time. She wore a pair of oversized sunglasses – a dark shadow peeped out the bottom of the glasses under her left eye. Her bottom lip was split and her right arm was lined with dark bruises. All this was obvious even in muted light emitted by the street lights.

'Can I stay with you?' Alex's voice was void of emotion.

John wrapped his arms around her and held her for what seemed like an eternity. He took her bag from her and put his left arm gingerly around her and walked them both inside.

CHAPTER THIRTY-EIGHT

Kate nervously pressed the call button. She wasn't going to be distracted again. Especially not by that dickhead Jake.

'Kate!'

It was a woman's voice. Why was a woman answering John's phone? Did he have a girlfriend? Who was it? 'Ahh...'

'Kate, it's Alex.'

'Alex?' Why was Alex answering John's phone? This didn't make sense at all. 'Um... hi... can I talk to John?'

'He's in the shower.' Alex panicked. Why had she answered his phone? Why had she said that? She didn't want to explain to anyone what had happened with Daniel. She just wasn't ready. And it would be clear to Kate that something was up – why would she be at John's house while he was in the shower? 'I'll get him to call you back.' Alex hung up without waiting for a response from Kate.

****

'Have you spoken to Kate lately?' Alex swallowed hard. She hadn't passed on Kate's message yet. Did they know the hand she had played in breaking them up? She felt so incredibly guilty. Every single day. But if they weren't already talking, and she passed on that message, and they found out... It would all end. Neither of them would ever want to speak to her again. She couldn't lose them. Not now. She'd never needed anyone as much as she needed John right now.

'Yes. Sort of. Not really, though... you know she kissed me?'

'What? When?' Alex felt jealously like a bolt of lightning running through her.

'After Fi Fi's bachelorette thing.'

'Why didn't you tell me?' She was trying to sound excited, but her voice came across a little too deadpan.

'I guess I've had other things on my mind.' He shot Alex a grim smile. 'I figured she was just drunk, and it didn't mean anything to her. After last time – ending things without an explanation – I just don't think I mean anything to her at all... So, she hasn't said anything?'

Alex clenched her teeth and lied. She couldn't lose John now. 'No. I haven't spoken to her. I don't want to have to explain what happened. Not to anyone. Ever.'

She had planned on passing on Kate's message. She really had. Maybe even confessing to her earlier lies – in a way that didn't make her seem too bad – she'd got the wrong end of the stick, said the wrong thing. Something like that. But she felt like John was hers. Right now she needed him too much. She just couldn't share him with Kate now. She knew it was wrong – selfish – but she'd done it anyway. And once the lie was out of her mouth, there was no going back.

'You're eventually going to have to tell people that you've left him, you know.'

'I know. I'm just not ready yet. But I don't want to ever have to explain why.' Alex winced. Her whole body was still aching.

John exhaled audibly. He was wracked with guilt. He should have done something the moment he had met Daniel. He knew that Daniel was no good, and yet he'd done nothing. And Alex was hurt because of his own inaction – his cowardice. He felt so guilty. But there was nothing he could do now to change that. All he could do was help Alex as best he could. Support her, and try to help her get back on her feet.

'You can't stay holed up in my apartment forever.' John's voice was gentle. He was worried. She hadn't left his apartment and didn't seem like she planned to anytime soon. He didn't want her to become a hermit who couldn't cope with the outside world. She needed to get out. She needed to stop crying.

Alex knew he was right. Initially she had planned on staying with John until the bruises faded, and then she would go back to Brisbane and stay with her parents. But the longer she stayed locked up in his apartment, the more she felt afraid of the outside world. Afraid of the judgement, the questions, the explanations, of being alone, of having to act as though everything was normal – as though she was normal, and, most of all, she was afraid of Daniel. Daniel had called persistently, leaving pitiful apologies on her voicemail, until John had taken her phone and blocked Daniel's number.

CHAPTER THIRTY-NINE

Michelle walked into the office, takeaway coffee in hand. She'd only had one glass of wine the night before, but was feeling disgustingly hung over. Despite having given up on IVF and her alcohol-free ways, she had really only had a drink at the bachelorette party (well, more than *a* drink). And then last night. Her system must really be out of practice at dealing with alcohol for her to be feeling hung over from one glass. She did kind of enjoy being a teetotaller – she felt so much more productive on the weekends, and she had been feeling so fit, maybe it was worth staying on the wagon.

When Michelle took a sip of her coffee, she gagged. There was something wrong with this coffee. It seemed strange for her usual coffee shop to make bad coffee. They must have given her one with almond milk.

A partner meeting was first on her calendar for the day. She sat in the meeting, her stomach churning; her mouth full of excess saliva. She swallowed hard, trying to neutralise the uneasy feeling in her stomach. Michelle fought the feeling as best she could and tried to concentrate. The rest of the day continued much as it had started. She skipped lunch – the thought of eating made her stomach lurch. By the end of the day, she had concluded she had a stomach bug. Or maybe it was the sushi she ate the day before. She certainly couldn't have an all day hangover from one measly glass of wine.

Michelle left work early and went to bed as soon as she got home. This upset stomach had left her feeling exhausted.

When her alarm went off the next morning, Michelle rolled out of bed and staggered to the bathroom. She felt good again. It was such a relief – she had far too much that she needed to get done that day, to waste it feeling lousy. She bent over to lift the toilet lid, her other hand already reaching for her knickers, but before she could turn around, a tidal wave of vomit erupted from her mouth. It was so entirely unexpected, she felt too shocked to register that she was instantly feeling sick again.

As Michelle splashed her face with water and brushed her teeth, a thought occurred to her. She frowned at her reflection in the mirror. Surely not. It seemed crazy to even consider it – if she couldn't get pregnant via IVF, she surely couldn't *accidentally* get pregnant from a one night stand.

Michelle opened the top drawer in her bathroom vanity and pulled out a pregnancy test. She shrugged. She didn't really believe that she could be pregnant, but there was no harm in checking. Peeing on the stick, Michelle had myriad thoughts running through her head. If this was it, what would she do? She didn't even know Beard's name. How would she track him down? Would she track him down? If she really was pregnant, how far along would that make her? She would certainly be further along than last time. Even still, there was such a high risk of miscarriage, she shouldn't get too excited.

Miscarriage. The fear of losing something she didn't even know for sure existed caused her chest to tighten. She'd had a glass of wine. She'd had sushi. Guilt, fear and sickness muddled around in her stomach.

Partly filled with excitement, partly filled with dread, Michelle placed the stick next to the bathroom sink and waited.

CHAPTER FORTY

Alex had avoided her three friends for nearly two full months. Apart from her brief phone conversation with Kate, she hadn't had any contact with them. And now today was the day. The wedding. They could no longer be avoided. She would have to see them. And she would need to tell them the full story.

If Alex had her way, she would have spent the last two months in John's apartment, never leaving. But John had other ideas. He said she had to tell her parents. And she had to leave the apartment every day. According to him, staying indoors for weeks on end was unhealthy.

Alex had been broken. Years of emotional assaults had left her a different woman. She would never be the same again. And if it weren't for her black eye, she probably would be back with Daniel already. The fear that had rocked her wasn't going anywhere; the mental image of her husband punching her in the face was confronting. He had, in the past, given her bruises – grabbing her arm and throwing her against a wall wasn't a new development – although she refused to admit that to John. The cracked ribs could be explained – he was angry and jealous because he loved her; he had pushed her; he didn't really mean to hurt her. He had never hit her. Never.

Until now. Punching her in the face – giving her a black eye – was deliberate, brazen; there was no way to explain away his actions, saying that he really loved her. She knew he had meant to hurt her. They weren't going to repair their relationship. She wouldn't – couldn't – forget. She didn't want to forget. She didn't ever want to be that person again. And for that to happen, she had to remember. She had to be strong. And she had to be honest. Telling people that it was a mutual split – or that they had fallen out of love – or that they were just in different places – left a bad taste in her mouth. Her family – and her friends – had to know. They had to know the truth. She couldn't live with the lies anymore.

So, almost a month and a half after leaving Daniel, Alex got on a plane to Brisbane. Her bruises had faded and finally disappeared. The two cracked ribs were still giving her a little bit of trouble, but not so much that it was easily recognisable in her movements. She went to see her mother. She sat on the couch and told her mother in a matter-of-fact tone that Daniel had hit her. That he had emotionally abused her for years. That he had broken her ribs on several occasions. And her mother looked at her as though she was a child telling tall tales to get out of doing her homework. Alex cried. Her mother hugged her; not quite believing her, thinking it was the exaggerations of a broken hearted girl, but trying to support her anyway.

Telling her sister had been cathartic. Telling her father had been scary. But both had been compassionate and, surprisingly, her father hadn't threatened to kill Daniel, though Alex felt sure that his safety wouldn't be guaranteed if her father happened to run in to him.

Despite now feeling quite practiced at explaining the circumstances surrounding her leaving Daniel, Alex was not looking forward to having the conversation with her three friends. She contemplated speaking to them before the wedding. But dismissed that idea – unlike with her family, she didn't want to have to explain every little detail of her relationship, her weakness, her broken self. She wanted to quickly drop the bomb and move on to sighing in awe at the beautiful vows, dress, flowers, anything.

Alex arrived at the church exactly on time and quickly found Rachel, Kate and Michelle.

They chatted briefly on the lawn outside the church until ushers announced to the crowd that they must now take their seats inside. As they made their way inside, Alex steeled herself. Hopefully she could make her announcement just before Fi arrived – she was set on limiting the discussion.

The four women sat near the centre of the church, Michelle taking the aisle seat. Alex spotted John and waved. They hadn't spoken since she left for Brisbane two weeks earlier, save for a few text messages here and there.

'Oh Kate, have you and John talked yet?' Michelle whispered loudly, as she leaned across Alex.

'No.' Kate sounded hesitant. She still wasn't sure what was going on with John and Alex, so was a little unsure what she should say. She was quite sure that they weren't together, but almost felt as though Alex knew John better than she did. It felt like she might say something wrong in front of her.

'So, ahh, I've got some news.' Alex paused. *Just do it. Like ripping off a bandaid. Get it done quickly.* 'Daniel and I broke up.'

Kate's mind raced. Maybe she was wrong. Maybe Alex and

John were together. Maybe Alex had left Daniel for John. It sounded insane, but it kind of made sense.

'Oh my goodness. Are you alright, sweetie?' Rachel reached across Kate and grabbed Alex's hand.

Alex grimaced and gave a short, sharp nod. *Don't cry. Don't cry. Don't cry.*

Michelle raised an eyebrow. She knew that Daniel was no good. She felt it in her bones. That dick had done something to Alex. This wasn't going to be a nice amicable breakup (if there was such a thing). 'What happened?'

'I don't really want to talk about it. But the short version is: he's a dick, he treated me like crap, and one day he snapped and hit me.'

All three women's jaws dropped, almost at the exact same moment. Kate gasped. Rachel squeezed Alex's hand harder.

'I wanted you three to know, but as I said, I don't really want to talk about it.'

'I think you should talk about it.' Kate turned to see Isaac walking to the front of the church. 'Obviously not here, but I think you should.'

'I've got the name of a really good counsellor who might be able to help you.' Rachel's voice was gentle and full of concern.

Kate cocked her head to one side. Something didn't sound right about that. Why would Rachel know of a good counsellor? Maybe Rachel's prim and perfect life wasn't quite so perfect after all. It was probably marriage problems. That husband of hers probably couldn't live up to the expectations of someone who was just so perfect in every way.

A cello began to play Canon in D Major. The crowd,

including the four friends, were silenced. The doors at the back of the church were flung open and the bridesmaids began to make their way down the aisle, one by one. They each wore floor-length midnight blue gowns, with lace covering the décolletage and shoulders and coming into a small cap sleeve. The back of the gowns plunged to just above the waist. *Lucky they've all got perky boobs and don't need to wear bras,* Michelle thought to herself. Each of the bridesmaids carried a small bouquet of loosely gathered, small ivory flowers, with the stems exposed.

The noise from the crowd toward the back of the church hummed above the cellist. Kate, Michelle and Alex craned their necks trying to get a peek of the bride. Rachel, however, a wedding lover, locked her eyes on Isaac. She wanted to witness the look on his face when he saw his beautiful bride for the first time. And it was priceless. Before he set eyes on Fiona, his face was a mask, trying to hide the nerves and undulated anticipation; the mask slowly dropped from his face as he caught sight of Fiona; his blue eyes sparkled with unshed tears; a grin lighting up his face; in that moment, he may have been the happiest he had ever been in his life.

Fiona glided down the aisle on her father's arm. The champagne dress was magnificent; the bodice was embellished with pearls and metallic rose-gold beading; the sweet-heart neckline of the dress gave an ever-so slight emphasis to Fiona's curves; however the embellishments on the bodice continued above the fabric of the dress, covering her décolletage and shoulders, in a similar way to the lace on the bridesmaids' dresses, however these embellishments were not attached to lace. It wasn't clear how they were held to

Fiona's dewy skin, Kate imagined a dressmaker painstakingly spending hour after hour gluing them onto Fi. The embellishments were heavier around Fiona's waist, and across her neckline. From the waist, the dress extended into a mermaid style, the silk fabric clinging to her hips and flaring out slightly from just below the knees to fall loosely to the ground and form a small train behind her.

The bride's bouquet was the same as that of the bridesmaids'. It was simple and understated, which fit perfectly with the romantic, feminine and intricate dress. Fiona's hair was styled into a classically sleek up-do; her makeup was soft, in feminine pinks; she wore no jewellery, save for her engagement ring on her right hand. She was breathtaking.

A fat tear ran down Alex's face. She cried out of happiness for Fiona; out of sadness for herself; fear for her future; and relief at her newly found freedom from the terror that she had lived amongst for too long.

The Minister asked the crowd to be seated and began the service. Michelle's prayers had been answered – the service was short, unlike some church weddings she had attended in the past. The vows were not personalised, rather they were the standard words used in church weddings; a touch that Rachel mentally marked them down for; everyone prefers to hear funny, heart warming sentiments, but Rachel knew that some churches do frown on that. Making up for lack of personalised vows, was the look on Fiona and Isaac's faces as they pushed the rings on to each other's fingers. Anna, the maid of honour, gently pressed a folded handkerchief into Fiona's hand, and Fi dabbed at her tears trying not to smudge her makeup and swallowed hard in an attempt to bid back any further tears. The sight of Fiona struggling not to cry was too much for Michelle; her eyes began to well with tears. Michelle never cried at weddings, but for some reason she was in a particularly teary mood today.

Alex watched the ceremony and thought back to her own wedding. She hadn't had any bridesmaids. Actually, she hadn't invited any of her friends. She wasn't quite sure how it had happened. They had decided on a small wedding and when she had written up the guest list, Daniel had picked it apart over the course of several months. He hadn't wanted to invite Kate, Michelle, Rachel and Fiona because he'd never met them before. It seemed reasonable. And her closest friend in Sydney, Chloe, had been cut from the list because Daniel had said she was bad news – a little too loud and opinionated. Not that Daniel ever explicitly said she shouldn't be invited. He had said that she could *obviously* invite Chloe if she really wanted to – he wasn't going to dictate who she was friends with. At the time, Alex had supposed he was right – Chloe was really annoying sometimes. And it wasn't long before they completely lost touch. There were a group of workmates that Alex had wanted to invite, but Daniel had said that work friends weren't real friends. And it was going to be a small wedding, so it made sense to scrap them from the list. In the end, Alex had only invited her parents and her sister. Looking back, Alex had never realised before exactly how controlling Daniel had always been; how he had cut her off from the outside world. And in those early days, she had been so in love, that she hadn't minded not having any friends; it was just her and Daniel against the world. She didn't need anyone or anything else.

****

Kate had arrived early at the wedding (which was very unusual for her) in the hope that she'd have the opportunity to run into John before the ceremony. She really wanted to talk to him. He hadn't called her back, but... maybe, just maybe, there was a reason. Maybe he still thought about her. The further they got from that moment when she decided to give up on him for good – because he was a cheater – the more she began to question it all. She had definitely been too hasty. She should have talked to him about it. Found out the truth. She just couldn't stop thinking about him. She loved him so much. But was it too late now?

John had appeared briefly before the ceremony and then disappeared – he seemed to be handling some crisis with the flowers. Kate didn't see him again until they were seated in the church. She sat through the service willing it to be finished. She was so distracted thinking about John and thinking about Alex's news, that she honestly didn't even notice that it was finished until everyone around her stood and cheered. She mustn't have even heard the *I now pronounce you man and wife* part. Kate, a little zombie like, followed her friends and the crowd toward the back of the church, where the setting sun had lit up the stained glass windows, showering them all in dancing colourful lights, and onto the church lawn, where champagne glasses were being distributed to guests as they took in the gorgeous view of the river, the cityscape and the sky, all of which was bathed in the beautiful hues of oranges and purples from the setting sun.

Kate felt an enormous amount of guilt about Alex. She had instinctively known something wasn't right and yet, somehow, she'd let Daniel's smile – those dimples – fool her. How could she be so stupid? She felt like a failure as a friend. But more than that, she felt angry. Angry at herself – and Michelle and Rachel – for seeing a problem and dismissing it as nothing, for not doing anything; angry at Daniel for doing this to Alex. Kate wanted to hurl abuse at him, to call him names, but there were no words that could capture her anger or his abhorrent nature. Kate wondered if John knew. Probably. She suspected that they had some sort of relationship. That was why Alex had answered his phone. Had Alex passed on her message? Had it been some sort of failure in communication or had John made a conscious decision to not call her back? Even if he didn't get her message, she really thought he would have called her after their drunken kiss. Was Alex a threat or was John just being a supportive friend? She had – with a bitchy thought and a slight twinge of shame – previously concluded that Alex simply wasn't pretty enough to be a threat. And now she was feeling so incredibly guilty for thinking that way about her friend. How could she be so superficial? How could she be so blind? So self involved?

To think that Kate had actually envied Alex. She'd been jealous of the overseas holidays, the apartment, the Mercedes. Knowing what she now knew, Kate couldn't fathom how wrong she was. What she had known about Alex's life had been a facade hiding the horrendous truth. Everything that Kate had been jealous of was inconsequential when she knew the truth about Alex's life. Suddenly Kate felt very happy with her lot. Sure, she lived with her mother (again), and she had no money and she'd never travelled (apart from her two short overseas trips, which were almost regrettable because they were with men who were just a waste of her time). But she wasn't stuck in a horrible marriage. She had never had a man hit her. And she had confidence and happiness. It had been truly crazy to be jealous of Alex. Even the part of Alex's life that was on display for the world to see wasn't better than Kate's life. It was just different.

And now Kate was wrestling with her guilt and her outrage. And, if she was honest, her curiosity. She wanted to know all the gory details, despite knowing the pain that Alex was going through. But Kate's heart was breaking for Alex; she would try to get the information from John – assuming he knew – she just couldn't bear to ask Alex. And it gave her a good excuse to speak to him. Hopefully they could break the ice and have a real conversation about them. And find out for sure the real story about him cheating. Or at the very least she could gain some sort of glint of an understanding about how he felt about her. She was even willing – maybe – to go out on a limb and be forward with him; tell him that she wanted to be with him. But she probably wouldn't have the courage. She wasn't sure she could face rejection. Not from him.

'You look beautiful.' John smiled. He reached toward her to embrace her, but thought better of it; instead his hand just coyly – and a little awkwardly – brushed her arm.

And she did look beautiful. Her skin was glowing; her

hair was cascading over her shoulders in her signature loose waves. Kate had kept on the weight that she had put on while she and John were dating; and she had stopped partying and wasn't smoking at all. She wore a two piece emerald green and white ensemble. The bodice of the cropped green top had thick green straps crisscrossing across the bust and sitting off-the-shoulder, with cut out details at the back. The top looked almost as though she had been wrapped in a bandage made out of a gorgeous green fabric. The matching high-waisted pencil skirt was figure hugging and featured a green and white geometric print. The colour was gorgeous against her tanned skin. She looked radiant.

After they had broken up, Kate had nearly thrown out all the clothes that Jake had bought her. But when it came to the Louboutins, she couldn't quite bring herself to do it. Then she decided that there was really no need to throw any of it out. What's done was done; depriving herself of the clothes and – more importantly – shoes that had come from her bad life decisions wasn't going to change anything. Maybe they would be a memento of the failed relationship; serve as a reminder to never to be so stupid again. At least she could wear designer clothes while she worked in her menial job and lived with her mother.

'Thank you. You're not too shabby, yourself.' Kate paused. Not quite sure how to ask what she wanted to know about Alex. At the forefront of her mind wasn't just Alex though. She was also on the precipice of just blurting out her feelings for John. And of asking him point blank about cheating (although she bizarrely almost felt past caring about that – she just wanted to be with him so badly). Her three friends had seen John approach and had made themselves scarce. 'You know about Alex, don't you?' The words fell out of her mouth without much thought. Not the subtle tact that she was looking for.

John nodded silently, a shadow creeping across his face; his eyes thunderous.

'Do you know all of the details?' Her cheeks felt hot. She sounded like a gossip: someone who was going to delight in her friend's misery, purely for her own entertainment. 'I don't want Alex to have to go through the pain of reliving it all. But I want to know exactly what we're dealing with.'

John gave a brief account of what he had witnessed and what Alex had told him. 'This is probably not the place to go into a lot of detail.' His face was full of concern. 'You're right – she needs our support. And I think to give her the kind of support she needs, you need to understand just how bad it was. Not that I'm an expert. I wasn't there, but those bruises…' John shook his head as he trailed off.

Kate squeezed his hand. 'You've been a really good friend to her.'

'Kate, I –' John wanted to tell her that he loved her. But that seemed like jumping off a cliff – she had cut and run pretty quickly with no explanation the last time he had said that. Maybe it was worth it. What's the worst that could happen? Maybe he shouldn't lead with that though. He had no idea how she felt. Or why she had broken up with him. Or what was going on after that kiss. Or where their relationship was in the broader scheme of declarations of undying love.

Kate interrupted, words blurting out of her mouth awkwardly, 'I got a job. In fashion, I mean. It's nothing special

– just a starting point, really, but... I took your advice. You were right.'

They stood in silence for a moment.

'I've missed you.'

Kate felt the seed of hope that had sat wedged in her chest since she'd last seen John, bloom. And just as she felt that desire and anticipation and happiness grow within her, she saw the kid from the engagement party – what was his name? And he saw her and started walking towards them. *Crap. Crap. Crap.*

'Kate, how are you?' The kid gave her a smile and a wink.

Fuck. Can't he see that I'm trying to get back together with the amazing guy who is actually an appropriate age for me? And I definitely don't want to talk to some kid who I fucked once, like a year ago and whose name I don't even know. Don't fuck this up for me. John does not need to know that I slept with you. Just fuck off and let the grownups talk!

'Hey mate, it's Hayden, right?' John was pissed off at the interruption, but hid it very well. His voice was warm and friendly.

Hayden. That's his name.

'Hayden! How are you?' Michelle swooped in. She had seen the kid making a beeline for them and had literally run – clumsily in her stilettos on grass – from one side of the church lawn to the other. 'It's been so long! Let's go get some champagne.' She grabbed Hayden's arm and started steering him away from John and Kate.

Hayden was so confused. He had no idea who this woman was. Maybe a distant relative? 'Do you guys want one?' Hayden called over his shoulder to Kate and John.

John frowned. Michelle was being weird. It was an inopportune time to have to make small talk with that guy, but that seemed like a major overreaction. He was thankful nonetheless.

'I've missed you too.'

Tom, John's best friend, appeared at his side. 'John, you're needed for photos.'

John looked at Kate apologetically. 'Sorry. We'll talk later.'

Kate smiled and nodded. She drained her champagne glass as John and Tom walked off together. She just couldn't catch a break.

Once they were out of earshot, Tom put an arm around John's shoulder. 'Mate, you should be careful with that girl. I met her boyfriend the other day. Total dick. Kinda seems like she's only with him for his money.' Tom pulled a face. Kate was hot and seemed nice but no one likes *that* kind of girl. John could do better. Okay, his reference to *the other day* was a bit of an exaggeration. It had been a while ago. But John needed to steer clear of that bitch.

John frowned. Boyfriend? This was the first he had heard of a boyfriend. He doubted that Kate would be using a guy for his money. But that wasn't really the point. Somehow he'd completely blown it with Kate. And he thought – hoped – that kiss had meant something. She was just drunk. That's it. He felt dejected. And there he was about to profess his love for her. He felt like an idiot.

****

Kate joined Alex, Rachel and Michelle. 'Thanks Michelle. I owe you one,' she said grimly.

'What happened?' Rachel's voice was full of concern.

'We got interrupted before we had a chance to talk about us.' Kate pouted. She was sure the conversation had been going in the right direction. All she needed was more time with him. Damn Hayden! And Tom. He better not have said anything about Jake. Surely he wouldn't. Just because she was with someone *months* ago when she ran into him at the ball, didn't mean anything.

'You two will have a chance to talk properly later.' Michelle's eyes scanned the lawn. 'Now where is a waiter when you need one? I think we could all do with some champagne.'

Rachel frowned. 'I actually think that we should all go easy on the alcohol tonight. Kate, don't you want to have a clear head when you have this conversation with John?'

'Ummm... I would actually probably rather have a few drinks under my belt.' Kate looked sceptical. 'Bit of Dutch courage to take the edge off a bit.'

Rachel raised an eyebrow but didn't say anything else.

'Well, I need a drink.' Alex's voice was matter-of-fact; not at all like her world was crumbling around her.

'Rach, come help me get some drinks for everyone.' Michelle raised her eyebrows and looked at Rachel pointedly.

Rachel was confused; Michelle was clearly trying to communicate something with those eyebrows, but Rachel had no idea what. 'Okay.'

The two women walked across the lawn toward a drinks table that was set up near the entrance to the church.

'I'm pregnant.' Michelle didn't believe in beating around the bush. She hadn't planned on telling anyone until she'd passed the first trimester, but she couldn't contain it any longer. And Rachel seemed like the appropriate person to share her news with.

'What? Oh, my gosh! Congratulations!' Rachel's voice was high pitched. She flung her arms around Michelle.

Michelle quickly pulled Rachel off her. 'Shhh... I'm not telling anyone else yet. Keep your cool.' Michelle grinned slyly.

Given their discussion at the bachelorette party, Michelle had been a little hesitant to tell Rachel about the pregnancy. Rachel's own inability to conceive had caused her so much pain, Michelle hoped that this news didn't upset her. But Michelle knew that Rachel would be happy for her, even if it did hurt a little. And Rachel would be a good confidant. Michelle needed for *someone* to know. Rachel had been through a pregnancy herself and, despite her own fertility problems, was actually the most stable of her friends at the moment.

'I had no idea that you and Andrew had gotten back together.' Rachel started fanning her face. 'Sorry. I'm trying really hard not to cry. I'm just so happy for you.'

There was a part of Rachel – a part she tried to keep hidden even from herself – that wanted to shout *that should be my baby!* She felt the emptiness where her burgeoning womb should have been; an aching along that scar; she was incomplete and always would be. Rachel stamped down hard on that that thought – on that little part of herself; she kicked dirt over it; covered it as best she could, but didn't bury it – that just wasn't possible right now; at least it was hidden though. As always in these situations, Rachel was torn by feelings that were polar opposites. And she was mortified that she was – even if it wasn't the whole of her – jealous. What a dark, dank, mouldy part of her soul that was.

'Arh... thanks. But Andrew and I didn't get back together.' Maybe it was a mistake telling Rachel. Here comes the *holier than thou* look.

'So... does that mean you did the whole –' Rachel paused, looked around to make sure no one could hear her and whispered – '*sperm donation* thing.'

'Yes and no.' *You need to get comfortable with this. And quick. You're going to be explaining this for the rest of your life.* 'I tried IVF with donor sperm. But it didn't work.'

'Theeeennnn....' Rachel paused. How to put this without sounding rude?

'Who's the father?' Michelle asked the question for Rachel.

Rachel cleared her throat uncomfortably. She hadn't wanted to be so blunt, but, yes, that's what she was trying to ask. She gave a quick nod; eyes wide, waiting for the answer.

'No one important.'

Rachel couldn't help herself. She tssked and shook her head. 'He's the father of your child. He's important, whether you want him to be or not. He's going to be part of your life. Forever.'

'Well, that's going to be hard, considering I don't know his name and have no way of contacting him.'

Rachel's mouth dropped. She stood in silence and stared, mouth hanging open.

'Hmmm... I'm going to be dropping this little gem for a while. Do you think it would be better if I just lie and say that it was a sperm donor? In a way that's what he was, even if the insemination method was relatively cheap and low tech. I guess I could always say *none of your business.*' Michelle frowned, thinking, then shrugged 'Whatever. I'll need to really work on it, either way.'

'So you accidentally fell pregnant from a one night stand?' Rachel couldn't hide the judgement from her voice.

'Yep, those IVF hormones work a treat. I have no idea what went wrong with the condom though.' She was pretty sure there had been a condom. Maybe.

Rachel tried to compose herself. *Move on. There's no point focussing on this right now.* 'How far along are you?'

'Nine weeks. I wasn't really planning on telling anyone until I get through the first trimester. I lost – arh –' Michelle's voice wavered so slightly it was almost undetectable, but Rachel, acutely aware of these sorts of things, noticed – 'had a miscarriage before, so if that happened again, I don't want everyone knowing. You know?'

'I had no idea. I'm sorry.' Rachel grabbed Michelle's hand and squeeze briefly before Michelle snatched her hand back, conscious that they might be making a scene.

In that moment, Rachel recognised the insanity of her jealousy. Michelle had had a miscarriage. She wanted a child so badly that she was willing to do it without a partner. The father of her baby was a stranger. And for some reason Rachel had felt jealous. Michelle's life was no better than hers. As much as Rachel yearned for another child, she was so happy with her little family. She had no need to feel jealous of her friend.

'I had a scan though. There were heartbeats.' A smile danced across Michelle's lips. Her eyes misted over just a little. 'It was amazing.'

Remembering the morning that she'd had her first ultrasound had Michelle on the brink of tears. Up to that point, she hadn't allowed herself to get excited. She tried so hard to keep her emotions in check. There was no day dreaming about tiny pink dresses or dimples. This would not be like the speck. She couldn't go through that again. She just couldn't.

Michelle had booked in for the dating scan – which was supposed to tell her how far along she was in the pregnancy – at the earliest time the doctor recommended. She had to see with her own two eyes that this was real before she could possibly celebrate. She had sat on the edge of the chair – literally – in the waiting room, leg jiggling nervously, willing it to be her turn next. What was taking them so long? She had an appointment for fuck's sake. The sonographer eventually called her name. Michelle had been so nervous, her hands shook. She didn't meet the man's eyes for fear that she'd burst into tears. Who the fuck was this crazy, emotional woman? This wasn't her. But she wanted a baby so badly. Please, please, please let there be a baby in there. Let the baby be ok. Let there be a heartbeat. And then most amazing thing had happened – the sonographer had squeezed her hand and pointed out the *two* distinct hearts flickering on the screen. Just thinking about it gave Michelle that tight feeling in her chest all over again. It felt stupid to even think – crazy, overemotional, like those women (Rachel) who were overly clucky and had always lived their lives just waiting for the moment they could get knocked up – so much so, that Michelle didn't like to admit it even to herself, but the truth of it was: seeing those heartbeats was the single greatest moment of Michelle's life to date.

'Heartbeats?'

Michelle pressed her lips together, then broke into a huge grin. 'I'm having twins.'

Michelle had been shocked and a little scared at the news she was having twins. Being a single parent with two children sounded more than a little daunting. But she felt confident she could handle it. She had always excelled at everything that she'd set her mind to. And this would be no different. She wanted a baby. And now she was getting two. Just like her to have an overachieving womb.

The nausea had subsided a little bit, but still came back in waves some days. And the smell of coffee made that sick feeling come rushing back a little too quickly. Michelle had had a few incidences of spontaneous vomiting; no warning signs at all, feeling great one second, and projectile vomiting the next. Thankfully it had never happened at work, and – the thing that she was absolutely most grateful for – Michelle had never actually vomited *on* anyone. The three times it had happened had been at home, in a taxi (which had been expensive and seriously embarrassing) and while walking down the street on her way to work (she had managed to not get any vomit on herself; once done, she had sidestepped the spray of puke on the sidewalk and had continued walking as though it hadn't happened; she was sure she'd gotten a few looks, but she didn't give a shit).

Interrupting Michelle and Rachel's conversation, John approached. 'Hey,' he smiled broadly at both women, and kissed them each on the cheek. 'I'm told that you're needed for a photo. School friends I believe this one is. Do you mind rounding up the other two and seeing the photographer's assistant over there?' He gestured towards the area where Fiona was standing, being photographed by three photographers and a few relatives like she was a Kardashian.

Michelle frowned. She knew John had been running around like crazy doing wedding errands, but it seemed strange he didn't want to tell Kate himself that she was needed by the photographer. Kate was only about twenty metres away.

'Sorry, I've got to go see someone about the champagne. The word is that they've run out.' John rolled his eyes and gave a good natured grin. 'I'm Fi Fi's errand boy today. Fingers crossed I'll be allowed some time off to actually enjoy myself sometime tonight.'

The four friends went and had their photograph taken with Fiona and then a group shot with all of the wedding guests. The gorgeous view of the river and Brisbane city lights behind them, making the perfect backdrop for the photos. Rachel, the wedding connoisseur of the group, had initially been surprised by the late start to the ceremony, but after seeing the stunningly lit view at night, completely understood. It was perfect.

After the group photo, the guests slowly made the short walk from the church to the restaurant perched on the Kangaroo Point cliffs, high above the river. The view was nothing less than spectacular. The restaurant had been styled for the cocktail style reception, with an overall theme that was understated vintage romance and a little eclectic. Crisp white linen tablecloths covered the dry bars; each table featured assorted posies of loosely gathered white flowers, with midnight blue ribbons and lace wrapped around the mismatched array of vases, perfectly complementing the bridesmaids' dresses; the bar was adorned with a round terrarium the size of a soccer ball, containing a small plant with delicate little white flowers. A four tiered cake took pride of place on a table overlooking the river. The cake was topped with a plethora of white flowers and covered in white chocolate ganache, rather than fondant, with ripples of imperfections, adding to the overall theme that encompassed simply beautiful imperfection. Waiters walked around the room with trays of mojitos and whiskey sours in mason jars.

Rachel let out a long sigh. 'This is incredible, isn't it?' She wasn't talking to anyone in particular.

'Mmmm....' Kate wasn't really listening; she scanned the room looking for John.

'I've gotta go to the loo.' Michelle piped up.

Rachel gave Michelle a knowing look and discreetly raised her eyebrows, which wasn't quite so discreet as to go unnoticed by Alex.

'Oh, Kate, there's John,' Alex said as she nudged Kate gently in the ribs. Alex had decided she would atone for her hideous and selfish behaviour by getting Kate and John back together. She was worried about what it would mean for her friendship with them both, but she couldn't stand the guilt.

Kate took a deep breath. 'I'm just going to do it. How do I look?'

'Gorgeous, as always,' Rachel smiled.

Kate made her way through the crowd toward John. John caught a glimpse of her making a beeline for him and disappeared into the crowd. Kate scanned the room, looking for where John had gone. Could she have really seen that right? Had he seen her walking toward him and left? Last time they spoke, he had said he missed her. It seemed like he was going to say more than just that, and now he was running away. She briefly felt confused and hurt. Then she imagined what could have happened over the course of the last hour or so. It must be Hayden. That stupid fucking kid had said something to John. And now John thought she was a hoe. Kate fumed. But, she reasoned, there was really nothing for John to be upset about. Sure, she had slept with the kid, but that was before anything had happened between her and John. And she's an adult; a woman who is perfectly within her rights to sleep with whomever she damn well pleases. But... he *was* probably feeling a bit sensitive given the end to their relationship, so maybe just that little nudge was enough. Plus John was very old fashioned. A real gentleman. So maybe Hayden would be a bigger deal for him. No. John is a reasonable guy. He might be a bit weirded out to begin with, but he would come around. Or would he?

'Fucking stupid kid,' Kate muttered to herself.

'Who are you talking about?' Alex had walked up behind Kate and handed her a mojito.

Kate blushed. She didn't know if she should have this conversation with Alex. There was obviously a closeness between Alex and John that Kate didn't really understand. Alex had gone to him when her world had fallen apart; Alex possibly knew John a lot better than what Kate did. *Wait. Alex knew John better than Kate.* 'Do you know why John never called me back?' Embarrassment was forgotten. Kate needed to know. Kate couldn't beat around the bush. She *had* to know.

It was now Alex's turn to blush. 'Argh... I – yeah – umm...' Alex couldn't meet Kate's eyes.

Kate spoke slowly, deliberately. 'You have to tell me. Spit it out.'

She felt so guilty for not passing on Kate's message. She had been so selfish wanting to keep John to herself. Kate was a really good friend and Alex had reciprocated by being an incredibly shitty friend. She wished she could take it back. She wished she had told John. She wished that she hadn't lied about the cheating thing in the first place. She really hadn't meant to. It had just happened. Alex looked everywhere but at Kate.

'Is it me? Did I completely blow it with him? I never even broke up with him properly. I never gave him the chance to explain about the cheating thing.'

Alex was amazed that Kate could ever blame herself or think that a guy wouldn't be interested in her. Kate was the most confident person she had ever met. Or at least she seemed to be. Maybe Kate wasn't all that she appeared to be. Alex remembered, what felt like a lifetime ago, John had said about Kate: *it's all smoke and mirrors.* Maybe Kate wasn't as confident as she came across. And maybe Kate's life wasn't as perfect as it seemed to be.

Alex gave a huge sigh. 'I never passed on your message. He doesn't know that you called.'

'What?'

'I umm...' There it was. She was a terrible friend; a terrible person. It was over. Kate now knew. And Alex had just lost a friend – probably two friends – at a time when she needed them most.

'Of course, of course, you've had so much on your mind.' She gave a small strangled yelp and hugged Alex excitedly. 'This means that he didn't not call me back – he was just waiting for me to call him, which totally makes sense, given that I just cut all contact when we broke up.' Kate rolled her eyes. 'I'm such a dick.'

Alex rolled her eyes in response and grinned. 'Just go talk to him.'

'That's what I was going to do, but I think he's hiding from me.'

'I don't think he's hiding from you,' Alex said sceptically. 'He's probably just really busy running errands for Fi. I'm sure he'll catch up with you once things have calmed down a bit.'

'I'm going to ask him about the whole cheating thing.' Kate couldn't contain her excitement. She was talking a million miles an hour. 'I should have listened to you all in the first place. I should have talked to him about it. And, as *everyone* pointed out to me, he didn't cheat on me. So –'

'Kate,' Alex interrupted. She was thankful that Kate seemed to remember the whole thing incorrectly, and seemed to think that she had been amongst the people who were urging Kate to contact John and just get back together with him. 'I think that maybe,' Alex paused. This had been so much easier when she had practiced it in front of the mirror, 'Maybe he never cheated at all. I think maybe I just got the wrong end of the stick?' Alex posed the last part as a question. She was so unsure of her lying abilities and how Kate would take this.

Kate gasped. 'Oh my God.'

'I'm so sorry.'

'So, I broke up with John for absolutely no reason? I'm such a fucking idiot! Assuming every guy is going to be like Peter – what a fuckhead.' Kate closed her eyes and put her head in her hands. Suddenly she looked up. 'I've got to find him.'

****

The four friends stood around a bar table, champagne glasses in hand. Alex had drunk several mojitos, in a bid to forget some of her own sorrow and show her friends that she was okay. It had, in fact, done the opposite. She seemed like she was turning to alcohol to numb the pain. And Michelle, Kate and Rachel were all worried.

Rachel too had been drinking beyond her usual limits. Michelle's news had rocked her. It had reminded her of her own inability to conceive. She had reasoned away the jealousy, but she still had that hollow incomplete feeling sitting just below her stomach. She was determined to drown that feeling with alcohol.

Apple juice was all that was in Michelle's glass. She had volunteered to go to the bar to get refills for everyone each time they were needed, and had discreetly asked the bar staff to fill hers with juice. No one had seemed to notice so far. Michelle had always been adamant that alcohol while pregnant, as long as it was in moderation, was fine. But now that she was here, pregnant, and scared shitless about losing another baby – babies, there was no way she would take any risks whatsoever. Each day she braced herself for another loss; and as each day passed, the tiny glimmer of hope – of excitement – grew within her. And that night, she felt as though this might really happen. She really might have a baby in her arms in thirty-one weeks.

Rachel registered Alex's excess drinking, and was drunk enough herself to comment. 'Alex, do you think maybe you want to talk about it?'

'Not really.' Alex's reply was curt.

'Something so horrendous has happened to you – been happening to you for goodness knows how long. We're your friends. We're here for you.' Rachel pushed. She genuinely thought that it was in Alex's best interest to talk about it. She meant to be loving, caring, a good friend. Her intentions were good. 'Don't you just want to get it off your chest?'

'No. I want to forget it ever happened.'

'Was it just the one time?'

Alex threw back the rest of her drink; she swallowed hard, trying not to cry. *You will keep it together.* Alex knew that there was no avoiding it. She would eventually have to explain the whole fucked up story to her friends. She had naively hoped that they would just leave it alone. Let her be. But that clearly wasn't going to happen. They were intent on picking away at the scab of her broken life, her ruined marriage. 'He's hurt me before. But he's only ever hit me once.' Alex's voice was like stone. No emotions were visible on her face. She was a blank slate. She needed to be to get through this conversation.

'Oh, Alex.' Rachel wrapped her arms around her friend.

'Why didn't you leave that piece of shit the first time he hurt you?' Michelle was sympathetic, but sincerely didn't understand her friend's plight. It didn't make any sense to her. Why do women stay with men who treat them badly – who hurt them?

'I didn't have a job. Or money. Or any friends. I didn't have any options. What was I going to do? What *am* I going to do?' Cracks were forming in Alex's stony veneer. 'I felt as though I deserved it. And he apologised. And he said he loved me.' A flint of emotion had crept into her voice. 'I'm weak.' Her voice was despondent.

Kate's heart broke for her friend. 'You *are not* weak,' Kate said slowly, deliberately. 'He's the weak one. He's the gutless shit who treated you like that – and hurt you – to feel better about himself. And you could never deserve to be treated like that.' Kate turned to Michelle, anger written all over her face. 'Michelle, why the fuck do you think she didn't leave? He made her feel as though she couldn't. He made her feel like shit – like she deserved it. Don't be so fucking insensitive. And keep your stupid fucking questions to yourself,' Kate barked at her friend. All her frustrations, guilt and anger about not recognising the problem and not doing anything to help her friend, were aimed squarely at Michelle.

Michelle ignored Kate and turned to Alex. 'I'm sorry. I didn't mean to upset you. Of course you're not weak.' Michelle's voice was rigid. She wasn't used to apologising. She did think that Alex was weak. She felt for her, but that didn't change the fact that Michelle believed wholeheartedly that Alex should have left – that Alex could have just left at any time. Either way, the worthless piece of shit that Alex was married to deserved to be castrated. And that was something that they all could agree on.

****

John stood by the bar, looking back at the dance floor. Kate was in the middle of it, skyscraper shoes discarded, dancing to *Baby Got Back*. Her tiny, round behind stuck out, shaking. She was a bad dancer. A terrible dancer, in fact. But she had didn't take herself seriously at all, and had enough confidence to get away with it. She was laughing heartily at her own impossibly bad dance moves.

God, she was beautiful. She was a beautiful dork. All the spray tan and designer clothes in the world couldn't hide her dorkyness from John. She was the same girl she had always been. The same girl he had a crush on when he was twelve.

He had thought that maybe she wanted him. That maybe that kiss had meant that she wanted to get back together. That drunken kiss. He really had thought that it might have meant something. But then she hadn't called him. He supposed that he could have called her. But now she had a boyfriend. Did that mean that she just saw him as a friend? Maybe she had been so drunk she didn't even remember the kiss. Maybe it meant nothing other than that she was drunk.

The words *All the Single Ladies* reverberated around the room, met with squeals of delight. John wondered to himself whether Beyonce had envisaged her song would be used for this purpose at every single wedding for the rest of eternity.

What seemed like hordes of women went rushing to the dance floor, to form a huddled mass in front of Fi Fi, all fighting for a prime position to catch the bouquet. And there was Kate in the middle of the pack. She stood out, being taller than every other woman in the group.

From his vantage point, John could see the women jostling, some good naturedly, others not so much, with their elbows out. He was surprised that he couldn't see Michelle amongst them – she was usually the first in line for a competition – the fiercest competitor, regardless of whether she gave a shit about the prize or not.

Fiona turned her back to the crowd of women and threw her bouquet over her right shoulder, back into the throng behind her. Fi had thrown the bouquet high. Very high. Kate, being the tallest by miles, and having no shoes on to aid in her jumping prowess, leapt up, throwing her long slender arm into the air to snatch the bouquet.

John smiled at Kate's victory. She was all limbs and awkward as hell, but that girl could jump. John watched, as, out of nowhere, his cousin, Stacey, came at Kate. Stacey was a short, dour woman in her late forties, who lamented, bitterly, about her divorce at every opportunity. Her divorce had happened more than a decade ago, but the sour resentment never seemed to have abated. And all the years of hostility, resentment and jealousy of anyone in a happy relationship were written all over her face. She looked mean spirited. Stacey barrelled toward Kate, hunched over, right shoulder squarely aimed at Kate's middle. They collided. Stacey's attack to Kate's centre of gravity was enough to knock them both to the ground, Kate's long legs seemingly everywhere. The bouquet was still clutched in Kate's hand, but Stacey was determined it wouldn't be for much longer. Kate, knowing full well what Stacey was after, was gripping the bouquet tighter – not because she wanted it – she honestly couldn't care less about the tradition, she didn't even want to get married – but because she was pissed off that this bulldog of a woman had attacked her, and Kate just didn't want that woman getting what she wanted. Stacey tried to wrench the flowers from Kate's hand, with no success, all the while, the two women still writhing around on the floor. Stacey then pressed her weight into Kate's chest, and prised Kate's fingers from the bouquet. Stacey had it, and, with all the grace of an overweight older woman with bad knees, stood and held the bouquet over her head in victory.

Kate hopped to her feet, brushing off her clothes, pulling down her hemline and smoothing her hair with her hands. She took a sidelong glance at the victor and burst out laughing. Although a little indignant, she honestly couldn't be mad – the woman clearly wanted that bouquet like nothing else. And the sight of the dishevelled Stacey, grinning and pounding a squashed bouquet against her chest in triumph, was just too much for Kate to bear. It was hysterical. Besides which, Stacey looked like the kind of woman who was in desperate need of a win, so Kate just let it go.

John felt his heart tug a little at the sight of Kate's grace in defeat. She really had class. Not everyone would laugh off an incident like that so easily. John decided he didn't care if she had a boyfriend. He didn't care if she rejected him. Again. He had to tell her how he felt. He would regret it if he didn't. He began to walk toward her and felt a tap on the shoulder.

'Grandma's ready to leave now. Can you please be a sweetie and help her get a cab?'

Despite the bad timing, John couldn't help but smile at his beautiful older sister. She was a beaming, euphoric ray of sunshine. They say that a wedding day is the happiest day of your life, and it clearly was for Fiona. She couldn't contain how ecstatic she was to have just married the love of her life. It was written all over her face.

'No worries, Fi Fi.' Kate would have to wait.

****

Michelle walked back to her friends after her hundredth trip to the bathroom. 'Why is John avoiding you, Kate?'

'I told you, Alex. He *is* avoiding me.' Kate pursed her lips and wrinkled her nose. 'I have no idea. You two are his best buds. Maybe you can shed some light on it.'

Michelle shrugged. 'I saw him earlier. He looked at you and practically ran in the opposite direction. He hasn't said anything to me. But we've hardly spoken lately.'

'Last I heard – and I'll admit it was about two weeks ago – he had suspected that you'd just kissed him because you were drunk. But...' Alex took a long sip of her drink and shrugged. She almost lied and said that she'd told John otherwise, but lying had already gotten her into enough trouble.

'Wait – you kissed him? When? Seriously, did I miss this while I was in the bathroom?'

'No.' Kate shook her head, exasperated. 'We kissed at Fi's bachelorette party. And what is with the four hundred and fifty-six bathroom breaks? Your spanx too tight or something?'

Rachel jumped in to detract attention from Michelle. 'Hang on – he was at the bachelorette party?'

'He came to pick Fi up. Because I was stuck with her *by myself* while she vomited in the gutter. Thanks for leaving early, by the way.' Kate rolled her eyes. 'When we were at the church he said he misses me. But something must've happened since then. I think that stupid kid must have let it slip that we slept together at the engagement party. But John will get over that. Right?'

'Umm… that's definitely not why he's avoiding you,' Alex said as though it was blindingly obvious.

'You said you didn't know why.'

'I don't. But he knew about Hayden ages ago.' Alex felt a little sheepish. John knew about Hayden because she had let it slip – sort of intentionally, when she was having a majorly jealous moment. *God, I'm a fucking shit friend. What kind of asshole tries to sabotage their friends' relationship like that?*

'Oh. Well why the fuck is he avoiding me then?'

'I think you just need to talk to him,' Rachel said gently.

'He's avoiding me. I can't.' Kate's voice was dripping with attitude.

'Fuck it. I'm going to find him and sort this shit out.' Michelle marched off.

It didn't take long before Michelle found John deep in conversation with his aunt.

'Hi Mrs Masters. How are you? It was a beautiful ceremony, wasn't it?'

'Oh yes, dear. And doesn't our Fi Fi look gorgeous?'

'She sure does. And that dress! Stunning.' Michelle smiled warmly. 'Do you mind if I steal John from you for a few minutes?'

Michelle ushered John toward a secluded table away from the dance floor.

'What's up?'

'What the fuck is the deal with you and Kate? The both of you need to sort your shit out.'

'Woah.' John put both hands up, palms facing Michelle. 'Calm down.'

'I don't know what the problem is, but you need to stop avoiding her and go talk to her.'

John looked at her quizzically. 'I don't understand – has she said something?' He exhaled loudly. 'I was going to, but I got distracted... And, well, what's the point? She's got a boyfriend.'

Michelle groaned and rolled her eyes. 'That's the reason you've been avoiding her? She doesn't have a boyfriend. Now go.' Michelle stared at John, waiting for him to walk off toward Kate.

'But Tom said –'

Michelle interrupted. 'Who gives a fuck what Tom said? She doesn't have a boyfriend.'

'So who was the guy that Tom was talking about?'

'I don't know. I don't care. And neither should you. She's been hung up on you since the engagement party. Put her out of her misery and go make up with her. And – quite frankly – insecure Kate is boring and annoying, so you would be putting the rest of us out of our misery too.'

PERFECT LIVES

****

Alex and Kate were talking intently about Fiona's amazing dress.

'I tried to get a good look when we had our photo with her. I wanted to see how that beading is –' Kate broke off mid-sentence. Alex's eyes had widened, she gasped as she inhaled and her hand jumped to her mouth; she was looking at something behind Kate. Kate turned and saw what had Alex's focus. Kate squared her shoulders and the corner of her mouth twitched. 'What the fuck?' Kate's words were said through clenched jaws.

'Alex,' Daniel reached a hand toward her, she flinched and stepped backwards.

Kate put herself between Daniel and Alex. 'What are you doing here, Daniel?'

Daniel sidestepped, so that he was facing Alex, without Kate in between. 'Alex – baby – I've missed you so much. I need to talk to you so badly. Your phone's not working. And the invitation for this –' Daniel gestured around him – 'was on the fridge. I just had to talk to you.' Daniel was stepping closer to Alex, and Alex continued stepping backwards away from him. 'I love you so much. I am so sorry. You have to believe me. I didn't mean it. I would never intentionally hurt you.' His voice was pleading – desperate. 'You believe me, don't you?'

Daniel was dressed like any other wedding guest. He wore a bespoke blue suit and a crisp white shirt, no tie. He didn't stand out amongst the crowd at all. Nothing at all seemed out of the ordinary to the other guests. No one was paying attention, despite Kate's desperate hopes that some burly man would step in and escort Daniel off the premises and out of Alex's life for good.

Kate put an arm in front of Alex, pulled Alex behind her, and kept a hand on Alex's arm behind her. 'Leave. Now.'

'I need to talk to my wife.'

'This isn't the time or the place.' Kate could feel Alex shaking. Kate was trying with all her might to keep level tempered. She didn't want to make things worse by losing her cool. Or to embarrass Alex by unnecessarily airing her dirty laundry in front of onlookers, though that was certainly a lesser concern. Daniel's warm breath smelt strongly of alcohol. Kate felt fear constricting her chest. Daniel was always a ticking time bomb, but right now he was drunk, desperate and a few wrong words from Kate away from being incredibly angry.

'Alex, you're the love of my life. One little mistake. I made one little mistake.'

Some of the other guests were beginning to stare now. Michelle and Rachel had noticed a minor commotion from across the room. Michelle's natural ferocity was fuelled by her hormones. She barged through the crowd. She, unlike Kate, didn't recognise the danger of the situation.

'One fucking mistake? You call beating the shit out of your wife a *mistake*?' Michelle had moved to stand next to Kate, the two women were shoulder-to-shoulder and blocking Daniel from Alex. 'Get it through your thick fucking head, Alex is NEVER going to forgive you. And she's never going to speak to you again. If you've got something to say, you can tell her lawyer.'

Something shifted in Daniel's expression. His face no longer belonged to the distressed husband who was begging forgiveness for a minor indiscretion; his face belonged to an angry man; the same angry man who hit his wife. He said in a low voice, 'Fuck off, you stupid, ugly cow. Alex belongs to me. Just get the fuck out of my way.' Daniel's arm flew at Michelle and knocked her to the ground with a thud. He hadn't meant to hit Michelle. He had planned on being discreet, but he realised it was too late for that now, and abandoned the idea. He grabbed Alex by the arm and pulled her close to him.

The sight of Michelle on the ground sent a scream, choking from Rachel's lips. The babies. Rachel clambered to the ground, to Michelle's side.

Without giving any thought at all to her own actions, Kate flung herself onto Daniel. She tried to pull Alex's arm from his grip. She kicked him hard with her Louboutins.

Rachel looked around wildly. 'Somebody help!' she screeched.

The crowd of guests looked on, but no one stepped forward to help. Even with alcohol to fuel an overinflated sense of their own abilities, everyone seemed happy to watch and not act. This was clearly none of anyone else's business – at least not so much that it warranted physically stepping in on what was obviously some sort of domestic issue.

Michelle tried to push Rachel's claustrophobically helpful hands off her. She clutched her belly, panic written on her face, as she stood.

John pushed his way through the crowd, with Tom in tow. John grabbed Daniel's shoulder calmly – but very firmly – and pulled so that Daniel turned to face him. 'Let go of her and leave.' John's voice was low and calm. He didn't want to fight. He didn't want to exacerbate the situation. He didn't want to make a big scene. He didn't want to be a hero. He just wanted Daniel gone.

Tom had expected a fist fight, and was geared up. He took his lead from John and stepped backwards, in an attempt to assist in calming the situation. However, his fists were clenched and he was ready to pounce if need be.

'You,' Daniel said accusingly to John. 'You're the one she's fucking.' He let go of Alex and turned to face John, front on.

'You need to leave.'

Kate had let go of Daniel as soon as John had arrived. She wrapped her arms around Alex and pulled her into a tight hug. Alex stood still, stony faced, no emotion registering. She was in complete shock. She knew she would need to face Daniel sometime. Though she had hoped that she would be able to go the rest of her life without laying eyes on him again. But she had never in a million years expected to see him here. For him to make a huge scene. For her friends to witness his insanity first hand. Up to now, no one she knew had ever seen Daniel act in any way other than as a perfect gentlemen, loving husband and all round nice guy. Well – apart from that one little drunken slip up in front of Michelle, and his insane jealous reaction on meeting John. But then again, up until recently, she'd never had any friends around her to bear witness to his cruelty. She was amazed that he had let his mask slip so publicly. Her leaving must have really unwound him. Maybe he did really love her. Why else would he be so upset about her leaving?

Daniel's cowardice outweighed his temper. He knew he

was outnumbered. He hadn't come here to fight. He'd come to get Alex. If it were just him and John, he wouldn't have backed down; his anger would have won; but now it was clear he'd get pummelled if he stuck to his guns.

'Alex, come with me.'

Alex stood in silence, a blank expression on her face, not a muscle in her body moved.

'I'm not giving up on us. I love you.' Daniel's words sounded ominous – more like a threat than a declaration of undying love. Realising that Alex wasn't going to come with him at that point, Daniel turned – tail firmly between his legs – and left.

All four of the friends stood in silence and watched Daniel leave. Once he was out of sight, Rachel was the first to speak.

'Michelle, I think we need to get you to a hospital.'

Kate's brow furrowed. 'Are you okay?' Her voice was full of concern.

'Yeah, I'm fine, I think. Just in shock, I guess.' Michelle's voice wavered in a way her three friends had never heard before. She didn't sound fine. Not even close.

The crowd of guests was still encircling them; most with their mouths agape; a few loudly explaining their own understanding of the situation to their friends.

John wrapped an arm protectively around Alex. 'Let's go somewhere private.' John glared at some of the guests who seemed to be treating the altercation as some sort of wedding entertainment. 'There's a storage room out the back that I'm pretty sure we can use.'

John ushered the four women into the small windowless room.

'Alex, are you okay?' John enclosed her hand with both of his and gave her a look filled with so much pity that Alex couldn't bear to look at him.

Alex averted her eyes, gave a short, sharp nod and remained silent.

Momentarily Kate's mind flickered to what Daniel had said. Were John and Alex really sleeping with each other? John hadn't denied it. Kate dismissed the thought – there was no time to be jealous right now – Alex needed her. Instead, she filed the thought away to contemplate further later.

Rachel looked at Michelle. Shock had turned to worried panic. Michelle was terrified for those flickering flashes of heartbeats she had seen on the screen. Her heart raced. She didn't have a clue what to do.

'We need to get you to a hospital.'

Wide eyed, Michelle nodded silently in agreement.

'I thought you were alright. What's going on?' John turned, concerned, but mildly irritated at additional, seemingly unnecessary, drama. Michelle was not usually the type. But for some reason she appeared to be bordering on hysteria even though she didn't seem to be hurt in any way.

'I'm pregnant.' The words just jumped out of Michelle's mouth. She hadn't intended to say anything, but those two little words had been expelled by her mouth into the air of the small box-room, before she had a chance to think about it. Her face was ashen and wore a look of frank vulnerability that surprised her friends.

John, Kate and Alex all turned to face Michelle.

Jarred from her introspective state of mortification, shock and fear, Alex was the first to speak. 'Congratulations?' It was said as a question. Manners had been lost with Daniel's appearance, and Alex had no idea that Michelle had badly wanted a baby.

Guilt hit Alex. What if something had happened to Michelle's baby because of Daniel? It would be all her fault. Michelle would never forgive her. Alex would never forgive herself. Frenzied thoughts raced through Alex's head.

'Okay...' Kate pushed aside all emotion. This was no time for congratulations; there might not even *be* something to congratulate anymore. *Fuck.* Kate had to think about what they needed to do. 'We need to get Michelle to the hospital. I don't think we should wait.'

'I can take her,' Rachel said, without a second's hesitation.

'I –' Alex hesitated, she blushed – 'This is all my fault. I should be the one to take you.' Alex looked at Michelle, registering the panicked expression, and Alex looked intently at Michelle with eyes full of sympathy and guilt. 'And I really want to be there for you, whatever happens.'

Kate imagined what would happen if the news was bad, and Alex was the only one there to comfort Michelle. Alex needed someone to be there for her; she didn't need to be responsible for Michelle's grief as well. 'I'm going to come too. I think that you both need some support right now.'

'Guys, I don't think that all four of us can leave. Today is Fi's big day. We can't just leave without a pretty darn good excuse.' Rachel realised the implications of what she just said. 'I mean – this is obviously a really good reason to leave and Fi would completely understand, but that would mean *telling* her which Michelle doesn't want to do just yet.' *Especially now* she thought, but didn't say it out loud. 'I think that only one of us should go with Michelle. I think it should be Kate.'

Rachel had decided that she should stay with Alex, because Alex seemed to need a friend even more than what Michelle did in that moment. Michelle was strong. Whatever happened, she would be able to cope. But Rachel wasn't sure the same could be said for Alex. Not that Rachel was willing to say it out loud, but she felt that she was better at being there for a friend in need than what Kate was.

Alex hugged Michelle. 'Everything's going to be alright.'

Rachel joined the hug, wrapping her arms around Alex and Michelle. Kate rushed to join the embrace. The four friends stayed like that, while John watched on, awkwardly.

'Okay, let's get going,' Michelle said, as she tried to extract herself from her friends' arms. She didn't want to wait any longer. She just wanted to know, either way. This wasn't like last time. She'd seen their heartbeats flickering on the monitor. They weren't specks. They were more than that. Her two little babies had fingers and toes already. Michelle could feel rising waves of hysteria building inside her. She couldn't stand still any longer. The air in the box room felt thick, heavy, dense – it was getting too hard to breath. She needed to get out. She needed to move. She charged out of the box room.

Alex and Rachel followed Michelle, single file. Kate started after her friends, but before she got through the door, John caught her wrist and gently pulled her back into the room. He pulled her toward him, so that they were face to face, their mouths just centimetres apart. He stared intently into her eyes, silent. Then he leaned in and kissed her. The kiss was unlike the kisses they had shared in the past. It was intense, yes, but urgent, pleading; the longing that had built up over the past months merged with loneliness; the desperation to be together melded into the terror they had both felt in trying to protect Alex earlier that night and their fear for Michelle.

'I never stopped loving you,' John said in a low voice.

An image of Michelle's frightened face flashed through Kate's mind. She had to be there for her friend. Michelle needed her. She didn't have time to do this with John now. She opened the door and turned to leave. She took one step through the open door and quickly turned to John.

'I love you.' Kate's voice was frank, slow and quiet. She kissed him quickly, hard, on the lips. 'I'm so sorry about everything. I'm never going to let you go again. I have to go with Michelle.' Kate stepped away from John again, then, hesitating briefly, turned back toward him and kissed him once more.

CHAPTER FORTY-ONE

'What the fuck is taking so long?' Kate chewed on the inside of her mouth. She was trying to remain calm – for Michelle's sake – but was failing miserably. Her face was slightly contorted with anxiety. She'd broken the skin inside her mouth where she'd been absentmindedly chewing, and her senses were enveloped by the metallic taste of blood. Kate was surprisingly level headed in emergencies. But this waiting around was not her forte. She'd tried to keep Michelle's mind off it by reminiscing about old times and telling jokes, but it hadn't worked at all. So, she resorted to waiting in silence, holding Michelle's hand and chewing the inside of her mouth.

Michelle lay on a bed, with a crisp white sheet across her abdomen and thighs. She was coping with the situation much better than Kate – mainly because her brain simply couldn't process anything at that moment. The fear was far too much for her, so her mind had shut it down, ending the *what ifs* and thoughts of the speck and memory of the two flickering grey images she had watched on a screen in a room very similar to this one. She was lying – mind blank – staring at a crack in the ceiling. Her mind only in the present; only taking in what was physically in front of her; only thinking of the crevice where the plaster had cracked. It was only small – about twenty centimetres, Michelle would have estimated, although she was never great at judging those sorts of things. There were a few smaller lines creeping, jagged, from the crevice – they weren't quite crevices yet – fine as a hair, barely noticeable, but imperfections in the plaster, nevertheless. Michelle wondered what caused a crack like that. The building shifting, she supposed. Would the crack get bigger? Would those tiny lines coming off the main crevice become gaping holes one day?

'Sorry to keep you waiting. Now let's have a look, shall we?' A young woman in blue scrubs said, as she bustled hurriedly into the room. The woman looked tired, drained.

Michelle just stared blankly and clenched her jaw. Had anyone else noticed the cracks in the ceiling?

The woman looked up from the screen she was examining, and briefly caught Michelle's eye. The woman momentarily forgot about how hard and long her day had been. In that moment, the look in her eyes wasn't professional or harried, it was the look of a woman bearing witness to the anguish only a woman can understand.

'This might feel a little cold. I'm sorry.' The woman's voice was gentle. She pulled down the sheet to expose Michelle's stomach and pushed the probe into Michelle's belly.

Kate held her breath and squeezed Michelle's hand hard.

The woman moved the probe around and pressed it harder against Michelle's belly, causing her to wince.

'How far along are you?' The woman asked distractedly, still staring intently at the screen in front of her.

'Nine weeks, three days.' Michelle's voice was quiet.

The woman continued to angle the probe, pressing harder and harder.

Would that crack be plastered over? Had there been more cracks in that ceiling that had already been filled and re-painted?

'I can see one...' The woman said distractedly, as she continued to move the probe and examine intently the screen.

'One what?' Kate sounded fretful. She looked as though she would jump up at any minute and shake answers out of the woman. 'One heartbeat?' She was on the verge of screaming at the woman: *For fuck's sake! Don't you understand how important this is? Just tell us!*

A few moments passed – although those moments felt like a lifetime – before the woman looked up. She gave a tight smile, distracted. 'Yes, just give me a minute...' She turned back to the screen and continued to look.

Michelle remained staring at the crack in the ceiling, jaw slack. One heartbeat. Did all of the rooms have ceiling cracks like this? Were those ceilings worse? One heartbeat. Or did those ceilings have cracks below the surface? Cracks that weren't visible to the world yet? Were there other people in the other rooms staring at the cracks in those ceilings?

The woman exhaled loudly. 'And there's the other one.' She turned to face Michelle, a broad grin plastered across her tired face. 'Two strong heartbeats.'

Kate made a strange sound – like a strangled yelp – and pressed her hand to her mouth, as tears began streaming down her face.

Michelle's shoulders slumped. Her jaw was still slack and she felt her throat tighten and her eyes begin to sting with tears. All of the feelings that she had been trying to keep at bay came crashing over her. The corners of her gaping mouth turned upwards and she buried her contorted face in her hands; Michelle shook with terror, joy, relief.

Kate wrapped her arms around Michelle and pulled her close. 'You're going to be a mum.' Kate gave a strange laugh. 'Holy fucking shit. You're going to be a mum.'

CHAPTER FORTY-TWO

Watching Fiona and Isaac waving from the backseat of a vintage Mercedes, Alex breathed a sigh of relief. It had been a long and emotional day. Alex had honestly had enough before Daniel had even shown up. She'd wanted to leave when Kate and Michelle had left for the hospital, but Rachel had said it was bad manners to leave early. And, in any case, it would be much more noticeable if all four of them had left early. So Alex had stayed, out of obligation – because Rachel had told her to. She'd felt a weight lifted from her shoulders when they received the text message from Kate saying that everything was okay with the babies. At least that was one less thing to feel bad about.

Rachel and Alex hugged goodbye and Rachel went outside to wait for her Uber. Alex needed a quick bathroom pit stop before leaving – she'd really had far too much to drink. She wobbled in her low kitten heels. She wasn't used to wearing anything other than flats. Stuff it. She took off her shoes and walked barefoot to the street. Most of the guests had dispersed. A few were still standing around waiting for their rides, presumably. Alex pulled out her phone to order an Uber.

'Hey.'

Daniel. The expression on his face was gentle, calm. His eyes were bloodshot from what looked to be a combination of too much alcohol and crying.

'Hi.' Alex's voice sounded wary, but she felt a lot more at ease than she had all night.

'I love you. I love you so much.' Daniel reached for her hand. 'Please forgive me.'

'You really hurt me.' Alex's voice was meek. Her gaze hovered somewhere around his shoulders. She couldn't look him in the eye – that just felt too confrontational – too real. God, she was tired.

'I know. I'm sorry. But you know it was an accident. You know I would never hurt you on purpose. I just love you so much.'

'I –' Alex's voice faltered. Did she know that? No, she didn't think she did. He had hurt her.

'I know you've got these new friends. I think they're putting ideas in your head. I don't think *you* want to leave me.'

'No. That's not true.' Alex's voice was a whisper, barely audible. But she wasn't quite sure of herself. She was scared. Lonely. Tired. So, so very tired.

'What will you do without me? Get a job? Who's going to employ you? You don't have any skills.' Daniel spoke gently. He was concerned about her future, he wasn't being mean. He was just being honest.

Panic started rising in Alex's stomach. Who *would* employ her? She hadn't worked in years. She hadn't even finished her degree. What would she do? She didn't really get along with her mum *that* well. She would need a proper job to be able to afford to live somewhere – anywhere – that wasn't her parents' house. It all sounded really hard – overwhelming – and exhausting. Just thinking about it was exhausting.

'I'm not trying to hurt you. I just want you to face up to reality. It's a really tough world out there. You don't really know that because you've always had me to look after you.'

Daniel *had* always looked after her.

'And that bloke –' A sneer briefly broke through to Daniel's face, then it was gone – replaced by his gentle, concerned expression. 'That bloke doesn't love you. He's not going to spend the rest of his life with you. He's not going to marry you. No one could ever love you the way that I do. You know that. I love you for you. I don't care if you're overweight. You don't need to be pretty for me. I love you anyway.'

Alex's heart felt like it had turned to lead and was sinking to her feet. No one would ever love her. She was fat. Ugly. Who *could* love her? John certainly didn't. He was in love with Kate. Alex was lucky to have anyone, let alone someone as gorgeous as Daniel.

'You love me. I know you do.' Daniel squeezed her hand. 'I think that this is all an overreaction. Those new friends of yours have convinced you to leave. You don't want to.'

Was he right? She did love him. She knew that for sure. She always had.

She felt fear wrap around her like thick tentacles, sliding around her torso, her arms, her legs; they squeezed her tight; she couldn't breathe; claustrophobia set in but she couldn't move; the tentacles tightened, dragging her down. Fighting it was draining – and she was just so very tired.

Daniel continued, 'They're just playing with you – with our lives. You know they're doing it just for fun. Pretty girls messing with the head of the weak, unpopular girl. You know you're easily manipulated, don't you? You know that they're manipulating you, don't you?'

No. He was wrong. They were her friends, weren't they? Kate was so beautiful. An image flicked through Alex's mind of Kate laughing. Laughing at her. It really didn't make sense why a girl like that would want to be friends with her. No. He was wrong. Kate was her friend. Kate liked her. Alex was sure of it. And John – he liked her too, didn't he? She had never understood why he spent so much time with her. But that didn't mean that Daniel was right. But what was there for John to like? Were they just doing it for a laugh? Were they about to drop a bucket of pig's blood on her head? No, he was wrong. Wasn't he?

'But you hit me.' Alex's voice was a defiant whisper. She stared at the ground. She wasn't quite up to an argument. She was so tired. And drunk. She didn't want to provoke him. A wave of exhaustion hit her. She was scared. Scared of him. Scared of being alone. Scared of the future.

Daniel's mouth dropped open. He wrapped his free arm around her waist, still holding her hand tight. 'Alex, what do you mean?' He sounded shocked. Horrified.

'You –' She swallowed hard. 'You hit me. You hurt me.' Her accusations stammered out of her mouth.

'I would never hit you, Alex. Never.' Daniel caressed her lower back. He continued, his voice still gentle but condescending, 'I can't believe you would say such a thing – think such a thing.' A tear slid down his cheek. 'You fell. I was angry and jealous – of course – *because I love you so much.* And then you tripped. It was an accident. How could you possibly think that about me? I'm your husband. I love you. I always have. I would never, ever hurt you.'

She did remember tripping. But she also remembered his fist. Or was that her imagination? She was so tired, she didn't think she could keep standing for much longer. She thought she remembered the whole night, but all of a sudden she didn't feel so sure. It all felt so blurry in the fog of alcohol and fatigue.

'Those pretty girls have really done a number on you. I can't believe you would let them convince you of such horrible things. About me. I can't believe you could be turned against me so easily.' Daniel looked into her eyes imploringly, his face a mask of hurt and pain. 'I'm your husband, Alex. I'm yours and you're mine. We belong together.'

Alex stared into his beautiful blue eyes. His long black eyelashes damp with tears. She did love him so much. And she knew for sure that Daniel was right about her being weak. She was a fat, ugly, weak person. Her mind felt numb with exhaustion. Why had she had so much to drink? She tried desperately to piece together the memories from that night. There were fragments – bursts of a movie reel and still frames in her mind; but which were real and which were her imagination. Had John told her some of these things? She remembered John telling her about Daniel hitting her – asking if Daniel had, probing and pushing. Had her mind filled in the blanks? She was just so tired; it was really hard to think. It was as though her memories and thoughts had been torn apart, and the ripped shreds were floating through the air – light like confetti – and she was swinging her arms, grasping, trying to catch the pieces as they fell. But even if she could catch them, how could she sew them back together to make sense of it all? She felt crazy. Was she crazy? She didn't remember what was real. It all felt so confusing and overwhelming.

Daniel was right though – it didn't make sense that such beautiful, popular girls would want to be her friend. Why were they friends? What did they see in her? She wished with all her might that she could be like them – gorgeous and confident and sexy like Kate, strong and smart and driven like Michelle, pretty, petite and perfect like Rachel. But Alex wasn't any of those things. She was fat. She was awkward. She was boring. She was unemployed. She was ugly. There was nothing about her that measured up to those other three. She had nothing going for her. She had nothing... But she did have Daniel.

'I love you, Alex. So much. The wedding's over. It's all over. Let's go home.'

CPSIA information can be obtained
at www.ICGtesting.com
Printed in the USA
LVOW11s2009140617
538109LV00005B/922/P